PENG

BBC

NO BANANAS

Peter Cave was born in East London, and now lives in Torquay, Devon. After leaving school at seventeen years old, he pursued a career in journalism, although his major ambition was to write. His bestselling novel, *Chopper*, was published in 1971 and was followed by three equally successful sequels. He became a full-time freelance writer in the mid 1970s and has written over fifty novels since, published under both his own name and some pseudonyms. Among his thrillers are *Foxbat*, *Siege* and *Fireflood*, and his television work includes novelizations of *The New Avengers* and *Taggart*.

Peter Cave is married with two daughters, Tina and Holly, born exactly nineteen years apart. His favourite pastimes include skiing, gliding, riding on rollercoasters and driving through America. His current unfulfilled ambitions are to survive into the twenty-first century and to repeat his mid-70s coast-to-coast trek across the USA on a Harley-Davidson, and to find a publisher who would subsidize it!

NO BANANAS

Peter Cave

SERIES CREATED BY
GINNIE HOLE

PENGUIN BOOKS
BBC BOOKS

PENGUIN BOOKS
BBC BOOKS

Published by the Penguin Group
Penguin Books Ltd, 27 Wrights Lane, London w8 5tz, England
Penguin Books USA Inc., 375 Hudson Street, New York, New York 10014, USA
Penguin Books Australia Ltd, Ringwood, Victoria, Australia
Penguin Books Canada Ltd, 10 Alcorn Avenue, Toronto, Ontario, Canada m4v 3b2
Penguin Books (NZ) Ltd, 182–190 Wairau Road, Auckland 10, New Zealand

Penguin Books Ltd, Registered Offices: Harmondsworth, Middlesex, England

Published in 1996
1 3 5 7 9 10 8 6 4 2

BBC BBC used under licence

Set in 9.5/12 pt Sabon Monotype
Typeset by Datix International Ltd, Bungay, Suffolk
Printed in England by Clays Ltd, St Ives plc

Below, in the distance, the undulating shape of the River Medway looked like a huge golden-scaled serpent, its gently rippling surface refracting back the ruddy, slanting rays of the late afternoon August sun. The air was still and sultry, with virtually no breeze. With September now only three days away, the summer of 1939 continued to be one of the hottest on record for many years, yet it was more than just the weather which contributed to Harry Slater's sense of oppression.

He sat on his army tunic, spread out on the meadow grass. With one shirtsleeved arm draped around Kaye's shoulders and the other hand toying idly with a clump of rye grass, he stared moodily down the hill, trying to pull his turbulent thoughts into some sort of order.

He should be feeling at peace, Harry thought, almost bitterly, here, in the heart of the Kentish countryside, on a near-idyllic day, and close to the beautiful girl who had virtually idolized him for the past three years. At any other time, under different circumstances, it would have been a young man's dream.

Sensing his mood, Kaye half turned towards him, her bright eyes clouded slightly with worry.

'What is it, Harry? What's wrong?' she murmured concernedly. He had been oddly distant all day, and she just didn't understand.

There was no answer. Harry plucked a long stalk of grass, thrusting it between his teeth. He nibbled at the sweet, crisp white tip of the inner shoot, sucking on the rest.

'Do you want to . . . you know?' Kaye prompted, in an embarrassed little voice. Lowering her eyes, she pulled away from him slightly. Raising her fingers to the top buttons of her thin cotton frock, she began to unpick them somewhat awkwardly.

There was longing in Harry's eyes as he took in the creamy swelling of her firm young breasts, but there was a deep sadness too. He looked away, returning his gaze to the river without really seeing it.

The rebuff struck Kaye like a physical blow. Her pretty face creased into a hurt expression which was part confusion, part shame. Her bottom lip trembled slightly as she spoke again.

'What, Harry? You always wanted to.'

Harry spoke at last, his own voice choked with emotion. 'It's different now,' he muttered thickly.

There was a long, and very heavy, silence between them, in which they could both hear the faint, distant rumble of summer thunder.

Or was it thunder, Harry wondered, unsure whether the sounds of practice firing from the coastal batteries at Shoeburyness could carry this far? This thought, and all it implied, increased his sense of gloom.

Kaye was speaking again, pulling him back to the moment.

'Is it because you don't love me any more?' she asked plaintively. The question itself begged a denial.

Harry's chest heaved convulsively. Something between a laugh and a sob burst from between his lips as he shook his head, slowly and sadly.

'No, it's not that.'

'Then what?' Kaye was almost pleading with him now.

Harry gave a helpless, hopeless shrug. 'It could be any day now. You could be called up any time too. What if you got pregnant?'

A tear bubbled from the corner of Kaye's eye and rolled slowly down her face. Filled with compassion, Harry kissed it away and laid his cheek against hers, then hugged her tightly. A silence descended again, but this time it carried all the things they could not, or would not, say to each other.

Eventually, as people do, they filled the void with words, not conversation.

'Perhaps it won't come to it,' Kaye suggested hopefully. 'Perhaps old Hitler will back down, after all.'

There was still some optimism left, largely fostered by the popular press. Only a few days previously, the *Daily Express* had even carried an advertisement for family holidays in the Belgian seaside resorts. 'Parliament is taking a holiday – why not you?' the ad had read. 'Visit the Belgian coast, where everyone is happy, peaceful and smiling.'

Harry sighed deeply. 'Yes, perhaps,' he muttered, without conviction and unable to even share Kaye's faint hope. The reality was that German troops were gathering in force on the Polish frontier. The British fleet had already been mobilized. All over London, and much of its outskirts, the air-raid sirens had already been erected, wired up and tested. Despite the dire warnings of Winston Churchill and a handful of others, only the politicians seemed to still believe that war was not inevitable.

The sun was dipping now towards the western horizon. Through the gathering dusk, the faint rays of searchlight beams could be seen scanning the evening sky. It was yet another reminder of the menacing threat which hung above their heads.

'I wish you was on them,' Kaye murmured wistfully, nodding towards the sweeping sheets of light. 'Then you wouldn't have to go away. It'd be all right between us, then.'

Her words ended abruptly in a bitter and hopeless sob. She began to cry openly, the tears rolling down her cheeks.

Harry's heart surged, feeling the desperate need to join her but trapped and isolated within the archetype of his own masculinity. Grown men didn't cry, an inner voice told him. Even now, when, God knows, the whole world was poised on the verge of tears.

Tom Slater stepped gratefully through the small steel door set into the massive wooden gates of Wormwood Scrubs prison and contemplated the outside world. Standing on truly free ground for the first time in nearly five years, he paused briefly to brace himself against an initial and overpowering surge of elation as the door clanged shut behind him. The sound rang in his ears like the peal of some great bell, heavy with portent. The chime of freedom, Tom thought fancifully to himself, grinning. He stepped forward, breaking into a brisk trot, anxious to place some physical distance between himself and the site of his incarceration.

Only when he had turned a corner, and was shielded from the high prison walls, did he stop again to fully savour his new status as a free man. He drew in a long, deep breath of the early morning air through his nose, sucking it into his lungs. It tasted good, pure, finally free of the all-pervading odours of urine and carbolic soap which seemed to permeate the confines of His Majesty's prisons, including the exercise yard.

Tom delved into the small haversack he carried over his shoulder. Fishing out a folded grey cap, he shook it open and pulled it over the dark stubble of his severe prison haircut, setting the peak at a jaunty, defiant angle. He began to walk again, less quickly but with equal purpose. There were several things he needed urgently, but they were arranged inside his head in order of strict priority. There were calls to be made, people to contact, the odd favour to be called in. After that, and hopefully with a few bob in his pocket, the most important thing in the world was a pint pot in his hand just as soon as the pubs were open.

*

The reek of beer fumes, tobacco smoke and human sweat assaulted Tom's nostrils as he turned in to the Who'd Ha Thought It public house in the back streets of Chatham. He drank it all in greedily, as if it were some expensive and particularly stimulating perfume. It was a *good* smell, Tom reflected. The smell of life.

The place hadn't changed much in five years. Still largely the haunt of out-of-work labourers, casual dockers and the local criminal fraternity, the clientele matched the shabby paint-work and the phlegm-stained sawdust on the plain wooden floor. Harry, standing just inside the door dressed in his clean and crisply pressed army uniform, looked oddly out of place.

A somewhat guarded smile of welcome spread across his face as Tom walked in. Turning towards the bar, Harry picked his way past tables of stout-drinking grannies and tattooed merchant seamen, taking his place at the counter beside a bruised-looking woman collecting a jug of ale to take home. He ordered two pints of mild from the purple-nosed landlord and carried them back to where Tom had found himself a comparatively quiet corner.

Tom took a long and grateful draught of beer from his glass before he said a word. Finally, wiping his lips with the back of his hand, he grinned broadly.

'Well, little brother. It's good to see you.'

Harry sipped at his own beer, nodding. 'You too, Tom.' He raised his glass in a toast. 'So – here's to freedom, eh?'

Tom jerked his own glass into the air. 'Heil bleedin' Hitler,' he announced, in an embarrassingly loud voice.

A worried look clouded his brother's face. The buzz of conversation which had been filling the pub suddenly died away, giving way to a few low, menacing rumbles. The atmosphere was suddenly hostile.

'Blimey, Tom, watch what you're saying,' Harry hissed warningly. 'You're a bit out of touch. Old Adolf isn't exactly over-popular around here.'

Tom dismissed the warning with another cocky grin. Raising his glass again, and turning to address the pub in general, he qualified his unusual toast.

'Well, he got me off the last three months of me stretch, didn't he? No sense in having able-bodied men banged up behind bars when there could be a war on,' he announced.

The ominous grumblings died away. Knowing smiles replaced frowns of suspicion. Everybody relaxed, and the atmosphere in the pub settled back to normal.

Tom returned his attention to Harry, eyeing his uniform. 'Well, fancy you joining up, then. Thought it was against your principles to go in the Army.' There was the faintest note of sarcasm in his tone.

Harry shrugged off the implied rebuke. 'It was,' he conceded. 'Then I saw some of the refugees who've come over.' He paused to take another sip of beer. 'Mind you, Mum was a bit upset.'

A warm smile of affection washed across Tom's features. 'Ah, good old Mum,' he murmured fondly. 'How is she, by the way? How's everybody?'

Another vague shrug. 'They're all right, I suppose. Tell you the truth, I haven't seen as much of them as I might, what with training camp and being called up. Mum's fine, but Dad and Clifford are having to work twelve-hour shifts at the dockyard now.'

Tom's brow momentarily furrowed at the mention of their father. Then he brightened. 'Well, if the old bugger's out of the house all day, maybe I'll pop in.' Serious again, his voice took on an edge of bitterness. 'Do you know, he never even visited me once?'

Harry was embarrassed, suddenly placed in the position of having to apologize for his own father. 'He'll come round, Tom. It's just that he always had such high expectations – of all of us.'

Tom registered a thin, rueful smile. 'Yeah. Well, at least you always come up to them, don't yer?'

The remark sent Harry's thoughts spinning away, back to the sense of depression which had haunted him for weeks now. His voice was oddly distant as he replied, 'I wouldn't bank on that, Tom.'

Tom eyed him curiously, sensing a hidden message of some kind but unable to put his finger on it. Always the deep one, he thought, remembering how he had never fully understood his younger brother, even when they were kids.

'Anyway, I'm going to show the old bleeder this time,' he announced, returning the conversation to their father. 'I'm going to go straight, make something of meself.'

Harry dragged himself back to the present, managing a faint smile. 'Get a job, you mean?'

Tom snorted derisively. 'Good chance of that, with all the unemployment,' he muttered sarcastically. 'Who's going to want me, not even good enough for cannon fodder?' He paused, draining his pint. 'Still, you get a lot of time to think when you're sewing mailbags. I reckon I can set meself up all right.'

Harry reached for the glass in Tom's hand. 'Look, I have to leave in a minute. Let me get you another one before I go.'

Tom held on to his empty glass, shaking his head. 'Don't bother.' He nodded towards the pub landlord. 'Reg'll see me right for a couple of pints. He owes me. Besides, we got some business to discuss.'

'Business?' Harry looked dubious.

Tom nodded. 'What I was saying – about setting meself up. Reg has this old lorry that needs fixing up. If I can get it back on the road, he'll let me use his back yard to do repairs. Get a few readies together and I can open me own little garage.'

It all sounded a little over-optimistic, Harry thought. As ever, his elder brother saw only the dream of instant riches, not the reality. As gently as he could, he voiced his doubts.

'A lot of cars and vans are being commandeered for ambulances and such.'

Tom refused to see a problem. 'Well, then – they'll want 'em all in good order, won't they?' he said cheerfully. 'There should be even more of a call for repair work.'

Harry let it go, nodding an unenthusiastic agreement. 'Yes, I suppose there will.' He finished his beer, setting the empty glass down on a nearby table. 'Look, I really do have to go,' he muttered apologetically. He opened the pocket flap of his army tunic, pulling out five separate one-pound notes and thrusting them rather self-consciously towards his brother. 'Maybe this'll help, in the meantime.'

Tom accepted the money without shame or hesitation. 'Ta, mate.' He crumpled the notes in his fist, transferring them to his trouser pocket. Withdrawing his hand, he slapped Harry on the shoulder. 'Well – be seeing you, eh?'

Harry nodded. 'Yeah.' He turned away towards the door.

'Well, I'll be blowed. Tommie Slater, as lives and breathes. Five years up already, is it?'

Harry regarded the newcomer with equal distrust and dislike. He didn't know the man, but he knew the type. Everything about Bernie Silver screamed out 'wide boy' – from the slicked-back hair, the lurid tie and the white silk scarf to the brown and cream two-tone shoes.

Tom, however, greeted the man like a long-lost friend, embracing him with a warm smile. 'Bernie, you old bugger. What you doin' these days?'

Bernie's eyes flickered shiftily over Harry's khaki tunic. He had an innate distrust of any kind of uniform. 'Oh, this and that, yer know. This and that,' he muttered evasively.

It was definitely time to go, Harry thought. He walked towards the door without another word, without looking back.

Bernie looked relieved. 'So – when d'yer get out?'

'This morning,' Tom said.

'Then you'll be needing a little earner, won't you? Still a whizz wiv motors, are you?'

Tom beamed with enthusiasm. 'You bet. Got something needs a bit of fixing, have you?'

Bernie winked, shaking his head. 'Nah – but I could use a driver for a couple of hours. Little removal job – know what I mean?'

Tom knew exactly what he meant. His eyes narrowed slightly. 'So what's in it for me?'

Bernie shrugged. 'A nice easy pony, maybe a few hundred ciggies and somewhere comfortable to hole up for the night.'

Tom didn't have to think about it. The offer of a decent bed after five years on a prison bunk was enough temptation in itself. He fished one of Harry's pound notes from his pocket, dragging Bernie towards the bar.

'A drink on it,' he suggested with a grin.

3

The smell of burning privet greeted Mary Hamilton's nose and stirred childhood memories as she turned into the driveway of Albourne House. It was this, as much as the sight of the slightly weatherbeaten frontage of the old house, that gave her a strange sense of coming home after a long absence, even though it had actually been little over a year. Transferring her single suitcase from one hand to the other, she walked up the side of the lawn towards old Dovey, the family gardener and handyman, who was busy heaping fresh hedge cuttings on to a bonfire at the side of the old tennis court.

Hearing the sound of her feet on the gravel, Dovey looked up, his craggy features registering first surprise, then cracking into a smile. He pulled his ever-smouldering pipe from between his teeth to welcome her.

'Hello, Miss Mary. Nobody told me you was coming.'

Mary smiled warmly at him. Dovey was like part of the family. 'I didn't know myself until a couple of days ago, Dovey. But with all the London schools being evacuated to the coast, I'm out of a job.'

Dovey wasn't sure whether this was good news or bad news. Strictly of the old school, he had his own fairly rigid views on class structure, and it was still unusual, even slightly outrageous, for young women of Miss Mary's background to go out to work – let alone leave home and live in somewhere like Lewisham.

'Well, welcome home, anyway,' he said, avoiding the issue altogether. He tidied up the bonfire and stepped away from it, wiping his hands on his calico apron. 'Here, let me take your case into the house. I'll tell your mother you're here.'

'Thank you, Dovey.' Mary handed the heavy case over gratefully, but did not follow him immediately. Instead, she turned slowly around in the drive, taking in the house and grounds as if to re-establish severed connections. It was a way of life as much as a place, she reflected, idly.

The house itself, impressive despite its faintly run-down appearance, seemed smaller than she remembered. Other things seemed the same – the rusting garden swing on the lawn, the neglected tree-house built between the two large sycamores at the end of the garden and the old barn, which had never been fully converted to its present use as a garage.

The gardens looked as neat as ever, evidence of Dovey's continued loving care. Once a sizeable country farm, the land surrounding Albourne House had shrunk as the village of Chittenden had grown. Now consisting of little over one and a half acres, the grounds were still a small, but significant, reminder of stately England.

Mary stepped into the house, heading straight for the drawing room. Her mother rose from her work – sewing blackout sheets – and held out her hands in welcome. It was a warm, but not effusive, greeting. Evelyn Hamilton was not a woman much given to overt displays of emotion.

'Mary, darling – this is a surprise.'

It was a perfect opportunity, Mary thought. There didn't seem much point in delaying the inevitable.

'Actually, it's not the only one, Mummy. I'm getting married.'

It was a shock, rather than a surprise. Temporarily speechless, Evelyn backed away to the chesterfield and sank onto it, gaping up at her daughter blankly.

'His name's Harry – Harry Slater,' Mary expanded. 'You remember I wrote to you about him. He saved me from a police horse.'

Evelyn found her voice at last. 'That's hardly a reason to get married, dear,' she murmured, managing to make it sound like a mild rebuke.

'We've been seeing each other for months,' Mary said, as if justifying herself. 'It's just that he's been called up, so we decided not to wait.'

Evelyn frowned slightly. 'Presumably he hasn't spoken to your father?'

A flash of irritation crossed Mary's face. A born rebel, she instinctively rejected what she considered to be old-fashioned and outdated niceties. There was an edge of sarcasm in her tone as she replied, 'Oh, sorry. Not proper form. But he is marrying me, not Daddy.'

William, Mary's fifteen-year-old brother, came bounding in through the French windows at this point, defusing the tension between the two women.

'Hello, Mary. Dovey told me you were home.' William broke off, catching the somewhat strained expressions on the faces of his mother and sister. 'What's up? Has the war started already?' he demanded eagerly.

Evelyn forced a look of enthusiasm on to her face. 'No, it's good news, dear. Mary's getting married.'

William looked suitably impressed. 'Gosh – when?'

Mary shook her head. 'I'm not sure. This week, probably.'

Her mother sagged in the chesterfield under this second shockwave. '*This week?*' she repeated, parrot-like.

William didn't seem too pleased, either. 'Well, it had jolly well better not be on Saturday. I'm playing in the cricket team against the airbase.'

Evelyn struggled to regain her air of calm control. 'We'll have to telephone the vicar at once,' she said firmly.

Mary drew a deep breath before dropping the next bomb-shell. 'No need,' she announced. 'We're getting married in a registry office.' She caught the expression of horror which crossed her mother's face. 'People do,' Mary added, defensively.

Evelyn's response was indignant rather than angry. 'People like Mrs Simpson do,' she muttered heavily. A sudden and horrible thought struck her. 'He's not been married before, has he?'

Mary shook her head. 'Nothing like that, Mum. It's just that Harry's an atheist.'

Already reeling under the sustained attack on her sensibilities, Evelyn found this final revelation too much to comprehend.

'Maybe he is, Mary, but at a time like this we all need God on our side, even if He doesn't exist,' she said, lamely.

As owner and editor of the *East Kent Echo*, Arthur Hamilton was used to analysing all news, good or bad, with quiet stoicism. As a father, it was not quite so simple. Even at twenty-two, Mary was still the little girl he had pushed on the garden swing, built the tree-house for.

'Are you sure about this, Mary? It's a huge step, pledging the rest of your life.'

Mary let out a slightly sardonic little laugh. 'Well, that might not be very long, might it?' she pointed out.

A sad smile crossed her father's face. 'And is that it?' he asked.

Mary shook her head with sudden vehemence. She seemed about to say something else, then fell silent.

'You have to believe in the future,' her father went on.

Mary nodded. 'I know. And I do. That's why. Please try to understand, Daddy. I'm grown up now.'

Arthur made the effort to smile reassuringly. 'You mean I can't stop you,' he said, managing to make it almost a joke. He looked serious again. 'What regiment's he in?'

'North Kents,' Mary told him.

Her father looked thoughtful. 'I wonder if Barney Gibbs knows him,' he muttered. 'I'm sure he could pull a few strings for a few extra days' leave.'

Mary smiled faintly. 'I doubt if he's even aware of his existence, Daddy. Harry's only a private soldier.'

'But you said he had a first-class honours degree,' Evelyn

put in, snatching at the single positive thing she had heard all day.

Mary turned on her mother irritably. 'That doesn't mean he either wants or can afford to be an officer,' she snapped.

Evelyn's face froze. She cast a helpless look at her husband. 'You try to talk some sense into her, Arthur. I'm going to make a nice cup of tea.'

Arthur waited until his wife had left the room. He regarded his daughter with a serious but warm expression, his tone not quite a plea.

'If the church is of no significance to you, Mary – would it matter so very much getting married there? To make your mother happy?'

Mary smiled cynically. 'Happy, Daddy? Or to make up for committing the faux pas of not marrying an officer?'

Arthur sighed, feeling a need to speak in his wife's defence. 'She's had none of your opportunities,' he pointed out. 'No proper education, let alone Cambridge. Please don't go out of your way to turn her world upside-down.'

4

Nelson Street, Gillingham was no different to hundreds of others throughout the south-east. Twin rows of flat-fronted, four-windowed terraced houses butted directly on to a narrow kerb and faced each other across a roadway just wide enough for two vehicles to pass each other.

Obviously the worse for drink, Tom Slater made his way along the street towards Number Seventeen. Stepping out from the kerb to avoid a window-cleaner's ladder, he lurched heavily against the side of a horse-drawn milk cart parked next door, making the empty bottles clatter.

Attracted by the noise, Ivy Collins poked her head out from the porch of Number Nineteen and eyed him curiously.

Tom grinned, treating her to a cheeky and suggestive wink. At thirty-five, Ivy was still an attractive woman, if a little on the tarty side. Dressed for housework in a floral pinafore and a colourful headscarf, her heavy make-up and permed and bleached hair suggested she was always ready for other things.

'Hello, Ivy. Still as gorgeous as ever?' Tom said, teasing her.

Ivy scowled at him, ducking back inside her hallway to pass on this minor piece of scandal to her husband Reg.

Tom staggered to a halt outside the front door of his family home. As ever, it was unlocked. Pushing it open, he stepped quietly down the brown-painted passageway. He stood silently in the kitchen doorway for several moments, watching his mother preparing vegetables at the sink.

Suddenly aware of a presence, Ellen Slater turned slowly in his direction. Her face registered first shock, then pleasant surprise and finally joy. She dropped the kitchen knife with a clatter, rushing towards him with outstretched arms.

Tom grinned sheepishly. 'Hello, Mum. Return of the prodigal, eh?'

Ellen hugged him silently, tears bubbling out of her eyes.

'Well, fancy them letting you out again.' Granma Slater hobbled out from the living-room, her old eyes glittering brightly.

Tom detached himself gently from his mother's embrace, seizing his grandmother by the shoulders. He kissed her full on the mouth. 'Hello, Granma – still alive then?'

'Cheeky bugger.' Granma grinned hugely, unable to conceal her delight at seeing her favourite grandson. 'So, when did you get out?'

'This afternoon,' Tom lied, having been on a two-day bender. He turned back to his mother, who had pulled herself together and was wiping the tears from her eyes. Unhooking his bulging haversack from his shoulder, he laid it down on the kitchen table. Delving inside, he pulled out packet after packet of Craven A cigarettes, piling them into a tower. 'These are for you, Mum.' Digging deeper, he brought out a bottle of port. 'And this is for Granma.'

Neither woman asked where the gifts had come from. Perhaps it was better not to know. There was a momentary silence, finally broken by the sound of the port bottle being uncorked.

'Time for a little celebration,' Granma suggested, grateful for any excuse to take a drink. A music-hall performer in her younger days, she still loved her tipple even more than she still loved to sing. She winked at Tom. 'I hate drinking on me own and yer ma's got a thirst like a bleedin' sparrer.'

Ellen brought over three glasses, which Granma promptly filled to the brim.

Thomas Slater brought his Rudge motor-cycle and sidecar to a halt outside the house. Switching off the engine, he dismounted and removed his cap and goggles, tucking them into his greatcoat pocket. A slightly puzzled frown crossed his face as he heard the sound of singing coming from inside the house.

Ivy Collins was lounging against her front door, a cigarette dangling from between her lips. She regarded Thomas with a knowing smile. 'Your Tom's home,' she informed him.

Never a man to smile much, Thomas's stern features hardened into a grim mask. He pushed open the front door just as his mother finished off a spirited version of 'You are the Honeysuckle, I am the Bee'.

Unaware that his father had entered the house, Tom was enjoying himself. He kissed Granma again, flirting with her outrageously. 'You should never have retired from the halls, Gran,' he told her.

Granma cackled gleefully. 'Me bones make more noise than me vocal chords these days,' she said, without bitterness. 'Anyway – who was it went and pawned me accordion?'

The sound of the front door closing broke into the air of gaiety, causing everyone's eyes to turn towards the hallway. Ellen's face took on a worried, apprehensive expression.

Thomas hung up his coat on the hallstand, pulling a folded copy of the *Evening Standard* from the pocket. Grim-faced, he marched silently into the living-room and sat down in his favourite chair, unfolding the paper in front of his face like a protective barrier.

'Hello, Dad,' Tom said in a soft voice.

Thomas ignored the greeting. 'What's he doing here?' he hissed in a tight, bitter voice, unable even to acknowledge his son's presence by referring to him directly.

Tom reacted instinctively as the years of antagonism flared up again. 'Visiting my family,' he snapped. 'Law against that now, is there?'

Ellen jumped in, desperate to build bridges between the two men. 'He's got all sorts of good plans to start an honest business, Thomas. Doing up old cars, opening up a little garage.'

Thomas cut her short. 'I've told you. I don't want him in my house.'

Obstinate and narrow-minded, Granma Slater thought. Just as he had been as a boy. 'Thomas, he's your own son, whatever he's done,' she muttered, scoldingly.

Thomas folded the paper slowly and carefully, placing it on the floor. He glared defiantly at his mother. 'No son of mine goes breaking into folks' houses,' he said firmly.

Granma glared at him. 'Well, if you want to make him do it again, you're going the right way about it.'

Thomas jumped to his feet, his eyes blazing. 'Stay out of this, Ma,' he warned her, angrily.

Ellen tried again to calm matters down. 'Please, Thomas – that's no way to talk to your mother.'

Tom rose to his feet, slipping his arm around his mother's shoulders. 'It's all right, Mum, I'm going. Don't want to cause any more trouble than I already have done.' He moved towards the hallway, not even attempting to say goodbye to his father.

Granma glared scornfully at Thomas. 'I suppose you're proud of yourself now, Mr Lily White,' she muttered scathingly, before hobbling after Tom.

She caught up with him just outside the door, clutching at his arm. 'Where you going to go?' she asked, concernedly.

Tom shrugged. 'I'll be all right. I got friends.'

Granma fished in her purse, drawing out two half-crowns and pressing them into his hand. 'Here, find yourself a room for the night and don't go wasting it on booze.'

Tom would have refused the money, but it was obvious that she wanted to make the gesture. 'Thanks, Gran,' he said, hugging her. 'And tell Clifford I'd like to see him, will you? Perhaps he could meet me tomorrow night after work, in the Who'd Ha Thought It.'

Granma nodded. 'I'll tell him,' she promised. A faint sparkle of mischief glowed in her eyes. Eager to send him off on a brighter note, she broke into an awkward little dance routine in the middle of the pavement.

'I am your honeysuckle . . .' she trilled out loud.

Tom grinned, despite himself. 'I am the bee,' he sang, responding to her lead. He began to dance away down the street, as though he didn't have a care in the world.

Granma's eyes followed him. 'Yeah, and you'd sting me for every last penny,' she muttered to herself, with a wry smile.

The tea room was quiet, with a scattering of couples and single women seated around the tables. Harry and Kaye were seated by the window. Both had fancy cakes on their plates; both were untouched.

'We just don't know what's going to happen,' Harry was saying. 'It's best you feel free.'

Kaye didn't understand. She looked at him with moist eyes, just short of the point of tears. 'Why?'

'Suppose you meet someone?' Harry asked.

Kaye gritted her teeth. 'I don't want to meet someone. I want you.'

Harry was silent, a sad, almost apologetic look on his face.

'What you're really saying is you don't want to carry on, isn't it?' Kaye asked, drawing her own conclusions. 'I'd sooner know.'

Harry sucked in a deep breath, swallowing it. 'Yeah,' he sighed miserably.

She could hold back the tears no longer, but Kaye would not cry in public. She pushed her chair back, jumping to her feet and heading, almost at a run, for the door.

Harry stared after her in abject misery. 'I do love you, Kaye,' he murmured, but she was already out of earshot, even if he had really wanted her to hear.

5

As the youngest son, Clifford Slater had grown up in the shadow of his three brothers yet had never felt really close to any of them except Tom. Frank had always been too much a carbon copy of his father, plodding, reliable – and dull. Harry had been some fun when he was a kid, but after the age of twelve always seemed to have his nose stuck in a book, or some school homework.

But Tom was different, exciting, always good for a laugh, or a prank – Tom who had given him his first cigarette at the age of nine, Tom who had bought him his first strictly illegal drink shortly before he went inside. To his father, Tom was a 'wrong 'un', a despicable criminal. To Clifford, he had always been Dick Turpin, Robin Hood and Raffles rolled into one. An adventurer, a pirate, a loveable rogue. A hero.

It was no different now. Clifford sat at a table in the Who'd Ha Thought It, sipping at a pint and drinking in his brother's every word about his grand plans to open up a garage.

'Sounds smashing, Tom,' he enthused. 'And you reckon you've got work already?'

Tom nodded over his shoulder towards the bar. 'Promised Reg I'd fix up his old lorry. Only trouble is, it needs welding, and I haven't got half the tools and equipment I need.' He leaned further over the table in conspiratorial fashion, lowering his voice to a murmur. 'So what I was thinking was maybe I could borrow 'em from the dockyard, just for a couple of weeks. They got more stuff than they could possibly miss, and Dad's got all the keys to the stores.'

Clifford stared at his brother, aghast. 'Blimey, Tom – you know Dad'd never agree to a scheme like that.'

A crafty grin spread across Tom's face. 'Maybe not – but

you could help me, couldn't yer? Get hold of the keys, make a re-cut. It'd be simple.'

Tom paused, studying his younger brother's face shrewdly. His voice took on a distinctly wheedling tone as he spoke again.

'I just need this one little break, Cliff. Wiv all the clapped-out vans being used for towing ambulances and such, it can't go wrong. I'd be serving me country and making me fortune at the same time.' He broke off again, piling on the pressure. 'Besides, this is my one big chance to make Dad see I'm all right, show him I can make something of meself. Just think how I felt last night, Cliff, being thrown out of the house like a piece of rubbish.'

The look in Clifford's eyes told Tom that the barb had struck home. He was almost convinced, but just a little scared.

'It's not as though we're talking about the Crown Jewels, Cliff,' Tom went on. 'Just a couple of gas cylinders and a few drills and suchlike. You could borrow Dad's bike, sneak the stuff off the docks in the sidecar.'

Clifford looked incredulous. 'Fat chance of that – you know how Dad loves that bike.'

Tom snorted derisively. 'Yeah, more than his bleedin' family, it seems to me.'

Clifford felt obliged to say something in his father's defence. 'That's not fair, Tom. Him and me might not always see eye to eye, but he's done his best.'

Tom let out a short, bitter laugh. 'What's fair, then? He won't let me in his house. He won't let me see me own mum or gran. And now he's even managing to turn you against me as well.'

Clifford looked hurt. 'I'm not against you, Tom. I'd never turn me back on you, you know that. I'm scared, that's all. What about the military police guarding the dock gates?'

Tom grinned reassuringly. 'Everyone on the docks knows

Dad,' he pointed out. 'Good old honest Thomas. Who's going to search his son, the bright young apprentice?'

Clifford chewed nervously at his bottom lip, on the verge of agreeing. 'Well, you might be right about that – but how do I get the bike in the first place?'

Tom grinned again. 'I've already thought of that.' He pulled a copy of the *Evening Standard* out of his pocket, spreading it out on the table and pointing to a short article on page three. 'There's a recruiting rally for the Red Cross in Maidstone termorrer evening. You could tell Dad you want to go, that you're thinking about volunteering. He'd go for something like that.'

The last card was on the table. Tom fixed his brother with a final, pleading look. 'Well, what do you reckon? Will you help me? Think of the times I helped you out of a scrape when you was a kid.'

An appeal like that didn't leave him much choice, Clifford thought – little realizing that he'd never had one anyway. His face grim and tight, he gave his brother a curt nod.

'All right, I'll do it – but don't ever ask me to lie for you again.'

Tom smiled with relief. Seated at the next table, so did Bernie Silver, who had been eavesdropping on the conversation with great interest.

Ellen Slater was in the kitchen rolling out pie dough as Clifford entered the house. He kissed her on the back of the neck and sat down to join Granma at the kitchen table, finishing off Tom's bottle of port.

'Evenin', Gran.'

She grinned at him knowingly. 'How's Tom?' she asked.

Clifford regarded her in amazement. 'How did you know?'

Granma tapped the side of her nose, giving out a wheezy laugh. 'Bleedin' Sherlock Holmes, me. And the smell of that boozer ain't changed in all these years.'

Ellen had overheard the conversation. 'Just don't tell your father,' she warned him over her shoulder.

His father's absence suddenly registered with Clifford. 'Where is he, by the way?' he wanted to know.

His mother nodded out of the kitchen window. 'He's out in the garden. Your brother Frank came round to help him put up the Anderson shelter.' She suddenly stopped what she was doing, turning round to face her son. 'He's a good man, Clifford. A fair man.'

'He's not fair to Tom,' Clifford muttered obstinately.

Ellen sighed. 'He's hurt, that's all.'

Clifford was unconvinced. 'And you think Tom isn't?'

There was no real answer to that. Ellen turned back to her work, folding the rolled-out dough over a meat and potato pie. Popping it in the oven, she stared out through the kitchen window into the backyard to where her husband was still working on the shelter. Yes, he was a good man, she reminded herself. Uncompromising, perhaps – and maybe he kept a shade too tight a check on his emotions – but a good man nevertheless.

A delighted whoop from Granma snapped her out of her thoughts. She turned to see Harry walking down the hallway towards the kitchen. He looked very serious, Ellen thought, and her heart sank. She wiped her hands on her apron and moved to greet him, fearing the worst.

'What is it, son? Received orders, have you?'

Harry forced a thin smile. 'Nothing like that, Mum. Not yet, anyway.'

'They've found out he's bloody useless and demobbed him,' Clifford put in, grinning.

It wasn't a bad joke, but Harry didn't laugh. 'Actually, you're the one I really came to see, Cliff. The thing is, I'll be needing a best man. I'm getting married.'

'Blimey.' Clifford was thunderstruck.

Ellen's own shock was swamped by her sense of relief. She hugged him, laughing. 'Well, that's a bit of nice news for a change.' Releasing Harry, she ran to the kitchen window and opened it, shouting out into the garden. 'Thomas, Frank – come in, quick. Harry's here and he's got some good news.'

Granma Slater had been unusually silent, trying to read Harry's face. 'You look like you'd be happier going to a funeral,' she observed, finally.

Ellen looked shocked. 'Gran – what a thing to say,' she scolded.

Granma shrugged. 'Well, if it's a celebration, we ought to be having a toast.' She picked up the port, checking its contents. 'Cliff, get us some more glasses.'

Thomas burst in through the kitchen door with Frank close on his heels. His normally dour face lit up at the sight of his favourite son.

'So what's this good news, then?'

Ellen took a glass from Clifford and allowed Granma to splash a few drops of port into it. She handed it to her husband, smiling. 'He's only come to tell us he's getting married,' she said proudly.

'Blimey, Harry – you always were a dark horse,' Frank Slater put in, joining the queue for a drink.

'Congratulations, son,' Thomas said. In a rare show of affection, he threw one arm around Harry's shoulder and hugged him.

Granma had climbed to her feet and was raising her own glass in the air. 'Ain't we forgetting someone here?' she pointed out. 'Here's a toast – to Kaye.'

Harry scanned the room, taking in all their faces. He looked awkward, even guilty. 'It's not Kaye,' he announced flatly. 'She's called Mary. Mary Hamilton.'

There was a stunned silence, which seemed to last forever.

6

Mary was waiting outside the barracks gates as Harry came out, flashing his pass at the two guards. She ran to greet him, wrapping her arms around his waist and smiling brightly.

'Everything okay?'

Harry nodded. 'Better than I expected. They gave me five days. "Passionate" leave, as my corporal insists on calling it.'

Mary giggled. 'Well, there's nothing wrong with that.' she rose on tiptoe to kiss him lingeringly on the lips.

Harry pushed her away, gently. 'Not here, people are looking,' he muttered, obviously embarrassed. 'Anyway, I suppose we'd better get going, get it over with.'

Mary cast him a slightly reproving glance. 'You make it sound like an ordeal of some kind.'

Harry grinned ruefully. 'I do feel a bit like I'm being sent to the front line, meeting your family for the first time.'

Mary clutched at his arm, squeezing it and flashing him a reassuring smile. 'Nonsense. You'll love them. Mummy's sweet, even if she does fuss a bit, and Daddy's an absolute darling.'

Harry took this information at face value. Taking her hand, he began to walk down the street. 'So, how did they take the news?'

The faintest frown crossed Mary's face. 'I'm afraid they've gone rather overboard. Mother's determined it's to be in the local church.'

Harry stopped dead in his tracks, glaring at her. 'And you agreed?' he demanded. Her silence was all the answer he needed. He let out an exasperated sigh. 'Bloody hell, whose wedding is this?'

Mary looked up at him pleadingly. 'Please, Harry – don't be angry. I just wanted to make things easy.'

She looked like a little hurt schoolgirl, Harry thought, relenting. He squeezed her hand, starting to walk again. 'Come on, then. I want to show you the ring I've chosen. It's in a little jeweller's shop just down the road from here.'

'Well, do you like it?' Harry asked.

Mary nodded happily, beaming down at the plain golden ring adorning her finger. 'It's lovely.' She giggled nervously. 'But it's bad luck to keep it on. You'll have to take care of it.' She tried to pull the ring off again, but it refused to move. She half turned towards the shop window, seeking better light to see where it was sticking.

'Here, let me help you,' Harry offered. He took her hand, starting to ease the ring off her finger and suddenly froze as he saw a familiar face gaping at him in shocked disbelief through the jeweller's window.

In a matter of a few seconds, Kaye's world had fallen apart. One moment she had just been strolling down the street, idly window-shopping – and the next she had seen the man she loved apparently in the act of slipping a wedding ring on a strange young woman's finger.

Harry had never seen such hurt on a person's face before, and it shocked him to the core. Guilt, shame and the most bitter sorrow crowded in on him, numbing all other feeling. Dropping Mary's hand, he stared hopelessly through the glass, transfixed by Kaye's ashen face as her tears began to flow.

'What's the matter, Harry? What's wrong?' Mary begged, alarmed by the horrified, haunted look in his eyes.

Receiving no answer, she turned slowly towards the window, following his gaze. The two women confronted each other for several seconds, then Kaye turned away from the window and broke into a run down the street, not even knowing, or caring, where she was going.

There was confusion, doubt, even fear on Mary's face as she turned back to Harry. 'Who was that?' she asked, in a strained little voice.

Harry drew in a long, slow, deep breath, fighting to compose himself. 'Someone I used to know,' he managed to grate out, finally.

It was not really an answer, but Mary let it go, afraid to pursue it any further. She tried to brighten, as Harry slowly recovered himself. 'Well, I didn't think you'd been a monk before I met you,' she told him, slipping her arm through his.

Knowing her doubts, but grateful for her outward appearance of control, Harry forced a smile. 'Come on, then, we've got a train to catch,' he muttered. 'Can't keep your parents waiting.'

It was not quite peace, not quite a truce, between them. Merely a pretence that nothing had ever happened, even though they both knew this to be untrue. The shadow of Kaye had entered their lives like a ghost, and would not be easily exorcized.

Harry was somewhat overwhelmed by his first sight of the Hamilton family seat. He gazed at Albourne House, the grounds and the expensive-looking Talbot open tourer parked in the gravel driveway, in awe.

'Blimey. Talk about the stately homes of England,' he breathed. 'You might have warned me.'

Mary looked slightly embarrassed. 'It's just a house.'

Harry nodded towards the tennis court, where her brother William and their cousin Rose were playing. 'You could fit my house into one end of that court,' he observed, rather pointedly. 'And the car's a bit flash, too.'

Mary giggled, even though she was less than happy to see the Talbot.

'Yes, it is, isn't it? But Auntie Dorothea thinks it looks nice parked outside the house in Belgravia. Mummy's younger sister. Looks like she's come down to stay for the wedding, worse luck.'

'Skeleton in the family cupboard?' Harry asked, reading between the lines.

Mary giggled again. 'Sort of. Dorothea's the most ghastly snob and Edward, her husband, is a bit right-wing. He's a friend of Oswald Mosley. I think he even met Hitler once.'

Harry looked shocked. 'You mean he's a Fascist?'

Mary frowned. 'We tend to avoid that word, if we can. Just try not to get involved in any political discussions with him, will you? If he says anything outrageous, just humour him.'

Harry glared at her, his eyes flashing a warning. 'I say what I believe, Mary – and I'll not make polite small talk with anyone, just for the sake of it.'

An invisible barrier had sprung up between them. Mary tried to smooth it away. 'Of course, Harry – and I wouldn't want it any other way. Just try not to let either of them upset you, that's all.'

Only slightly mollified, Harry couldn't resist a sarcastic jibe. 'Any other little do's and don'ts as far as your family is concerned?'

Mary saw a chance to end the conversation on a lighter note, and took it. 'Just keep your eyes off my cousin Rose,' she told him, smiling. 'She's only eighteen, but she's infuriat-ingly gorgeous and a real man-eater.'

Harry glanced over towards the couple on the tennis court again, confirming this assessment. 'Boyfriend?'

Mary laughed. 'No, but I think he dreams about it. That's my brother, William.' She took Harry's hand again. 'Come on. I can't wait to introduce you to everyone.'

She led him towards the front of the house, as a small long-haired Pomeranian launched itself out of the front door and scurried towards them, yapping furiously. It was closely followed by the most glamorous and elegant woman Harry had ever seen.

'That's Auntie Dotty now,' Mary hissed in warning. 'Prepare yourself for the onslaught.'

Dorothea Grant caught up with her precious lapdog and bent down, scooping it up into her arms. Straightening up, she seemed to notice the two figures walking up the drive for the first time. Her face congealed into a smile of rapturous welcome, as false as her new eyelashes.

'Mary, darling – what thrilling news,' she gushed. Stepping forward, she bobbed her head either side of Mary's cheeks like a pecking bird, making loud and exaggerated kissing sounds.

Stepping back, Dorothea ran her eyes up and down Harry like a butcher appraising a fresh carcass. 'And this must be your dashing young soldier. Harry, isn't it?'

Harry nodded, starting to offer his hand, then pulling it back rather awkwardly and self-consciously when it became apparent that Dorothea was far too busy cuddling her dog.

'I just had to bring Napoleon,' she announced, as if by way of explanation. 'It's an absolute massacre in London. Everyone's putting them to sleep.'

Introductions appeared to be over as far as Dorothea was concerned, Harry realized. Turning her back on them, she began to walk back towards the house, issuing orders like a drill sergeant. 'Well, come along, the pair of you. We're all waiting to have dinner just as soon as your father gets back from some silly ARP meeting.'

Evelyn, Harry, Dorothea, Rose, William, Mary and Edward sat around the large oblong dining-table in that order, an empty place setting for Arthur left at the head. Mrs Dovey busied herself laying out plates of shepherd's pie and tureens of steaming vegetables.

Rose fixed Harry with a pair of large, blue cow-like eyes. 'I think men look so handsome in a uniform,' she informed him. 'So, when did you join the Terriers?'

Harry fidgeted awkwardly in his chair. 'About a year ago.'

'I'm planning to join the Female Auxiliary Nursing Yeomanry,' Rose announced proudly. 'I'm going to be driving ambulances.'

This idea was not approved of by Dorothea, as she made patently obvious. 'Let's hope that won't be necessary,' she murmured, with a slightly pained expression on her face.

Edward Grant frowned at his daughter, conveying his own disapproval. He was a much older man than Harry had imagined, well into his sixties and at least twenty years older than his wife. 'It won't if the Government see sense,' he put in.

Mrs Dovey scowled at him. It was obvious that she had little time for the Grant family. 'It's Hitler who's meant to see sense,' she muttered darkly.

Edward ignored her, turning his attention to Harry. 'So, what made you join up? A wave of patriotism?' he asked, managing to inject the faintest note of mockery into his tone.

Harry faced him squarely. 'The Government was allowing Hitler to do as he pleased. It seemed the only stand I could make.'

Dorothea flashed her husband a warning glance across the table. She smiled at Harry. 'How did you meet Mary?' she inquired.

'We were both at a demonstration against British recognition of Franco. She got a bit too close to a mounted policeman and I pulled her back.'

Edward had ignored his wife's warning. 'So you think we should let the Bolshies just overrun Europe, do you?' he demanded aggressively.

Evelyn attempted to defuse the situation, snatching up a tureen of carrots and thrusting them under Edward's nose. 'Carrots, Edward?'

Someone more trained in social niceties would have recognized Evelyn's ploy and seized upon it gratefully. Harry did not.

'If we hadn't given the Fascists in Europe so much encouragement, I don't think we'd be facing a war now,' he said forcefully.

Evelyn, Dorothea and Rose were all glaring at Edward now, but he was on his favourite hobby-horse. 'So you wouldn't support trying to pursue peace with Germany?' he demanded. His mouth curled in a faint sneer. 'It's just a concept to you, isn't it? I was a surgeon at the Somme. Nothing justifies those deaths and mutilations – nothing!'

The women's eyes switched to Harry, but he was equally caught up in the heat of argument.

'I don't *want* war, killing and dying. Too many of my friends lost their fathers. But this is about the spread of nationalism, and what's happening to the Jews and minorities inside Germany and it has to be stamped out.'

Finally tired of subtle warnings, Evelyn took direct action. 'Harry was at London University,' she announced suddenly, cutting through the conversation.

Dorothea picked up her lead adroitly. 'Oh, really,' she breathed, as though it was the most fascinating piece of news she had heard all year. She beamed at Harry. 'That's supposed to be rather good, isn't it? What did you study?'

Harry had been shut up, and he knew it. He felt awkward, a social outcast. 'Physics,' he mumbled, looking down at his plate.

'Ah.' Dorothea was a bit thrown for a moment, confronted with something she knew absolutely nothing about. 'Evelyn tells me your father is in some sort of shipbuilding,' she said finally, abruptly changing the subject.

Harry looked up at her, his face clouded with confusion. 'My father is a storehouse-man at the Chatham dockyard,' he informed her flatly.

There was a long and pained silence, finally broken by the sound of the front door opening.

Evelyn breathed an audible sigh of relief. 'Oh, good. That will be Arthur. Now we can start dinner.'

Harry rose to his feet as Arthur Hamilton entered the

dining room, smiling apologetically at the assembled gathering. Evelyn effected the introductions. 'Arthur, darling, this is Mary's fiancé, Harry Slater.'

Harry stepped forward, extending his hand politely. Arthur took it, shaking it warmly. 'Hello, Harry. Sorry not to be here when you arrived.' He paused, tapping the ARP armband on his sleeve with a slightly self-deprecating smile. 'Matters of state, you know? Anyway, I'm delighted to meet you.'

Mary's father, at least, appeared genuinely friendly, Harry thought. He warmed to the man immediately. He sat down again, feeling more at ease as Arthur moved round to the head of the table and took his place. 'How much leave did they give you in the end?' he asked, as Mrs Dovey served his dinner.

'Five days,' Harry told him.

Arthur smiled knowingly. 'Oh, good. Barney Gibbs must have done his stuff, then.'

Harry didn't understand. 'I beg your pardon, sir?'

'Brigadier Gibbs – an old chum of mine,' Arthur said by way of explanation. 'Asked him to pull a few strings with your CO.'

Harry cast a baleful stare in Mary's direction, but she had already averted her eyes. He returned his attention to his plate as everyone started eating.

With the head of the household in place, Edward was more subdued, and the meal progressed with no more than harmless conversation and social chitchat. Nevertheless, Harry was greatly relieved when Mrs Dovey finally came to clear away the dishes and he was free to retire into the garden with Mary.

In silence, they strolled across the lawn, past the old treehouse to a small duckpond at the bottom of the garden and well clear of the house.

Finally, Harry stopped, a sullen expression on his face. 'Sorry if I embarrassed your mother, but I never learned the art of small talk.' It was more a complaint than an apology.

Mary regarded him with surprise, unable to understand why he was so upset. 'Don't be beastly,' she chided. 'She was only trying to help.'

The defence only seemed to incense Harry even more. 'Oh, yes – they're good at that, your family,' he went on, bitterly. 'Arranging our wedding, pulling a few strings with my CO – even moving my father a few rungs up the social ladder. Some sort of shipbuilding . . . Barney Gibbs . . . who do they bloody think they are?'

Mary looked hurt. 'They were only trying to be nice.'

Harry refused to be pacified. 'And that makes it all right, does it?' he demanded petulantly.

He seemed to be deliberately looking for trouble, Mary thought. Taking it personally, a flash of anger surged through her. 'They're not me, I'm not them,' she blazed defiantly.

Doubt simmered in Harry's eyes. 'Aren't you?' he asked, accusingly. 'You are when you're here. I thought we at least had things in common.'

The wall was up between them again, seeming thicker and higher than before. Perhaps even too high to even try to climb, Mary thought, all the fight suddenly knocked out of her.

'If you're looking for a way out, just tell me,' she sighed, miserably. 'We can still call it off.'

For a fraction of a second, Harry looked almost relieved. Then his face clouded over again. He shook his head, wearily. 'No,' he muttered, flatly. 'It's too late for that.'

They faced each other silently for a long time, each looking equally lost and hopeless as though at the mercy of something they neither understood nor controlled.

Finally, Harry's eyes softened. An almost tender smile played at the corners of his lips. 'Oh, Mary love,' he murmured, spreading his hands in the air.

Fighting to control a sob, Mary threw herself into his arms. It was going to be all right, she told herself. Everything was going to be all right.

7

As ever, Kaye had turned to her Aunt Ivy in times of trouble, knowing that she would receive more sympathy than from her own mother. She sat in the kitchen of Nineteen Nelson Street, her eyes red and puffy from hours of crying. A little more in control of herself now, she virtually chain-smoked from a packet of Player's Weights left open and ready on the kitchen table.

Ivy Collins had been dismayed by the news, but not really surprised. Years of experience had convinced her that men were a pretty worthless species. They were either after one thing and then off, or they were like her husband Reg, more interested in his marigold, rather than his marital, bed.

Nevertheless, she clucked sympathetically as Kaye recounted the confrontation at the jeweller's shop.

'After all them years courting? Just out of the blue?'

Kaye nodded miserably. 'I was with him only a couple of days ago. He seemed a bit distant, but he didn't say a word. I thought he was just worrying about being called up.' She stubbed out her cigarette, drew out and lit another. 'Perhaps I kidded myself. We never actually talked about marrying, but I sort of took it for granted.'

Ivy sighed, finishing off the heel of a much-darned silk stocking on an electro-magnetic Vitos machine. 'Have you told yer mum yet?'

Kaye shook her head. 'She'll only blame it on me for joining the WAAF, and perhaps she's right. But I always thought he wanted a girl wiv a bit of go about her.' She paused, eyeing her aunt suspiciously, finding it difficult to trust anybody any more. 'I thought maybe Ellen might have said something to you, given you a hint at least?'

Ivy shook her head firmly in denial. 'Not a bloody word. And I always thought we were really close.' This thought seemed to suddenly strike her personally, breeding anger and resentment.

Eyes blazing, she climbed slowly to her feet, her shiny cold-creamed face setting into a mask of grim determination.

'Right, that's it,' she muttered heavily. 'I'll just put me face on, then I'm going next door to have it out wiv 'em.'

Kaye clutched at her hand, restraining her. 'No, Auntie – please! It doesn't matter.' She put on a brave, defiant smile, qualifying this last statement. 'Leastways, I'm not having them think it does.'

The Slaters' kitchen looked more like a Chinese laundry, with washed and starched white shirts and freshly pressed clothes hanging everywhere. Granma sat at the table, reading a copy of the *Daily Mirror* with the aid of a magnifying glass as Ellen walked in, wearing her new wedding outfit.

'Well, what do you think?'

Granma did not look up from the paper. 'I think everybody's getting their knickers in a twist for no reason,' she observed. 'Cassandra's quite convinced there'll be no war.'

Ellen clucked her teeth with nervous impatience. 'I mean my new outfit. Do you think I look silly in it?'

Granma lowered the paper, running a rheumy eye over Ellen's two-piece. 'Oh, very posh,' she muttered, with just the faintest hint of sarcasm. 'I just don't know what you're all getting so worked up about.'

Ellen sighed. 'Yes, I'd sooner it was Kaye too, Gran. But it's no use crying over spilt milk. It's Harry's life, after all.'

Granma merely grunted, conveying her disapproval. Relenting, she forced a thin smile. 'Yes, you look very nice.'

Ellen looked relieved. 'I wanted to show Thomas. Is he in the garden?'

Granma nodded. 'Frank's helping him and Cliff finish off the shelter. Another waste of time, if you ask me.' She climbed to her feet, following Ellen as she hurried out to show off her new clothes.

The shelter was virtually finished. Frank shovelled the last of the excavated earth over its domed top, banging it down hard.

Thomas stood back, taking his breath. 'Thanks for your help, Frank. Couldn't have done it all on me own.'

Frank shrugged. 'Glad of something to do, Dad. There's not much call for building work lately, when everyone thinks they're about to be bombed out.'

'When's the family leaving for Ramsgate?' Clifford wanted to know.

Frank frowned. 'I'll take the kids after the wedding, but Phyllis is going down early to help with the evacuation.'

It was obviously a sore point, Clifford realized. It was no secret that his brother's marriage had been shaky for years, and additional strain wasn't going to help. He dropped the subject abruptly, letting out a low whistle of appreciation as he caught sight of his mother dressed up.

'Don't be vulgar,' she chided him, but grinning with secret pleasure.

Frank paused in his work, leaning on his shovel. 'You look smashin', Mum,' he told her.

'Which is more than can be said for that godforsaken hole in the ground,' Granma Slater muttered in the background. She stepped forward, peering dubiously down into the shelter entrance. 'If Mr Anderson thinks I'm going to get out of me nice warm bed and crawl down there in the middle of the night, he's got another think coming.'

Frank laughed. 'You might change your mind when the bombs start dropping, Gran.'

Granma shook her head emphatically. 'Not on your nelly,' she vowed. 'I'd rather catch me death from a bomb than from pneumonia.'

Thomas was finding it hard to get a word in edgeways. He was about to compliment his wife on her appearance when

Ivy's head suddenly bobbed up over the garden fence. Grim-faced, her voice was cold as ice.

'I thought we was friends,' she spat at Ellen venomously. 'You might at least've bleeding told us. That little rat of a son of yours didn't even have the guts to tell our Kaye the truth.'

With both his wife and his son under attack, Thomas whirled on the woman angrily. 'You've no call to speak of our Harry like that. Your niece might have set her cap at him, but he never made her any promises.'

Ivy turned splenetically on him, her face contemptuous. 'The sun may shine out of Harry's bleedin' arse as far as you're concerned, Thomas Slater – but as far as I'm concerned he can rot in hell.'

Having said her piece, she stormed off back into the house, leaving everyone stunned.

Finally, Clifford let out a rather nervous little laugh. 'Well, let's all hope that this Mary Hamilton's not like her,' he joked.

It did nothing to dispel the tension. Thomas threw his shovel angrily to the ground. 'Bugger Ivy,' he muttered bitterly, knowing in his heart of hearts that she was right.

It was left to Ellen to pick up the pieces. 'Come on, let's all go back in the house and have a nice cup of tea,' she suggested, with what little enthusiasm she could muster.

8

Dorothea looked on with great amusement as Frank's battered old building lorry ground to a halt just beyond the church lych-gate, bearing the Slater family to the wedding.

She glanced aside at her daughter, rolling her eyes in mock horror. 'Really, you'd have thought they could at least have hired or borrowed a car.'

Rose said nothing, watching Frank as he jumped out of the cab to let down the lorry's tailgate. Clifford and Frank's two sons, Geoffrey and Billie, jumped down and helped Granma alight. Returning to the cab, Frank let Ellen out of the passenger side.

'That must be his mother,' Rose observed.

Dorothea giggled maliciously. 'Then why is she dressed like a bus conductress?' She turned away and began to walk toward the church, unaware that Granma had overheard her last remark and was glaring at her balefully.

Ellen looked round anxiously. 'I can't see any sign of Thomas's motorbike,' she said, in a worried voice.

Clifford wrapped a reassuring arm around her shoulder. 'Relax, Mum,' he told her confidently. 'He's coming straight from work. It's only the best man gets to take the whole day off for a wedding.' He gave Ellen a quick peck on the cheek. 'And speaking of that, I'd better go and find Harry.'

He shot off as Frank ushered the group towards the church entrance, Granma taking the opportunity to pause and take a large nip of brandy from a hip-flask. Smacking her lips with appreciation, she tucked it back into her bloomers and followed the family into the church.

Harry was seated on a tombstone in the side church-yard,

his head in his hands. He looked like a man with all the woes of the world on his shoulders, Clifford thought, and said so.

'Blimey, Harry, you look awful,' he said, grinning. 'Night out with the boys you didn't tell me about?'

The joke failed to lift Harry's spirits. More serious now, Clifford nodded his head knowingly. 'Last-minute doubts, is it?' he inquired, sympathetically.

Harry let out a long, deep sigh. 'It's more than that, Cliff. I don't want to go through with this.'

Clifford stared at his brother in shocked incredulity. 'Blimey. *Now* you tell us.'

Harry pushed himself to his feet, turning his back on the church. He began to walk slowly towards the end of the church-yard with Clifford on his heels.

'You know all that "for better, for worse" stuff? Well I just don't feel like that. I just got carried away, thought I was in love. But she's not the one, Cliff – it's Kaye. We grew up together. She's part of me, somehow.'

Clifford glanced nervously over his shoulder towards the church. More and more guests were pouring in now, and the vicar was standing out on the front step, looking around anxiously for signs of the bride or groom. The Talbot, festooned with white ribbons, was just turning into the church drive, bearing Mary and her father.

Clifford grasped Harry's shoulder, pulling him round. 'They're here, Harry,' he muttered, the faintest note of panic creeping into his voice. 'You're going to have to make your mind up pretty damned quick.'

Harry watched the Talbot roll slowly up the drive. Even from a distance, Mary looked gorgeous. 'I keep telling myself that Mary's more interesting, more clever, more fun,' he murmured, more to himself than for Clifford's ears. 'But I just can't keep Kaye out of my mind.'

Clifford shook his head in exasperation. 'I always knew you was crackers, but not that bleedin' crackers,' he muttered heavily. 'Then why, for God's sake?'

Harry stared down at his boots. 'Mary's pregnant,' he announced in a quiet voice, finally releasing the secret which had burdened him for nearly two months.

The bombshell took a few moments to sink in. Clifford gazed over towards the Talbot as Mary and her father climbed out and stood awkwardly in front of the church door. Finally, he turned back to his brother.

'Well, it seems to me you've got three choices,' he said flatly. 'You can go over the wall, you can go and tell her how you feel – or you can walk into that church and no one'll ever know better.'

Harry nodded. 'Yeah,' he muttered miserably. He fished in the top pocket of his tunic, drawing out the wedding ring. 'Here, you'll need this,' he said, handing it to Clifford. Pulling himself up stiffly, he began to walk towards the church.

Inside the church, Ellen was becoming increasingly agitated. She cast yet another anxious glance back up the aisle towards the door. 'I wonder what can be keeping Thomas,' she whispered nervously to Granma.

'Relax, ducks. He probably had some trouble starting the bike.' Granma took another nip from her flask, which did not go unnoticed by Dorothea and Edward, sitting opposite. She took a quick look back up the aisle herself. 'Gawd's-trewth,' she blurted out, the expletive rolling round the hushed church like a minor thunderclap.

There was a creaking of wooden pews as all eyes suddenly turned towards the door. Tom entered the church with a grand flourish, looking resplendent in hired morning suit and carrying a top hat. His short prison haircut was flattened and plastered to his head with a liberal application of Brylcreem. He seated himself in an empty pew, flashing Granma a wink and receiving a salutatory wave of the hip-flask in return.

The congregation settled down again, as the vicar began intoning the familiar words of the wedding ceremony. Out-

side, the sound of a motor cycle announced Thomas's be-
lated arrival.

The drawing-room at Albourne House had been turned into
a bar and buffet, with the French windows opening out on to
a large marquee which had been erected in the garden.

Granma, with Tom on her arm, was already ensconced at
the bar, making the most of the freely flowing champagne.
Tom topped up her glass for the third time, glancing nervously round for any sign of his father.

'Don't worry, he won't cause a scene here,' Granma reassured him, reading his thoughts. 'Anyway, last I saw of him
he was going on at Clifford about something. Don't know
what it was, but it looked rather serious.'

'Well, you know Dad – he's always serious,' Tom muttered
jokingly, but a deeply worried frown had temporarily creased
his brow.

Granma missed it, having noticed Dorothea flitting nearby
and doing her social butterfly bit. Taking the opportunity to
wind the woman up, Granma added a few drops of brandy
to her champagne and raised her glass in toast, grinning fa-
miliarly. 'Bottoms up, ducks. Here's to our Harry.'

Dorothea blanched visibly, turning away with a shudder.
'What a ghastly old woman,' she complained to the nearest
guest. 'Did you see her knocking it back all through the ceremony?' Confident that Granma had overhead, she swept off
triumphant, nearly colliding with Clifford, who had come
hurrying in from the garden looking shocked and frightened.

'What's up, love? You look like you've seen a ghost,'
Granma said, but Clifford ignored her. He stared at Tom, his
eyes cold and accusing. 'Tom, I gotta talk to you – now,' he
hissed, urgently.

Tom glanced about nervously, worried that Clifford was
about to blurt out what was on his mind right there and
then. Grim-faced, he grasped his brother by the arm and
began to propel him towards the French windows. 'For God's

43

sake calm down, Cliff,' he urged. 'We'll talk about it quietly, in the garden.'

Reaching the lawn, he led Clifford round the side of the marquee, well out of earshot of the other guests.

'Now, what's this about?' he asked, forcing a smile.

Clifford glared at him, fear and anger fighting for control of his face. 'You bloody know, don't yer?' he accused. 'You know bloody well.'

Tom feigned innocence. 'I haven't got the faintest idea what you're going on about.'

'Dad told me about the burglary,' Clifford blurted out. 'Three hundred pounds taken from a safe, and a night watchman left injured.' He fell silent, studying Tom's face for a sign of guilt.

There was none. His brother continued to look as innocent as a newborn babe. 'Burglary?' he queried. 'I don't know nothing about no burglary, Cliff.'

'Then how come the police found tools from the dockyard left at the scene of the crime?' Clifford blazed. 'The tools that I took for you?'

Tom's eyes narrowed. There didn't seem much point in keeping up pretences any more. 'All right, I lent them to my mate Bernie,' he admitted. 'But I had no idea . . .'

Clifford cut him short, a look of betrayal on his face. 'I took them to help you,' he said bitterly. 'You said you wanted them for repairing cars. Now you've got me involved in a robbery. I'll lose my apprenticeship, probably go to prison.'

Tom shook his head. 'Not if you're innocent.'

Anger finally won the battle for Clifford's emotions. His voice rose, taking on an edge of desperation. 'But I'm not bloody innocent, am I? I took those tools.'

'Shush,' Tom hissed, fear beginning to show on his face. 'Don't tell the whole bloody wedding.' He paused, calming himself, finally grasping his youngest brother by the shoulders in a gesture of reassurance. 'Look, I'll sort it out, all right? It'll be okay.'

Clifford pulled free with a shrug of revulsion. He stepped back, staring open-eyed at his brother as though he had never really seen him before. The idol had suddenly turned out to have feet of clay, after all.

'Dad was right all along,' he muttered, hurt and sadness in his voice. 'He said you'd always let people down. I just didn't think you'd do it to me.'

He turned his back on his brother with a gesture which smacked of finality and began to walk back towards the bar. Suddenly, Clifford felt an overpowering need to get good and stinking drunk.

9

Tom jumped with alarm at the sound of footsteps entering the Hamiltons' dining-room. Quickly replacing the silver cigar box he had been handling on the mantelshelf, he turned towards the door, trying to disguise the look of guilt on his face.

It was a matter of only minor relief to see his father, who was regarding him with undisguised disgust. 'Come to pinch the family silver, have you?' Thomas muttered accusingly.

Tom stiffened in defence. 'I came to my brother's wedding, that's all.'

Thomas ground his teeth, fighting to control the bitter rage seething within him. 'And I nearly missed it altogether. I spent half the morning being questioned by a detective, feeling like a bloody criminal.'

Tom's eyes flickered nervously. 'I don't know what you're talking about.'

'Don't you?' Thomas spat out, disbelieving. 'Dockyard tools at the scene of a burglary? Tools from my stores?' He paused, shaking his head with impotent rage. 'God damn you. I didn't think even you could sink that low as to involve your own brother. Clifford's just a lad. He had a good job, a whole future in front of him.'

Tom opened his mouth to speak, but his father cut him short. 'No, don't say a bloody word. I don't want to hear any more of your lies. Just do me one favour, will you?'

Tom nodded. 'Of course, anything.'

Thomas's voice dropped to little more than a menacing whisper. 'Just leave – now,' he hissed venomously. 'Before I try to kill yer.'

*

Rocking noticeably on her feet, Granma stared over towards Clifford, who was standing alone and dejected by the French windows, staring blankly out into the garden. Dorothea brushed by on her way to the marquee, still loudly airing her views on the entire Slater family. 'I'm sure they're the salt of the earth and all that sort of thing, but they all reek of mothballs and hair oil.'

With the best part of two bottles of champagne inside her, Granma was sorely tempted to give the woman a mouthful, but her concern for Clifford overcame her anger. Staggering over to him, she nudged him gently in the ribs.

'Come on, wipe that long face off,' she told him, grinning tipsily. 'You'll spoil our Harry's day.'

Clifford let out a short, cynical laugh. 'He's already done that for himself.'

Granma's eyes narrowed suspiciously, her face becoming serious. 'What you talking about? What's going on I don't know about?'

Clifford regarded her moodily. 'I thought he was going to do a runner. Jilt her right there outside the church.'

Granma dismissed this information with a careless shrug. 'Well – nerves, you know.'

Clifford shook his head. 'No. He didn't want to get married. He still loves Kaye. But he's got this Mary girl up the spout, ain't he?'

Granma was completely stunned for a moment. She swayed noticeably – only partly from shock. 'Blimey!' she said finally, draining her drink at a gulp and staring at the empty glass for several seconds. 'Bloody miserable drink, champagne. It's all wind,' she observed at last. 'Reckon I need something a little bit stronger.'

She glanced out into the open marquee on the lawn, her eyes lighting on a decanter of brandy on one of the trestle tables. Frank's son Geoffrey stood nearby, helping himself to pieces of fruit cake. Granma called him over. 'Here, be a love and fetch that bottle of brandy over, will you?'

'Sure.' Geoffrey nodded, darting across to snatch the decanter off the table.

Edward's hand descended heavily on his wrist, restraining him. 'I really don't think you should be helping yourself to that,' he muttered, somewhat haughtily.

Geoffrey looked hurt at the implied rebuke. 'It's not for me, it's for me great-gran.'

Dorothea couldn't resist throwing in her two-penn'orth. 'Well, I should say your great-grandmother has had enough,' she observed cattily.

It was the straw that broke the camel's back for Granma. Her eyes flashing fire, she started to lurch towards the crowded marquee.

Evelyn, anticipating trouble, tried to pour oil on troubled waters, but it was too late. 'Really, Dorothea, she is our guest –' she started to murmur soothingly, but was cut short by Granma's strident indignation.

'Grudge us your bleedin' booze, do yer?' she demanded angrily. 'Too good for the likes of us, is it?'

Evelyn looked panicky, uncomfortably aware that every eye in the marquee was now turned towards the unpleasant little scene. 'Really, Mrs Slater – I think you have misunderstood what my sister was trying to say,' she muttered weakly.

Granma sneered at her. 'No, I ain't. I've heard her – all of yer – laughing behind our backs. Think yourselves all so much better than us, don't yer? Well, our Harry's worth ten of any of you. Which of your young men's going off to fight for his country? What of your family's got a First Class at the university? All you've got is yer money and yer high opinion of yourselves.'

Arthur rushed to defend the family honour. 'Please, Mrs Slater – we're proud to welcome Harry into the family.'

Granma cackled derisively. 'You can't kid me. You think your daughter's too good for our Harry. Well, I'll tell you something. He don't want her. He's got another nice girl, a decent girl. But because he's a gent, and because your daughter didn't have the nouse to keep her knickers on, he's lumbered wiv her for the rest of his life.'

A dropped pin would have sounded like a thunderclap as Granma finished her little speech. Turning her back on the hushed marquee, she tottered outside again, grabbing Geoffrey by the arm. 'Go and find yer dad, there's a good boy. I want to go home.'

It should have been Granma's finest hour, her grand exit to bring the house down, but it was not to be, for the day's fireworks were not yet over. Granma was hopelessly upstaged as a black Wolseley police car suddenly turned in through the gates, raced up the drive and pulled to a stop with a screech of gravel.

Detective Sergeant Howard jumped out, accompanied by two uniformed bobbies. He glanced around urgently, quickly locating Thomas and striding towards him, flashing his warrant card.

'Mr Slater,' he muttered, with a faint nod of recognition. 'I'm looking for my old chum, Thomas junior.'

Thomas hung his head in shame, confronted by the police for the second time that day. 'He's gone.'

Howard's face registered doubt. 'I'll just check that for myself, if you don't mind.' Pushing Thomas brusquely aside, he began to walk towards the marquee, flanked by the two bobbies.

Harry, seeing his father accosted by the police, had already jumped to his feet and was running out of the marquee. He glanced quickly at Clifford, who was still standing by the French windows, looking tense and nervous. 'Cliff? What's going on?'

His younger brother ignored him, his eyes transfixed by the sight of the three policemen apparently heading directly towards him. His sense of threat and panic rose to a peak, triggering off an ancient and inherited response. Automatically, the rational part of his brain shut down as his body galvanized itself for flight. He broke into a run, trying to skirt round the approaching policemen and make a dash across the lawn.

The nearest bobby was almost caught on the hop, but not quite. With commendable speed, he threw himself sideways, catching Clifford in a flying body tackle. The two men crashed to the ground together, Clifford struggling furiously and the constable raining blows upon his head in an effort to subdue him.

'You've got no right to do that.' Harry ran to his brother's assistance, trying to pull the policeman away. The second bobby joined the fray, grabbing Harry by the arm.

It was a reflex action, honed by months of combat training. Feeling himself under attack, Harry whirled in self-protection, Queensbury rules going by the board. He kicked the policeman in the groin, making him fall back with a scream of agony and a string of curses.

'Harry – no! Please, stop it.'

Harry turned at the sound of Mary's scream, seeing her struggling in her father's arms as he tried to restrain her. Thoughts of the baby – his baby – in her belly flashed through his mind.

Detective Sergeant Howard saw his chance and took it. He ran forward, slamming Harry heavily back against the side of the police car and driving a pile-driver blow into his solar plexus. Harry sagged, and began to slide down the car. Howard finished him with a rabbit-punch to the side of the neck and turned back to his two policemen. 'Cuff 'em both,' he snapped, wrenching open the rear door of the Wolseley.

Mary had stopped struggling now, numbed with shock. She turned in her father's arms, looking up at him with confused, frightened eyes. 'Make them stop, Daddy,' she pleaded like a little girl. 'They can't arrest him – not on our wedding day.'

There was nothing Arthur could say or do. As stunned and

helpless as his daughter, he could only watch as Harry and Clifford were bundled into the back of the police car and driven away.

10

The marquee had already been dismantled and taken away by the wedding contractors. Dovey busied himself folding up the last of the trestle tables and storing them away in the barn. William and Rose played a half-hearted game of tennis. The rest of the Hamilton family, supplemented by Edward and Dorothea, sat clustered round the radio in the drawing-room of Albourne House, waiting for the Prime Minister's promised broadcast to the nation. It was exactly 11.15 a.m., Sunday 3 September.

Precisely on cue, Neville Chamberlain came on air, his voice subdued and sombre.

'This morning the British Ambassador in Berlin handed the German Government a final note stating that, unless we heard from them by eleven o'clock that they were prepared at once to withdraw their troops from Poland, a state of war would exist between us.'

Arthur reached out to take Evelyn's hand as Chamberlain paused, briefly. Mary and Dorothea exchanged a quick, nervous glance. Edward, oddly detached and aloof from the rest of the family, merely stared at the wireless, a thin and almost sneering smile on his lips as the Prime Minister continued.

'I have to tell you that no such undertaking has been received and that consequently this country is at war with Germany.'

Chamberlain's voice droned on, but no one was really listening any more. Edward stood up slowly, fumbling in his jacket pocket. 'The fools,' he spat out contemptuously. He turned to his wife. 'Will you give me a cigarette, Dorothea? I seem to have mislaid my cigarette case.'

Evelyn jumped to her feet, glad of something to do. 'Here, Edward – have one of ours,' she offered, taking a box from the mantelshelf. Her hands were trembling as she handed it to him. Returning to Arthur's side, she drew a deep breath and let it out in an extended sigh.

'In a strange way, I feel almost relieved,' she murmured, to no one in particular.

William came bounding in from the tennis court, racquet in hand. He stopped just inside the French windows, reading everyone's face for a moment then grinning excitedly. 'War?' he demanded, eagerly.

'You may be taking your part in the fighting services or as a volunteer in one of the branches of Civil Defence,' Chamberlain was going on. 'If so, you will report for duty in accordance with the instructions you have received.'

'Lucky beggars,' William said. 'I wish . . .' He fell silent abruptly as Rose jabbed him viciously with her tennis racquet from behind.

'Don't be stupid, William,' she hissed in his ear.

He fell in, belatedly, the grin fading from his face as he looked across at Mary, already on the verge of tears.

Chamberlain's speech was drawing to a close. 'Now may God bless you all. May he defend the right.'

Arthur strode across to the wireless set, snapping it off. He moved to Mary's side, wrapping a comforting arm around her shoulder. 'I'll go and phone the police station, find out what's going on,' he told her, gently.

Grateful for his concern, Mary choked back her tears. 'Well, I suppose I'd better go and pack, just in case,' she said, with as much enthusiasm as she could muster. 'I might get a couple of days' honeymoon, at least.'

'I'll help you,' Evelyn offered. The two women went upstairs as Arthur walked out to the telephone in the hallway.

It seemed that everyone was making a supreme effort to get back to life as normal. Rose smiled at William. 'Come on then. I'm not letting you get away with beating me three-love.' She darted back towards the tennis courts with William on her heels.

Left alone, Edward and Dorothea looked at each other blankly, each trying to think of something meaningful to say. Finally, Edward picked up that morning's copy of the *Sunday Times*. The headline read: 'Mussolini still pursues peace'.

'At least Italy's remaining neutral,' he murmured. 'Mussolini may yet be our saviour.'

Dorothea made no response, although a concerned frown crossed her face momentarily. She strolled over to the mirror on the wall, appraising herself. Time to freshen up her make-up, she thought.

'Darling, have you seen my alligator-skin handbag?' she asked. 'I don't seem to be able to find it anywhere.'

Edward shook his head with a slight look of irritation. 'No, I haven't. But it's hardly the most important thing in the world right now, is it?'

Dorothea's face registered an expression of studied indignation. 'It's important to me, darling. It's got my whole world in it. Compact, address book, house keys, diary. I shan't even know where I'm supposed to be lunching for the next month.'

Edward dropped the paper with a weary sigh, regarding his wife almost pityingly. 'Good God, Dorothea. Is that really all you care about?'

Dorothea whirled on him, anger clouding her normally bland features. 'No. I wish you'd wake up to realities, Edward. Drop all this Fascist nonsense – right now. You're still in contact with Mosley, aren't you?'

Edward faced her squarely, unruffled and defiant. It was an answer in itself. 'I'll serve my country, Dorothea,' he said coolly. 'But I will not turn my back on either my principles or my friends.'

Dorothea might have responded, but Arthur re-entered the drawing room at that minute. He was smiling.

'Well, at least there's some good news,' he announced.

'They're releasing young Harry immediately.' He moved back to the door, shouting the news up the stairs.

Moments later, Mary came running down, finally smiling again. 'He's free? No charges?'

Arthur nodded. 'So I understand. But I'm afraid they're holding his younger brother.'

Evelyn came down the stairs, carrying a small overnight case and a gas mask. Putting the case down, she handed the gas mask to Mary with a rueful smile. 'Odd sort of thing to have as part of your trousseau, but I suppose you ought to take it.'

'Thanks, Mum.' Mary kissed her mother on the cheek. Somehow, the gesture didn't seem quite enough. She turned to her father, holding them both by the hand. 'Thank you both, for everything,' she added. 'And especially for being so understanding about that awful business yesterday.'

Arthur gave a vague shrug. 'I suppose Harry can't help his grandmother,' he muttered, nodding his head almost imperceptibly backwards into the drawing-room towards Dorothea. The gesture was an unspoken codicil to that last statement: 'Any more than we can help some of our relatives.'

He stooped to pick up the suitcase from the floor. 'Well, I suppose you'll be wanting to get on your way. I'll take this out to the car for you.'

Evelyn called into the drawing room. 'Dorothea, Edward – Mary's leaving now.' Slipping her arm around her daughter's waist, she walked her towards the front door.

Arthur was just loading the suitcase into the boot of his ageing Rover. 'Not the most luxurious transport for a honeymoon trip, but it should get you as far as Rye,' he told Mary. Dropping the case, he pulled out the starting handle.

Rose came running over from the tennis court, eyeing the object in his hand with childlike enthusiasm. 'Can I do that, Uncle Arthur?' she asked. 'If I'm going to be driving ambulances, I ought to get all the practice I can.'

Arthur handed it over with a smile. From the doorway,

Dorothea groaned. 'Please don't encourage her,' she complained. 'She can hardly even steer. The best way to win this war would be to second her to Hitler.'

The joke was not appreciated. Taking the starting handle, Rose bent down, slipped it into place and turned the engine over. The Rover coughed into life almost immediately. Rose stood up, grinning triumphantly. 'You see? First go,' she said proudly. She walked round to the rear of the car, dropped the handle back into the boot and slammed it shut.

Mary climbed into the car, winding down the window. Settling herself comfortably, she toyed with the steering wheel, obviously impatient to get going.

It was time for goodbyes. William stepped forward, kissing his sister on the cheek. 'You tell Harry to give those Jerries hell when he gets there,' he said, brightly.

He stepped back to make room for Rose, who flashed Mary an outrageous wink and giggled. 'I won't tell you not to do anything I wouldn't do because you've already done it,' she whispered.

Evelyn had produced a handkerchief from the sleeve of her dress and was mopping at her eyes. 'Try to enjoy yourself, dear,' she called, as though her daughter was about to embark on some long and dangerous quest. Dorothea and Edward were content to wave from the front door.

With a final wave, Mary slipped the car into gear and let the clutch out slowly. The Rover began to move down the driveway.

Arthur suddenly broke into a run, catching up with the car before Mary reached the end of the drive. Mary stopped, regarding him through the open side window.

'Look, there is just something I wanted to say without your mother hearing,' her father said, panting slightly. 'It's about Harry's brother.' He paused, trying to cope with a delicate situation. 'The thing is, he'll probably need a good solicitor, and I don't really know how the Slaters are fixed,' he blurted out at last. 'It's just that I know this chap, writes bits of legal advice for the paper. He's a Jewboy, but he knows his stuff. You could call it a sort of wedding present,' he finished off with an awkward little smile.

Mary smiled back at him, but her face carried traces of doubt. 'Thanks, Dad – but I'll have to ask Harry,' she said gently.

Her father nodded, understanding. 'Well, let me know, anyway.'

He stood back as Mary slipped the car into gear again and moved off. He followed it down to the gates and stood there waving until Mary had disappeared around the first bend in the road.

A lone figure on a bicycle came into view, pedalling furiously towards the house. Arthur groaned as he recognized Miss Cardew, the local WVS superintendent. Grim-faced, he retreated back up the drive towards the house.

'Miss Cardew's coming,' he informed Evelyn, as though announcing the Four Horsemen of the Apocalypse. Unable to face the old dragon himself, he pushed past Edward and Dorothea to seek the sanctuary of his study.

Miss Cardew pedalled up the drive, parked her bike against the old garden swing and marched purposefully in Evelyn's direction with an almost military gait.

'Good morning, Evelyn,' she bellowed heartily, although there was not the slightest trace of warmth or humour on her thin, angular features.

Evelyn forced a thin smile, reflecting that, in Germany, the woman would probably have been leading a division of stormtroopers. 'Morning, Miss Cardew.'

Pleasantries over, the woman got straight down to business. 'Well, action at last,' she announced briskly. 'They're arriving later this morning.'

Evelyn looked a little blank. 'Arriving? Who?'

Miss Cardew eyed her like an errant schoolgirl. 'Why the children of course. The evacuees. You promised to take some in, remember?'

Evelyn turned distinctly pale, vaguely recollecting a brief conversation in the village stores some weeks previously. 'I didn't exactly *promise*, Miss Cardew,' she pointed out. 'I just happened to mention that we had one spare room and I'd think about it.'

Miss Cardew didn't seem to be listening. 'Anyway, you've been allocated two. They'll all be assembling in the cattle market at two o'clock.'

'How apt,' Dorothea murmured from the doorway.

Miss Cardew shot her a withering glance before turning back to Evelyn. 'So, I'd appreciate it if you would pick yours up promptly,' she finished off.

Having delivered her message, Miss Cardew returned to her bicycle, mounted it and pedalled off down the drive again, leaving Evelyn stunned.

Dorothea, as ever, had to have the last word. 'Oh dear, Evelyn,' she said in faintly chiding voice. 'What have you done?'

11

At exactly 11.35 a.m., less than twenty minutes after Neville Chamberlain had announced a state of war, the air-raid siren at the end of Nelson Street wailed into life, in concert with thousands of others all the way down from London.

Surprisingly, the initial reaction was one of curiosity rather than panic. Several doors in the close-packed terrace houses opened, disgorging their occupants to join those already in the street staring blankly up into the sky.

Thomas Slater dropped the Sunday paper he had been reading and rose from his easy chair, striding into the kitchen to where Ellen and Granma were seated around the table.

'Come on, we'd best get into the shelter,' he said firmly, forcing himself to remain calm for their sake.

Granma cackled derisively. 'Not on your bleedin' nelly,' she announced. 'I've still got me curlers in. Besides, I want to see what all this bloody racket's about.' Pushing herself up from the table, she began to hobble down the hallway towards the front door.

Thomas cursed mildly under his breath. For the moment, he concentrated his concern on his wife. 'You go on, love,' he urged her. 'I'll go and get the daft old bugger.'

Pausing until Ellen was on her feet and moving towards the back door into the garden, he went in pursuit of his mother.

Stepping out on to the kerb was like walking into the middle of a street carnival, Thomas felt, with a vague sense of unreality. Several small groups of people had already formed themselves into impromptu choirs and were heartily singing the National Anthem, or 'Rule Britannia'. From the far end of the street, a policeman wearing a tin hat came pedalling precariously towards him like a circus trick cyclist, one hand on the handlebars and one clutching a huge megaphone through which he bellowed orders to take cover. Next door, Ivy Collins watched contemptuously from the doorway as her husband Reg uncoupled the horse from his milk cart.

'I'm telling you again, Reg – you're not bringing that bleedin' horse into the house,' she warned him darkly.

Granma was out in the middle of the street, dancing a geriatric little jig and waving her clenched fists up into the sky. 'Come on, Jerry. Where's your bleedin' bombs, then?' she challenged the entire might of the Luftwaffe.

It was all too much for Thomas to take in. He shook his head as if to clear it, feeling a mounting sense of urgency. Glancing upwards, he saw Gladys Pym leaning out of the top window of Number Fifteen, grinning insanely and waving a small Union flag on a stick.

Thomas shouted up at her, 'Get under cover, Glad. This is an air raid, not the King's bloody birthday.'

'Air raid my backside,' the woman yelled back, ignoring his advice.

Thomas turned his attention to Ivy and Reg, still arguing over the horse. 'Come on, you two. Go and join Ellen in the shelter.'

Again, no one seemed to be listening to him. Thomas finally gave up. 'Bugger you all, then,' he muttered to himself, striding over to Granma.

There was no point in wasting further time with words. Wrapping his arms around Granma's bony hips, Thomas hoisted her frail body up over his shoulders in a fireman's lift.

'Oi, you cheeky bugger, what you doing?' his mother protested vigorously, pummelling his back with her fists.

Thomas ignored her, carrying her in through the front door and down the hallway towards the garden.

Ellen hovered anxiously at the entrance to the Anderson shelter, waiting for them. She breathed a quiet sigh of relief as Thomas finally burst through the back door and deposited

Granma back on to her feet again. Brooking no further protest, he pushed her forcefully across the yard.

Ivy Collins had finally come through into the back garden
to take up Thomas's offer of the shelter. She reached the gap
in their joint fence, turning briefly to shout angrily back towards the house, 'You should have married that bloody horse
of yours.'

'Bugger Reg. Just get into the Anderson,' Thomas
snapped, his patience totally exhausted. He moved back as
Ivy came through the fence and joined Ellen. Together, the
two women jumped down into the shelter.

There was a high, shrill scream, quickly followed by a
sticky splashing sound and a muffled curse.

Alarmed, Thomas stepped towards the shelter entrance,
peering down into the gloom. Ivy lay flat out on her back in a
black, slimy puddle with Ellen standing over her, calf-deep in
oozing mud. Both women looked shocked, but otherwise
unhurt. Relieved, Thomas turned back to Granma, who was
also inspecting the interior of the shelter with an expression
of distaste.

'Get in there, Mum – it's only a bit of mud,' Thomas said,
pulling at her arm.

Granma shook herself free. 'Not on your nelly,' she muttered emphatically. 'I told you it was a bleedin' death-trap.'

The wail of the siren suddenly cut out and began to die
away. In the ensuing few seconds of silence, Thomas could
hear Ivy giggling stupidly as Ellen pulled her to her feet.
Then the siren shrieked into life again, but this time it was a
single, continuous tone.

Ellen's face appeared in the shelter entrance. She began to
clamber up out of the mud. 'That's the All Clear,' she
breathed, a mixture of gratitude and disbelief on her face.

Granma grinned triumphantly, shaking her clenched fist at
the clear skies above. 'Well, where was you then, Jerry?' she
demanded. 'Not a bloomin' bomb in sight.'

Splattered with black mud, Ivy followed Ellen out of the

shelter, still chuckling to herself. 'Ruined me best pinny all for nothing,' she complained good-naturedly. She wrapped a wet arm around Ellen's shoulder. 'Still, you gotta see the funny side, ain't yer?'

Unaccountably, Ellen began to cry. Ivy's cheery grin faded, her face becoming serious and understanding.

'You're afraid – afraid for Harry, aren't you, love?'

Ellen shook her head hopelessly as the tears ran down her cheeks. 'It's everything, Ive.'

Ivy gave her a reassuring squeeze. 'We're all afraid, Ellen,' she reminded her quietly. She was silent for a while, choosing her words carefully. 'Look, I'm sorry for those things I said about your Harry. I didn't really mean 'em. I was upset for Kaye.'

Ellen nodded understandingly, grateful for the apology. She forced a thin, rueful smile.

'Actually, I think your Kaye had the last laugh,' she murmured. 'You should have come to the wedding. Would have done yer heart good, our Harry's send-off.'

With the air of a confirmed fatalist, Tom had ignored the air-raid warning. Yesterday's wedding suit thrown across his arm and his haversack over his shoulder, he strolled unhurriedly through the back streets of Gillingham, almost at his destination.

The pawnbroker's was on a street corner, the only building in a small, dingy row of shops which had not been boarded up and abandoned. The sign on the door read 'Closed', but Tom knew better. He ducked round the corner of the end terrace, making his way to the back entrance.

Inside, the place was an Aladdin's cave of clothes, household effects, jewellery and plain old-fashioned junk – most of it stolen. The most reliable fence in south-east London, Eddie Blunt was not the most generous payer, but could be trusted to keep his mouth shut.

He regarded Tom shiftily as he threw the wedding suit over

the counter and began to tip out the contents of his haver-sack. Dorothea's alligator-skin handbag, Edward's silver cigarette case, a pair of sapphire ear-rings, a carved ivory snuff-box and an expensive looking star-shaped diamond and emerald pendant.

Eddie seized upon the pendant first, screwing a magnifying glass into his eye-socket and examining it closely.

Tom grinned, feeling pleased with his little haul from Albourne House. 'Good stuff, eh?'

He was to be disappointed. Eddie lowered the pendant on to the counter, pushing it towards him. 'Them stones is paste. Besides, it's too distinctive, easily recognized. Give it to one of your lady friends, eh?' He poked through the remaining items, trying not to look too interested. 'Got anything else?'

Tom opened Dorothea's handbag, emptying it out. There was a gold compact and cigarette lighter, a silver-bound diary and address book and a matching alligator purse, which Tom had already emptied.

Eddie regarded the little cache without enthusiasm. 'Not bad stuff,' he conceded, finally. 'But hard to shift. I'll give you twenty quid for the lot.'

It was haggling time, all part of the game. Tom reacted in mock horror. 'Come off it, Eddie. It's worth three times that and you know it.'

The pawnbroker shrugged. 'Thought you wanted a quick sale, Tommie. All right – a pony, and that's my final offer.'

Tom slid his hand across the counter and clawed back Dorothea's address book, transferring it to his pocket. Someone like her would have some rich friends, he told him-self. He looked around the shop, his eyes finally falling on an accordion hanging up behind Eddie's head.

'Throw in the squeeze-box and we'll call it a deal,' he said, thinking of Granma.

Eddie smiled knowingly. Honour had been satisfied on both sides. 'Done,' he said. He scooped the merchandise off the counter and produced a thick roll of banknotes from his pocket. Peeling off five rather grubby-looking fivers, he handed them over and unhooked the accordion. 'Going into busking, are you, Tom?' he muttered sarcastically, passing it across.

Tom refused to rise to the bait. He slung the accordion strap around his neck, pocketing the money.

'Be seeing you,' he said, heading for the door.

'Sure,' Eddie called after him. 'Only don't make it too soon, will yer?'

12

Herded into the sheep and cow pens in the Chittenden cattle market, the children were making more noise than the animals which normally occupied them. Many of them away from the parents and homes for the first time in their lives and, after a long, hot and crowded train journey, they were tired, irritable and frightened. The sounds of sobbing, wailing and even the occasional fight filled the air.

Dorothea's nose wrinkled in disgust as she pulled the Talbot to a halt. She was already regretting her somewhat rash decision to stay on at Albourne House after Edward had gone back to London. The gesture had not been entirely altruistic, of course, since her London social life was becoming increasingly limited by her husband's known political affiliations.

'My God, Evelyn, I can smell them from here,' she complained. 'And all these people. It's like an auction at a Doctor Barnado's home.'

Her sister did have a point there, Evelyn had to concede. Hordes of conscripted foster parents milled up and down the rows between the penned-in children, seeking out the least grubby, healthiest or less aggressive-looking prospects.

'And whose fault is that?' she challenged. 'If we'd been here at the proper time, instead of turning the house upside-down searching for your things . . .'

Dorothea cut her short, huffily. 'Well, I'm very sorry, Evelyn – but I'm utterly lost without my bag, and that pendant was a present from a one-time fiancé of mine.'

'Break it off after the valuation, did you?' Evelyn asked, unable to resist the jibe. It was no secret within the family that the pendant was a fake, even though Dorothea liked to pretend it was real.

Dorothea was not amused. 'Really, Evelyn. I think that is in rather poor taste,' she muttered, in a hurt little voice. She glanced around the seething pens of children again, shuddering. 'This really is hell, you know. If you're really determined to go through with this, could we get it over with?'

It seemed that Dorothea was about to get her wish. Having picked Evelyn out in the crowd with her eagle eye, Miss Cardew came bustling towards them.

'Ah, Evelyn. Come with me,' she commanded. 'I have two very nice children picked out for you. A brother and sister.'

She led the way to the sheep pen at the very end of the row. The children in it all looked particularly scruffy and miserable. Obviously the rejects, Dorothea thought. She scanned them all with a pained expression, turning back to Evelyn with a look of horror on her face.

'Darling, they're filthy.'

Miss Cardew glared at her. 'Just travel stains. Nothing a good wash in paraffin and carbolic won't put right.' She opened the pen, pulling two particularly surly-looking children through the gate. 'Children, this is Mrs Hamilton, who's going to be looking after you,' she announced to them. She turned to Evelyn. 'Evelyn, this is –' she broke off, inspecting the name tags strung around each child's neck '– Janet and Philip,' she finished off.

The girl was about nine years old, Evelyn thought – her brother no more than six. They were a sorry-looking pair, both wearing cheap, much-darned clothing and their faces smudged with grime. Janet looked particularly belligerent, Philip merely miserable.

Evelyn had been hoping for a rush of maternal affection, but it didn't come. She struggled to fix a smile on her face as Miss Cardew thrust the children into her custody. 'Hello, children,' she said, as brightly as she could manage.

Philip began to cry. Looking on in total horror, Dorothea

noticed a spreading wet patch in the front of his short trousers. Janet glared at Evelyn. 'You're not my mum. I want to go home,' she announced, aggressively.

Dorothea's face brightened, seeing a way out. 'Well, there you are, then,' she said to Evelyn. 'There must be some other useful way of helping the war effort. Some of our friends are housing paintings from the National Gallery.'

Evelyn wasn't listening, concentrating on her efforts to propel two unwilling children towards the waiting Talbot. The temporary smile fading from her face, Dorothea followed them, wondering how she was going to disinfect the rear seats afterwards.

In the interrogation cell at Rochester police station, Clifford was receiving yet another grilling from DS Howard, as a uniformed PC stood guard by the door.

Howard was becoming increasingly frustrated and aggressive as his suspect refused to break. Because of his age, he had been hoping to force Clifford into an early confession, but the young man had maintained an obstinate defiance throughout.

'Right, let's go through this one more time,' Howard hissed. 'Where did you go after you left the dockyard?'

Clifford remained stubborn. 'Told you. Drove down to Maidstone, went for a drink.'

'Name of the pub?'

Clifford shrugged. 'Can't remember.'

'Talk to anyone?' Howard demanded.

'No.'

With a sigh of exasperation, Howard changed tack. He studied the sheaf of papers in his hand. 'According to the Marine Police guard's statement, you left the dockyard at seventeen minutes past eight.'

Clifford nodded. 'We're working late shifts now.'

Howard jumped on the statement. 'Yet according to your work card, you clocked off at seven.'

Clifford's face remained impassive. 'I told you. I had trouble with me dad's bike. Took some time to fix it.'

Howard sneered at him. 'And in the meantime, by total coincidence, those tools just walked from your father's store-house,' he suggested sarcastically.

Clifford shrugged again. 'I don't have access, any more than anyone else has.'

DS Howard leaned forward, his eyes no more than six inches from Clifford's, boring into them. 'Then perhaps you can explain why every single tool found by that safe had your fingerprints on it.'

Saliva filled Clifford's mouth. He gulped it down his throat. 'Sometimes I give me dad a hand cleaning 'em, tidying up the toolstore.'

Howard grinned triumphantly. 'But you just told me you didn't have access,' he pointed out.

'I meant I don't have access to the keys,' Clifford said, sullenly.

Howard sighed deeply, making a supreme effort to control his rising sense of frustration. Perhaps the nice guy approach might yield better results, he reflected. Forcing a friendly, understanding smile on to his face, he dropped his voice to little more than a murmur.

'Look, Cliff – more than three hundred quid went missing from that safe. And a man was injured. That could carry up to fourteen years, do you realize that?'

The fixed expression of defiance on Clifford's face faltered, replaced by a flash of fear. 'I wouldn't do a thing like that,' he blurted out, miserably.

Howard's eyes glinted, feeling he was at last getting somewhere. He nodded his head encouragingly. 'That's right, I don't think you would,' he agreed. 'You know what else I think, Cliff? I think you're covering up for your brother Tom – but he's not worth it, son.'

Howard fished in his pocket, drawing out a packet of Woodbines and offering them to Clifford. Guardedly, suspiciously, Clifford took one, accepting a light.

'He's used you, played you for a mug,' Howard went on, after a short pause. 'He spun you some story, persuaded you to nick the tools and now he's left you to carry the can. Some brother, eh? Not worth lying for, going to prison for.'

Howard fell silent, studying Clifford's face as he puffed nervously on his cigarette and choosing his moment. Timing was crucial, he reminded himself, psychology everything. Finally, he thought he had it right.

'All you've got to do is tell us the truth, Cliff,' he murmured, smiling. 'Tell us about Tom and you'll only be charged with nicking the tools. You're a nice lad, never been in any trouble before – probably get away with a suspended. We might even decide there's not enough evidence to charge you at all, and you could even keep your job.'

Indecision tore at Clifford's face. He chewed at his bottom lip, the cigarette burning down to a stub between his trembling fingers. On the verge of cracking, Tom's last words ran through his mind.

'Look, I'll sort it out. It'll be okay.'

Perhaps DS Howard was right, Clifford thought. Perhaps Tom had played him for a mug. But they were still brothers, there was still blood between them. Blood – and honour!

Clifford's features settled back into a grim, obstinate mask. He stared Howard straight in the eyes.

'I don't know what you're talking about,' he muttered firmly. 'I don't know nothing about Tom.'

Howard's frustration exploded at last. First into anger, then disgust and finally mellowing into pity.

'You're a bloody fool, Slater,' he spat out. He turned away towards the door, motioning for the guard to open up. He strode out without another word.

13

Harry and Mary sat in a hollow between the sand dunes, gazing down over Camber Sands to the sea beyond. Harry was silent and thoughtful, as he had been for most of the day.

'Thinking about what's over there?' Mary asked him, gently.

Harry shook his head. 'Actually, I was thinking of Cliff,' he admitted. 'I hated leaving him in there.'

Mary grinned. 'Well, at least you got to spend your honeymoon night with him,' she pointed out, joking. Her face became more serious. 'The best thing you can do for him now is to let Daddy appoint this solicitor.'

Harry sniffed. 'And Daddy will pay, of course?'

Mary clutched at his arm. 'He just wants to help, that's all. I don't really understand why you seem so against the idea.'

Harry fidgeted in the sand. 'It's just that I seem to get more and more beholden,' he said awkwardly. 'Your family don't even like me. I seem to have reinforced every bloody prejudice they ever had. Jailbird brothers, grandmother on the bottle – and I've even got their precious daughter in the family way.'

Mary giggled. 'I had a bit to do with that myself, if you remember. Besides, you're not married to them.'

'Aren't I?' Harry asked. He didn't sound too convinced. There was silence for a while.

'Well?' Mary asked, at length. 'Can I phone Daddy and tell him to go ahead?'

Harry thought for a long time, finally shrugging. 'All right, I suppose there's no harm done. It's just that I keep hoping they're just going to let him go.'

'You really think he's innocent?' Mary asked.

Harry shook his head slowly from side to side, letting out a little half-laugh. 'I honestly don't know. Last night when I talked to him about it, he said he was sorry for all the trouble he'd caused. When I asked him what sort of trouble, he said he didn't know a thing about any of it. I don't understand him any more.'

It was Mary's turn to be silently thoughtful for a while, running handfuls of sand through her fingers. There were things she didn't understand, too – and she needed desperately to be reassured.

'This other girl,' she murmured at last. 'The one your grandmother spoke about. Was it really serious between you?'

'We were kids together. We went to the same school, shared the same friends. Starting courting just seemed like a natural extension of that, that's all.'

It wasn't a full answer, Mary thought. 'But did you love her?' she prompted. 'Your grandmother seemed to think it was her you really wanted.'

Harry took her by the shoulders. 'Look, it's you I'm with,' he reminded her. 'And Granma was talking with the drink in her. She liked Kaye. I suppose she felt a bit disappointed, I don't know.'

The real question remained unanswered; Mary posed it again. 'But did you love her?'

Harry sighed. 'I thought I did,' he admitted. 'But I was wrong.'

There was just one last little cloud overshadowing Mary's happiness. She sought Harry's eyes. 'About the baby,' she started hesitantly. 'I didn't get pregnant to trap you, I want you to believe that.'

Her face was totally innocent of any guile. Harry *did* believe her. 'I know,' he said simply. He lifted her chin with his hand, kissing her tenderly on the lips.

Mary smiled, finally happy. 'That's not a honeymoon kiss,'

she scolded him. Rolling on to her back, she pulled him down on top of her.

They kissed with increasing passion until Harry finally pulled himself free and sat up again, panting heavily. 'I think it's time to go back to the hotel,' he pointed out, grinning broadly.

Mary leapt to her feet with enthusiasm, her eyes sparkling. 'That's the best idea I've heard all day,' she told him.

Hand in hand and giggling, they ran up the dunes towards the promenade.

The hotel desk clerk looked up as Harry and Mary entered the foyer. 'Oh, Mr Slater – a wire for you,' he announced. 'Came about an hour ago.'

Harry crossed to the desk, accepting the proffered buff envelope. Tearing it open, he read the brief message inside. The grin fell away from his face. His shoulders slumped.

'What is it?' Mary asked, urgently.

Harry repeated the message out loud. 'All leave cancelled. Report back to barracks 18.00 hours.'

Mary's face fell. She looked as though she was going to cry.

The hotel clerk stood up, leaning across the desk. 'On your honeymoon, ain't you?' he asked, a kindly smile on his face.

Harry nodded, miserably.

The man snatched the wire back out of Harry's hands and tucked it away beneath the desk. 'Well, ain't it a nuisance you didn't get that message until tomorrow morning?' he said with mock severity.

Both Harry and Mary were stunned for a few seconds as the unexpected reprieve slowly sank in. Finally, Mary smiled at the clerk gratefully. 'Thank you.'

The man shook his head, grinning. 'Don't thank me, miss. I ain't even seen you.' He nodded his head rather suggestively towards the stairs leading up to the bedrooms. 'Now get on out of here, the pair of you – before me conscience gets the better of me.'

Mary skipped over to him and kissed him briefly on the cheek. Rejoining Harry, she took his hand and tugged him towards the stairs. 'And that's the second best idea I've heard all day,' she said, giggling.

They reached their bedroom. Harry closed the door and locked it, crossing the room to pull the heavy blackout curtains. They undressed hurriedly in the gloom, knowing their time was short. Naked, Harry threw himself on the bed, waiting for her.

'I bought a new nightie,' Mary announced.

'Damn the nightie,' Harry muttered thickly, holding out his arms towards her.

Smiling, Mary crossed to the bed and lay against him, stroking the hairs on his bare chest with her fingertips. 'I love you,' she breathed, needing him to believe her.

Harry nodded. 'I know,' he said, turning on his side and pulling her against him.

They made love with a sense of urgency yet with gentleness, Harry acutely conscious of the unborn baby in her belly and afraid to harm it. Afterwards, they lay propped up against the pillows, Harry smoking a cigarette, Mary clutching his free arm.

'I'll write, of course. As often as I can,' he promised.

A twinge of pain passed across Mary's face. She turned her head away from him slightly, hiding it.

'I may not be at Albourne House,' she said quietly. 'I was thinking of trying to get my old teaching job back – for a while, at least.'

Harry gave a small start of surprise. 'Don't be barmy. You're having a baby.'

Mary turned back towards him, a pleading look in her eyes. 'Please try to understand, Harry. I want to be *doing* something – not just sitting around knitting bootees and worrying.'

Harry's expression made it clear that he did not understand. His frown was part worry, part censure. 'You always seem to be dashing around. As if the baby didn't matter.'

Mary hastened to reassure him. She smiled, kissing his cheek. 'Don't worry, the baby'll be fine,' she promised him.

She began to stroke his belly, anxious to make love again.

14

The early morning milk cart rattled along the streets of Deptford. Tom, hitching a free ride, sat on the back, scanning the house numbers as they passed.

Number Forty-seven was larger than most other houses in the street, with wide, ornamental concrete steps leading up to the front door and another bare stone flight plunging down to the basement.

Tom hopped off the milk cart, helping himself to a couple of bottles of milk as he did so. Hiding them under his jacket, he half turned to wave a cheery goodbye to the milkman, then headed down the basement steps where he rapped on the plain wooden door at the bottom.

The door opened almost immediately, to reveal a young girl dressed in a shabby night-dress and cardigan, clutching a four-week-old baby to her breast. She was no more than seventeen, although her face betrayed a world-weariness which suggested maturity beyond her years. She was pretty, despite a total absence of make-up and a liberal coating of grime on her face, and her swollen, milk-filled breasts tended to enhance, rather than detract from, her excellent figure.

Tom grinned at her, holding up the milk bottles. 'Early morning delivery,' he announced brightly. 'Now you can make me a cup of tea.'

Moira Barnes was not pleased to see her unexpected visitor. She glared at Tom with vehement hostility. 'What the bleedin' 'ell are you doing 'ere?'

Still grinning, Tom clucked his teeth reprovingly. 'Now, then – is that any way to greet your old dad?' he asked. 'Thought you might have a kiss for me.' Without waiting for an invitation, he pushed past her and stepped into the sordid basement room, smelling of damp, mould and soiled nappies.

Tom wrinkled his nose in faint disgust. 'Thought you might have had something a bit better than this – you being married an' all.'

Moira's eyes strayed towards a photograph on the bedside cupboard. Taken outside a register office, it showed her, flowers and a veil and heavily pregnant, with a smiling, fair-haired lad of eighteen.

'He's in the Merchant Navy,' she said defensively. 'He sends me what money he can.' She carried the baby over to a battered pram and laid it down, rocking it gently to sleep. 'Anyway, who bloody told you where I was?' she demanded, over her shoulder.

Tom nodded at the photograph. 'Your hubby. When he wrote to me for my consent.' He walked over to the pram, peering down at the baby with an unusual expression of tenderness. 'What's his name, anyway?'

'Hers,' Moira corrected. 'And it's Shirley.'

Tom smiled. 'She looks like you were,' he said, almost wistfully.

Moira snorted with derision. 'What, before you bloody ran off?' she said, bitterly.

The smile faded from Tom's face. 'I didn't run off. I was sent down. Look, I'm sorry if my coming here's upset you. I just wanted to see you, that's all.' He fished in his pocket, pulling out Dorothea's pendant. 'Here, I brought you a present – something special.'

'Bloody nicked it, more like,' Moira muttered scornfully. Nevertheless, she took the pendant, her expression softening. She allowed Tom to slip his arm around her shoulder, hugging her rather self-consciously.

'The thing is, you really shouldn't be all on your own like this,' Tom said after a while.

Moira pulled away abruptly, the contempt returning to her face as she confronted him.

'That's bloody it, isn't it? You're just looking for a place to stay, ain't you? Got nowhere else to go.' She sounded bitter, almost disappointed. 'I shoulda known!'

Tom looked genuinely hurt for a moment. 'That's not fair.'

Moira managed a resigned smile. 'Oh, don't worry. I ain't gonna throw you out. You're right, in a way. Even you's better than no one.'

A faint smile of relief returned to Tom's face. He crossed to the room's single bed, sitting down and testing its squeaking springs. 'Well, just till yer hubby gets back, eh?'

Ellen Slater was entertaining an unexpected visitor as well, and had got out the best Gamages tea cups for the occasion. Seated in the parlour, she smiled at Mary uncertainly, not sure of what to say. With only Harry in common between the two women, conversation was necessarily somewhat limited.

'Harry was very sorry not to be able to come and see you,' Mary said eventually, breaking the silence. 'But with his leave cancelled like that, everything was a bit hectic, you understand?'

Ellen tried, but was unable, to control a brief rush of resentment. It was hard to accept that her son's allegiance had changed, that his wife, rather than his mother, was now his first priority. 'Well, at least you managed to get to the seaside,' she said, making conversation. 'It was nice weather too.'

'Beautiful,' Mary agreed. She sipped at her tea, wondering what to say next.

'Anyway, it was very good of you to come,' Ellen went on. 'Let us know he's all right.'

Mary nodded. 'He's fine.' She paused. 'Actually, it wasn't just Harry I came to see you about. It was Clifford as well. My father's appointed a solicitor friend of his to try to help him. He seems to think he can get him out on bail, at least.'

Ellen looked surprised, then flustered. Talk of solicitors and legal proceedings were beyond her terms of reference.

'I'm afraid Mr Slater's at work right now,' she stammered uncertainly. 'I think you'd really need to talk to him.'

Seeing her confusion, Mary hastened to reassure her. 'I discussed it with Harry first, of course,' she explained. 'He said it was okay.'

The conversation was effectively terminated by the sound of the front door opening. Seconds later, Kaye's head popped round the door, smiling cheerfully.

'Blimey, Auntie Ellen – what you doing in the front par . . .?'

The sentence hung, unfinished, in the air as Kaye's eyes alighted on Mary and the smile drained from her face.

Mary, too, was stunned. The two women gaped at each other in silent hostility for a few seconds, reprising their earlier encounter at the jeweller's shop. Ellen's face was a study in embarrassment.

'Kaye, this is Mary, Harry's wife,' she managed to stammer out at last, trying to make the best of an impossible situation.

Surprisingly, it was Kaye who pulled herself together first. She stepped into the room, showing off her brand-new WAAF uniform. A bright, false smile fixed itself on her face. She moved forward briskly, extending her hand to Mary. 'Pleased to meet you.'

Mary took her hand, shaking it momentarily. 'Hello,' she murmured.

Kaye bubbled on – a little too quickly, a little too enthusiastically. 'Well, fancy bloomin' Harry not inviting me to your wedding. P'raps he was worried I'd spill the beans about his wicked past, eh?'

Mary's eyes were guarded, suspicious. 'Actually, I think he was more worried about how you might feel.'

Kaye let out a nervous laugh. 'Blimey. Thinks he's God's gift, does he? Can't say I'd fancy being stuck at home waiting for his letters to come.'

Ellen ran her eyes over Kaye's uniform. 'Been called up, have you, love?'

Kaye nodded proudly. 'Off today. I came to say cheerio to Auntie Ivy and Uncle Reg. Thought I'd pop in.'

Ellen smiled. 'That was nice. Have you had a cuppa tea?'

Mary climbed to her feet. 'Well, I suppose I'd better be getting along,' she announced.

'Oh, are you sure, dear?' Ellen asked, but it was not difficult to read the relief behind the words.

Mary nodded. 'I'm going to see the headmaster of the school I was teaching at, see if he'll take me back. Anyway, thanks for the tea.' She moved towards the door, turning back to flash a polite smile at Kaye. 'Goodbye. All the best.'

Kaye nodded. 'Ta. Same to you.' A slightly malicious smile flickered over her lips. 'Oh, and don't forget to give Harry a big hug and kiss from me – that's when you see him, of course.'

Mary did not give her the satisfaction of seeing that the little dart had struck home. Her face was impassive until she had closed the parlour door behind her. Only then did the word 'Bitch!' form silently on her lips.

Kaye eyed up the best set of china, the clean white cloth laid out on the parlour table. She looked at Ellen with a slightly mocking grin. 'I never used to get tea in the parlour,' she observed.

Ellen looked surprised, even hurt. 'You was family,' she pointed out, almost reprovingly.

15

Three days had passed since Chamberlain's declaration, and apart from one more false alarm at 2 a.m. on the morning of 4 September, the air-raid sirens had remained silent. Not a single bomb had fallen on British soil. For the civilian population, at least, the 'Phoney War' had started, and would continue for over nine months.

Returning from work, Thomas Slater climbed off his motor-bike to the strains of 'It's a Long Way to Tipperary', complete with musical accompaniment, coming from the front parlour. Mystified, frowning slightly, he let himself into the house to be greeted with a veritable party atmosphere.

Granma, fortified with several drinks from two opened bottles of port, squeezed away happily on an accordion, singing lustily while Frank, equally inebriated, added tea-spoon and biscuit-tin percussion. Even Ellen, who was not normally one for tippling, had a full glass in her hand and a somewhat flushed smile on her face.

Thomas glowered at them all. 'What the hell's going on?' he demanded.

Granma stopped singing, laying down the accordion to replenish her glass. 'What's it bleedin' look like? We're having a party, ain't we? Celebrating young Clifford getting out of the nick.'

Thomas's grim expression softened, momentarily. He gaped at his mother in disbelief. 'He's out? Where is he?'

Granma grinned at him. 'Where you'd be, if you was him. Out having a drink with his mates.'

Ellen stepped across, clutching at his arm and hugging it. Her face was radiant. 'Isn't it wonderful, Thomas? Mr Hamilton's solicitor managed to get him out on bail. As long as he stays here and reports once a week to the police station, he's free until his case comes up.'

Thomas's face clouded over again. 'Bail?' he repeated, heavily. 'That costs money. Where did it come from, you tell me that?'

Ellen couldn't understand why he seemed so upset, but nothing could take away her happiness. She smiled up at him. 'Mr Hamilton paid it,' she informed him. 'It was two hundred and fifty pounds, but he insisted. We thanked him, of course.'

Thomas reacted as though he had been physically struck. The colour drained from his face. He turned on his wife, fury working the muscles around his mouth like a demented puppeteer.

'You did *what*?' he screamed. 'You *thanked* him – for aiding and abetting our Clifford's lying?'

Frank struggled to mediate. 'It's not like that, Dad –' he started to protest.

Thomas cut him short, transferring his anger from his wife to his son. 'Then you tell me, what is it like?' he demanded. 'Him with his money and his fancy solicitors. Thinks he can buy my family, does he? Thinks he can make my son believe that cash will help him get away with dishonesty?'

Granma put her own two-penn'orth in, infuriated by this latest display of her son's narrow-minded intransigence. 'So you'd rather he rot away under lock and key, would you?' She paused, shaking her head sorrowfully. 'You great booby,' she added, sneering.

It was the pitying look in her rheumy old eyes which finally knocked the wind out of Thomas's sails. Feeling alone and vulnerable, outnumbered and apparently opposed by his own family, he lapsed into a sullen silence, trying to find something else upon which to vent his spleen.

His eyes fell on the accordion in Granma's hands, the two bottles of port. 'It's bloody Tom, isn't it?' he demanded petulantly. 'He's been here again – even after I said I didn't want him in my house.'

'He's not been here,' Frank said quietly. 'I'd have had something to say about it if he had.'

'They was on the doorstep when we got back from the court,' Granma put in. 'Guilty conscience, I suppose – but there's no sense in wasting good booze.'

Frank tried again to talk to his father calmly. 'Look, Dad – we all know that Cliff's covering up for Tom – but maybe having him home again will give us a chance to talk some sense into him. In the meantime, maybe the police'll pick Tom up, persuade him to admit the truth.' He paused, a determined look on his face. 'If not, I swear I'll find him myself, and beat it out of him.'

Ellen's earlier happiness had evaporated. She turned on Frank, a pleading look in her eyes. 'Please, Frank – don't you get involved as well. Isn't it bad enough that I have two sons in trouble and another one waiting to go off and fight?'

The party atmosphere was well and truly dead now. Granma reached for the port bottle, moodily. 'Well, if I can't have a drink to celebrate, I might as well console meself,' she observed philosophically.

Tom leaned against the park railings, covertly studying the row of elegant Georgian houses across the square from behind a copy of the *Daily Sketch*. The newspaper headlined the tragic sinking of the passenger liner *Athenia* by a German U-boat, but Tom hadn't bothered to read the story. He had spent most of the day casing Edward and Dorothea's Belgravia home, making frequent visits every few hours. This latest vigil was the longest, and the most encouraging. The square itself was virtually deserted, the only obvious sign of life being a housemaid shaking a feather duster from an upstairs window four houses down the street. The Grant house remained still and silent, with the blackout drapes closed exactly as they had been at 7.00 a.m. that morning.

Tom glanced at his watch with a little smile of satisfaction. It was now just after 8.00 p.m., and he was finally convinced that the house was empty and unattended. Folding the paper and tucking it into his pocket, he fished out Dorothea's front door keys and stepped jauntily across the street towards the front entrance.

Closing the heavy front door quietly and gently behind him, Tom stood rock-still in the darkened lobby, holding his breath and his ears pricked for the faintest sound. There was nothing. With a sigh of relief, he pulled out a small pocket torch and snapped it on, beginning to creep along the hallway.

He pushed open the door of the drawing room and peered in. Most of the furniture was covered in dust sheets, and Tom did not bother to investigate further. No doubt there were ornaments or other items of value in the room, but he was after small, quick and easily removable loot – things of immediate cash value which might not be missed. With the keys in his possession, he could always come back. He moved on quickly, investigating the dining-room and kitchen briefly before entering the last room on the ground floor.

The beam of the torch picked out rows of bookshelves around the walls and a large antique desk in the middle of the room, identifying it as Edward's study. The desk looked promising. Tom moved towards it, picking up a rolled-gold fountain pen laying across a sheaf of headed notepaper and slipping it into his top pocket. Edging around the desk, he tried the top drawer.

It was locked. A silver-handled paper knife on the desk top caught Tom's attention. Picking it up, he used it to prise the drawer open with an expert touch and flickered the torch over the contents.

A book of cheques went in his pocket at once, quickly followed by a silver cigar-cutter. There were a couple of medals of some kind, and Tom scooped them up hopefully. In the right-hand corner of the drawer, a pile of papers and letters merited attention and he lifted them up, about to spread them out on the desk top.

Tom froze, letting out a thin, surprised whistle through his teeth. Beneath the papers, glinting dully in the beam of the torch was the chamber and barrel of a Webley Service pistol. It was too good an opportunity to pass up. Tom picked the gun up gingerly by its 'bird's-head' grip and transferred it to his pocket, along with a small box of 0.455 calibre ammunition.

There was virtually nothing left in the drawer now except a small carved ivory photo frame, laying face-down. More out of curiosity than anything else, Tom lifted it into the light of the torch, turning it over.

It was an even bigger shock than finding the gun. Thunder-struck, Tom gaped at the photograph, hardly able to believe what he was seeing.

There were three men in the picture, seated around a table in a Munich café, and Tom knew them all. Edward, despite looking five or six years younger, had changed little. Next to him, smiling arrogantly as he had done in a hundred news-paper photographs over the past few years, was Sir Oswald Mosley. The third member of the group, however, had a face which Tom had seen mostly as a cartoon, yet was instantly and unmistakably identifiable. A shiver of excitement, almost fear, ran through Tom's body as he took in the infamous little moustache, the lank forelock of black hair, of Adolf Hitler himself!

16

It was just a scrap of paper with an address, followed by a question mark scribbled on it, but it was all Frank had to go on. Indeed, after the total bombshell which had rocked the Slater household just three weeks previously, it was about the only thing the entire family had which offered any sort of hope at all.

The paper spread out on the passenger seat beside him, Frank's lorry coasted slowly along the Deptford back street where Tom's young tart was rumoured to be living. This scant piece of information itself had only been gleaned under direct threat of physical violence, more discreet inquiries about Tom's whereabouts having met with a wall of silence. Up to only two days ago, Frank had tried to obey his mother's wishes that he leave well alone, but now the family crisis following Clifford's disappearance had precipitated him into action.

It was a rough-looking neighbourhood, Frank thought, this assessment appearing to be borne out by a loud and flaming fishwife-type argument between two women going on outside one of the houses. It came as something of a shock to realize that it was the very house he was looking for.

The row appeared to be coming to an end as Frank pulled the lorry to a halt and switched off the engine. On the pavement, at the bottom of the house steps, a young girl was hurling a last mouthful of abuse at the house's owner, a slovenly-looking bruiser of a woman in her early fifties. Beside the girl, in a battered-looking pram, a baby was screaming its head off.

'You thieving old cow,' Moira shrieked. 'Gimme my letters and money.'

The landlady had reached the top of the steps and was ducking behind the door. Half closing it, she shot back her own final comment. 'Bugger off and don't come back, you little tart. It's your own bleedin' fault for moving that flaming jailbird fancy-man of yours in wiv yer.'

The door slammed closed. Moira's shoulders slumped, and she began to sob. Turning to the pram, she began to rock it – as much to comfort herself as to console the crying child.

Frank climbed out of the cab, walking slowly towards her. For the first time, he noticed a torn and battered suitcase on the pavement, half-hidden by the pram's wheels.

Moira turned on him with fear and suspicion as he approached. 'Who the bleedin' 'ell are you?'

Frank smiled as gently as he could. 'Please, love, I don't mean you any harm,' he assured her. 'You looked like you were having trouble. I thought I might be able to help you.' He paused, nodding up at the house. 'Live here, do you?'

A flash of her previous fury crossed Moira's face for a second. 'I bloody did,' she spat out. 'Until that old cow threw me out.' The look of suspicion returned. 'Who the 'ell are you, anyway?'

'The name's Frank Slater,' Frank murmured. He was totally unprepared for the girl's sudden and violent reaction.

An expression somewhere between fear and loathing took over Moira's face. She lashed out viciously with her foot, catching him a painful blow on the shin. Bending to snatch up the suitcase, she bundled it on top of the baby and began to push the pram away down the street at a run.

Recovering himself, Frank limped after her, running around the front of the pram and forcing her to a halt. 'Look, I just want to talk to you,' he insisted. 'There's nothing to be frightened of.'

Moira glared at him, looking proud and defiant. 'I ain't bloody scared,' she insisted.

Frank smiled, feeling an odd sense of warmth towards the girl. He had been expecting some hard-bitten slag, probably in her mid-twenties. Moira was much younger than he had imagined, and although he had to admit she had plenty of spunk, there was a touching innocence about her too. Grubby-looking and foul-mouthed she might be, but she was no tart, he felt sure.

Still smiling, he looked at her thin, tear- and dirt-smeared face. Her eyes seemed sunken, with dark rings around them. She looked tired, and weak.

'When was the last time you had a decent meal?' he asked gently. 'I passed a nice little chippy just up the street. We could walk on up there – I'm buying.'

Frank had guessed correctly. It was over forty-eight hours since Moira had eaten. The offer of a free meal was enough of a lure to overcome her inhibitions. Moira's face brightened, although she was still guarded. 'All right,' she murmured, as though she was doing him a favour. 'But you ain't getting anything for it. I ain't no tart.'

Frank nodded reassuringly. 'I told you, I just want to talk to you.' He began to stroll unhurriedly up the street, Moira falling into step beside him.

Minutes later, they stood around the corner from the chip shop, Frank gently rocking the pram as Moira wolfed down fish and chips out of a newspaper.

'So, what was all that about back at the house?' Frank asked, conversationally.

Moira's face hardened. 'Evil old bitch threw me out,' she spat out through a mouthful of chips. 'Now she won't let me have my letters.'

'Because of Tom?'

Moira glared at him. 'Don't know what yer talking about.'

'So who was the "jailbird fancy-man"?' Frank pressed, quietly but insistently. 'It *was* Tom, wasn't it?'

The wary, guilty look in Moira's eyes gave him the answer he needed. She polished off the last of the chips. 'Look, I don't want nuffing to do wiv him – ever. Do you understand that?'

A rueful smile crossed Frank's lips. 'I'm his brother,' he said, nodding. 'If I wasn't, I'd want nothing to do with him either, but it's important I find him.' He paused, sighing. 'Look, my kid brother, Cliff, has jumped bail and run away. I think Tom knows where he is, or at least knows something about it. I have to speak to him. Someone told me he was living with you.'

Moira studied the anguish on Frank's face. He looked like a man in real trouble, she thought. It was equally obvious that he wasn't telling her the full story. Pity for him, and gratitude for the fish and chips, fought with what faint vestige of loyalty she still felt towards her father.

'All right – he did stay wiv me for a few days,' she admitted finally. 'But the police came looking for him while he was out, and he took off.'

'Any idea where he might have gone?' Frank asked, hopefully, but Moira merely glared at him in mute hostility. She was not going to offer any further information, he realized – at least, not without inducement.

'These letters you say your landlady's keeping,' he went on. 'I might be able to get them back for you, if they're so important.'

Moira was still guarded, but her expression softened slightly. 'It ain't really the letters. It's the money, see. What me husband sends me from the Merchant Navy.'

Frank was surprised. 'You're married?'

Moira's eyes blazed again. 'Yeah – why shouldn't I be?' she demanded sharply.

Frank felt embarrassed. 'I just thought . . . you and Tom . . .' he stammered out awkwardly.

Moira let out a short, bitter laugh. 'Yeah – well, you know what thought did, don't yer?' She was on the verge of blurting out the truth, but something held her back. She dropped her eyes to the empty newspaper wrapping in her hands.

'Still hungry? Want some more chips?' Frank asked.

Moira nodded. 'Wouldn't mind.' She looked up at him uncertainly. 'You ain't gonna hurt him – yer bruvver, I mean?'

Frank shook his head. 'I just need to talk to him.'

'Then you might try this boozer in Chatham,' Moira suggested. 'He said something about staying in the cellar underneath.'

Frank seized on the information greedily. 'The Who'd Ha Thought It?'

Moira nodded. 'Yeah, I think that was it.'

Frank smiled at her gratefully. 'Thanks,' he muttered. 'I'll go and get them chips.'

He walked round the corner to the chip shop. A small queue had built up, as the proprietor waited for a new batch to finish frying. It took nearly two whole minutes to get served, and by the time Frank emerged from the shop, Moira had gone. He thought, briefly, about chasing after her, finally deciding that there wasn't much point. She'd know the area, and he didn't. If she wanted to be lost, she'd already be where he wouldn't find her.

Besides, Frank told himself – he already had the information he'd been after and a more pressing appointment to keep. Picking at the greasy chips in his hand, he walked slowly back towards his lorry.

A single bare electric bulb dangled on a lethal-looking piece of flex from the ceiling of the dingy cellar. Between the stacked beer barrels and crates of bottles, an old mattress and a pile of blankets served as a makeshift bed. Besides the musty smell of stale beer, there was also the strong odour of petrol, coming from a pile of cans and oil barrels stacked against one wall.

Seated on two empty and upturned crates, Frank and Tom Slater faced each other like old enemies, not brothers. The threat of violence almost crackled in the air like static electricity.

Frank nodded at the stash of petrol, sneering. 'So this is your honest little garage business, is it? Black-market petrol?'

Tom refused to be goaded. 'A man's gotta make a living. The toffs'll pay through the nose for this stuff once they start to feel the pinch.' His eyes narrowed. 'How did you find me, anyway? I thought I could trust all the regulars in this boozer.'

'Honour among thieves?' Frank asked sarcastically. 'Don't worry, Tom – it wasn't any of your cronies who shopped you.' He fell silent for a while, before getting straight down to real business. 'Where is he, Tom?' he asked finally. 'Where's Cliff?'

Tom's eyes flashed guiltily. 'What makes you think I'd know?'

Frank clenched his hand slowly into a fist, brandishing it in the air. 'Don't make me, Tom,' he hissed with quiet menace. 'I could always give you a good licking when we was kids, and nothing's changed.'

The threat of direct violence had the desired effect. Frank was speaking the honest truth, and they both knew it. Tom slipped on to the defensive.

'All right, I'll tell you, since it don't make no difference now. Cliff's joined up – he's gone in the Navy. He couldn't face the possibility of going inside.'

It took a few seconds for the full implications to sink in. By the time it did so, Frank's body was shaking with anger, his voice verging on the edge of hysteria.

'And you *knew*? You bloody well helped him?'

Tom eyed his brother warily. 'It was his choice, Frank – believe me. I let him stay here for a week or so until his papers came through, that's all.'

Anger was futile, Frank realized, fighting to control it. He stared at Tom hopelessly. 'Christ, Tom – have you got any idea what you've done to this family?'

Tom stared back blankly. 'I was just trying to help Cliff,' he protested.

Frank didn't believe him. 'Protect your bleedin' self, more like. Dammit, Tom – didn't you realize that Mr Hamilton had put up two hundred and fifty quid bail?'

Tom shrugged carelessly. 'So? From what I saw of their posh house, they can afford it.'

'You bloody fool.' Frank spat the words out with contempt. 'You know what Dad's like. He's vowed to pay back every penny – and where the hell do you think he'll ever be able to find that sort of money? You've put him in debt for the rest of his bloody life.'

Tom's face fell. It was a possibility he had not even considered. He thought for a moment. 'Look, I'll sort it – all right? I'll get the money, pay Dad back.'

Frank jerked his head towards the hoard of stolen petrol again. 'What, with that?' he asked, scathingly. 'He won't even be able to use that, he's already talking about selling his bike.'

Tom shook his head, thinking of the Hitler photograph and formulating a desperate plan. 'No, that's just bread-and-butter money. I got something else lined up. A little business deal, gonna make me a lot of money.'

Frank regarded him pityingly. 'You? Lot of money? You've lived hand to mouth all your miserable life, Tom. You wouldn't know any other way. Besides, Dad wouldn't touch your dirty money, even if you had it.' Frank climbed to his feet, preparing to leave. 'I'm going now. The stink of this place makes me want to puke.'

Tom had no wish to change his brother's mind, but there was just one little thing he needed to know. 'Just out of curiosity – who did tell you where I was?' he asked.

Frank hesitated before answering, finally deciding that there was nothing to lose by telling Tom the truth. 'I met your little girl-friend,' he muttered. 'You've managed to bugger up her life, as well. Thrown out on the streets, because of you. No money, no place to go, and a baby. I hope you're bloody proud of yourself.'

Tom looked shocked. There was a nervous, panicky edge to his voice as he spoke. 'Moira? You've seen Moira? Where did she go?'

Frank frowned, finding his brother's reaction baffling. 'What the hell is it to you?' he said bitterly. 'You used her, same as you use everyone else. She was only a kid, for God's sake.'

Tom's hand dived into his jacket pocket, pulling out Edward's gun. 'Where is she, Frank?' he demanded. 'Tell me where she went.'

There was no fear, just total contempt on Frank's face as he regarded the gun, and his brother's face. 'She doesn't want anything to do with you,' he said coldly. 'And I wouldn't tell you where she was even if I knew.'

Tom waved the pistol menacingly. 'I'm warning you, Frank. You tell me where she is, or so help me . . .'

It was not the threat, but the sudden look of desperation on Tom's face which made Frank take in a slow, deep breath. 'Like I said, Tom – she's out on the streets somewhere, probably sleeping rough. She ran away, just because I was your brother.' He was silent for a long time, staring his brother in the eyes. 'Who is she, Tom?' he asked, finally.

The gun drooped in Tom's hand. His shoulders slumped, a look of terrible shame and guilt creeping over his face. 'She's my daughter,' he muttered, a distinct catch in his voice.

17

A log fire crackled cheerfully in the drawing room of Albourne House, in direct antithesis to the mood of its occupants. Arthur, grim-faced, sat poring over his business accounts, becoming increasingly despondent. The hefty bill for Clifford's jumped bail could not have come at a worse time. With harsh new Government restrictions on the supply of paper, and several of his editorial and production staff having quit to join up, the paper was down to little more than a four-page broadsheet, adversely affecting both sales and advertising revenue.

Evelyn and Mary both stared moodily into the fire, each with their own troubles. Ever a meticulous housekeeper, Evelyn had always kept a tight rein on the family budget. Now, with Arthur's dire warnings of the economies which would have to be made, she was worrying about how to make ends meet.

Mary was mostly just bored. With reinstatement to her old teaching job turned down, she was restricted to hanging about the house all day; the fact that Harry had not been granted so much as weekend leave for nearly a month only added to her sense of enforced seclusion. She felt like a nun, restricted to cloisters.

Dorothea had been unusually subdued for over two weeks, everyone assuming it to be because of the terrible business with the evacuee children, Janet and Philip. Janet had borrowed a silver inkwell from Arthur's study to write a letter to her mother. Catching her in the act, and still obsessed with the loss of her bag and pendant, Dorothea had accused her of stealing. Both children had run away that night, to be recovered only after narrowly missing being run down by a train.

In fact, Dorothea had other problems on her mind. Lord Haw Haw had started broadcasting nightly, churning out Nazi propaganda with his cultured and slightly affected call-sign of 'Jairmany Calling'. To most people, he was just a vile and traitorous Englishman who would be hung after the war was over. To Dorothea, recognizing his voice, he was a former house-guest, and she worried for Edward.

Only William and Rose had remained above it all, both sustained by the ebullience of youth. Seemingly oblivious to the mood of gloom all around him, William sat now in front of the fire, sharing a toasted tea muffin with the curled-up Napoleon.

The sound of the front door opening and closing made him jump to his feet, smiling brightly. 'That'll be Rose,' he announced cheerfully. 'I wonder what she looks like in her new uniform.'

The question was answered as the parlour door opened and Rose made a grand entrance, pirouetting into the room to show off her FANY two-piece. On her, it looked like a Paris original. 'Well, what do you think?'

'Very nice, dear,' Evelyn muttered politely, as William gaped at her with undisguised admiration. Dorothea merely winced slightly and said nothing.

'Had any patients yet?' William asked eagerly.

Rose sighed. 'No, but we will have next week. Some old bat in Parliament has been going on about all the people dying from cancer and things because of all the hospitals being cleared out.'

Arthur glanced up from his accounts, slightly peeved by his niece's inane prattlings. 'That's a bit inconvenient,' he observed sarcastically. 'Might interfere with your social programme.'

The jibe went over Rose's head. 'I just can't stand sick people,' she complained.

The incongruity of this statement raised even Evelyn's eyebrows. 'Isn't that a bit awkward if you're driving an ambulance?' she murmured.

Rose looked temporarily serious, shaking her head firmly. 'Oh, no – wounded's different,' she insisted.

'All part of the fun?' Dovey inquired, having just entered the room in time to catch the tail end of the conversation.

There was a pained silence. With a thin smile of inner satisfaction, Dovey turned his attention to Evelyn. 'Excuse me, Mrs Hamilton – but Miss Cardew rang a moment ago. Apparently, Janet and Philip got into another fight with the local village children and they've been taken up to The Grange. She'd like you to go and pick them up.'

Evelyn frowned. The thought of facing Miss Cardew was never pleasant – an irate Miss Cardew even less so.

Dorothea jumped up from her chair. 'I'll go,' she announced, stunning everybody. Seeing the look of total surprise on her sister's face, she looked hurt. 'Well, I did say I was staying on here to help out,' she added, with an air of wounded pride. 'It's the least I can do, considering everything.'

Evelyn was completely flummoxed. She had seen her sister in many moods – haughty, arrogant, spiteful, even downright bloody-minded – but a contrite Dorothea was something completely new to her.

'Are you sure, dear?' she inquired uncertainly. 'You know what you said about having them in the Talbot.'

Dorothea sniffed. 'Yes, well – they're a bit cleaner now, aren't they?'

Rose was equally astonished. 'Are you sure you have enough petrol, Mummy? You've been going through your ration as though there was no tomorrow.'

A flash of the old, familiar Dorothea re-surfaced. She fixed her daughter with a haughty, condescending smile. 'Really, Rose – I don't think my few shopping trips into town to the West End are going to bring the entire nation to a halt.' She broke off to smile sweetly at Arthur. 'Anyway, I'm sure your Uncle Arthur could spare a few gallons if I get stuck.'

If the comment was supposed to inspire Arthur to heights

of chivalry, it failed dismally. Ignoring her completely, he said nothing.

The smile faded from Dorothea's face. 'Well, I'd better get going, then.' Pausing only to pick up her new handbag, she swept from the room.

From the moment she turned out of the drive into the road, Dorothea was convinced that the Alvis coupé she could see in her rear-view mirror was following her. When she accelerated, it kept pace with her. If she slowed down, the driver showed no inclination to overtake.

More intrigued than frightened, Dorothea checked her mirror again as she turned off the main road into the lane which led up to The Grange at the top of the hill. Sure enough, the Alvis turned off after her.

Dorothea felt the first stirrings of concern now. She looked ahead, up the rise towards the big house and huge wrought-iron gates which marked its driveway. Feeling the sudden desire to be on private ground, she pressed the accelerator pedal into the floor.

The Talbot responded lumpily, first surging forwards and then giving a sickening lurch. The engine spluttered momentarily, misfired a couple of times and picked up again. It was with a great sense of relief that Dorothea turned into the Cardews' driveway, which curved some three hundred yards up to the mansion house. Her relief was short-lived. Just inside the gates, the Talbot's engine coughed again, back-fired, and died.

Dorothea consulted her mirror again nervously. The Alvis had followed her in and had come to a stop. The driver was getting out and walking towards her. She thought, briefly, of jumping from the car and making a run for The Grange, but quickly dismissed it. She was not exactly dressed for running, and such behaviour seemed spectacularly *undignified*.

Instead, she fixed a nervous smile on her face and turned to face the approaching driver. Her first impressions were quite positive. Snappily dressed in a blazer, slacks and sporting a trilby, the man looked quite respectable. Dorothea found the Old Harrovian tie particularly encouraging.

Then Tom spoke, and the illusion was shattered.

'Well, darlin',' he said with a cocky grin, 'looks like you could do wiv a knight in shining armour.'

Tom walked round to the front of the car. 'Open the bonnet up,' he commanded. 'And I'll take a look at what's wrong.'

Satisfied that he offered no immediate threat, Dorothea did as she was told. Still, the man's overly familiar attitude continued to bother her.

'Have we met before?' she asked, uncertainly.

Tom declined to answer, just flashing her another cheeky grin before lifting the bonnet and locking it in position. He bent over the engine, fiddling with the carburettor controls.

Dorothea decided that it would be most unladylike to attempt conversation through a car bonnet. In any case, her attention was caught at that moment by the sight of Miss Cardew pedalling furiously down the drive towards the two cars, waving one hand in the air and shouting angrily.

'I say there – don't you realize this is a private estate and you're trespass . . .?' Her voice tailed off as she recognized both the car and its occupant. Reaching the side of the Talbot, she dismounted from her bike and regarded Dorothea with an expression of vague disapproval. 'Oh, it's you. I suppose you've finally turned up to take those awful children home with you.'

The woman's haughty attitude rubbed Dorothea up the wrong way immediately. 'In case it has escaped your attention, Miss Cardew – this wretched contraption has broken down on me,' she retorted icily. 'I'll be up to the house to collect them just as soon as this Good Samaritan has mended it for me.'

Knowing she had met her match, Miss Cardew backed off slightly. 'Well, the sooner the better,' she said huffily. 'Savages, the pair of them. I would have thought your sister could have kept them under better control.'

Dorothea flashed one of her most disarming smiles. 'Then perhaps you could do a better job yourself,' she suggested. 'You and your brother must be lost with all those empty rooms at The Grange.'

It was time to beat a hasty retreat, Miss Cardew realized. She turned her bike back towards the house. 'Those rooms, Mrs Grant, happen to be accommodating art treasures evacuated from the British Museum,' she said by way of a parting shot as she remounted and pedalled off up the drive.

Tom's head appeared over the top of the car bonnet. There was a thoughtful look on his face. 'Wife of the local squire?' he inquired.

Dorothea giggled. 'Just the local busybody. Ghastly woman!'

Tom gestured over his shoulder towards The Grange and its spacious grounds. 'All this belong to her?'

'To her brother,' Dorothea corrected. 'He's a Member of Parliament. Abuse of power, if you ask me.'

Tom nodded. 'Yeah. Ain't right, is it? All that money in one family.'

Dorothea's eyes narrowed with suspicion. 'Are you a communist?'

'Let's just say I believe in a little redistribution of wealth,' Tom said, grinning. He slammed the car bonnet shut, returning to the driver's side door. 'Well, can't see anything wrong. I'd say you was just out of petrol. Lucky for you I just happen to have a spare can in the boot. Cost you, though.'

'Ten shillings?' Dorothea suggested, considering the offer over-generous, although Tom seemed singularly unimpressed. 'A pound?'

Tom shook his head, suddenly looking very serious indeed. 'I was thinking more like two hundred,' he muttered quietly.

Dorothea stared at him, aghast. 'For a can of petrol?'

'And something else I thought you'd be interested in

buying,' Tom said. He delved into his pocket, producing the Hitler photograph. 'Strange friends your hubby's got.'

Dorothea was frozen with shock for a moment. Recovering herself, she made a desperate grab for the photograph, but Tom was too quick for her. He pulled it away out of her reach.

'Now, now – don't they teach you toffs proper manners?' he chided. 'It's rude to snatch – especially from someone who's trying to do you a family favour. Blood being thicker than water and all that.'

With a sickening feeling, Dorothea suddenly realized at last why Tom seemed so familiar.

'I remember you now – at the wedding,' she murmured weakly. 'You're the brother. The convict.'

Tom clucked at his teeth reprovingly. 'That's not a very nice thing to say – especially since you're my auntie now.'

Dorothea shuddered. 'You broke into our house,' she breathed, horrified.

Tom waved the accusation away with a careless shrug. 'Let's just keep to the matter in hand, shall we? I got some letters to old Blackshirt Mosley as well, saying what a good bunch the Nazis are. I reckon two hundred's a bargain.'

In a last show of defiance, Dorothea attempted to call his bluff. 'I could go to the police,' she muttered, but her voice carried little conviction.

Tom merely smiled indulgently. 'Of course you could,' he agreed. 'Same as I could send some of those letters to Scotland Yard. Fancy seeing your hubby dangling on the end of a rope, do yer?'

Dorothea shuddered. She was beaten, and she knew it. What little composure she had left, collapsed. All she could do now was to play for time, hope that she could find someone who could help her. 'I don't carry money like that around with me,' she said helplessly. 'I'll need some time.'

She had feared that he might turn nasty, but Tom just looked thoughtful for a while. Finally working out that it would take him no more than forty-eight hours to round up Bernie and relieve The Grange of some of its art treasures, he smiled at her disarmingly. 'That's fine with me,' he told her cheerily. 'Two days enough?'

18

For millions, the Christmas of 1939 came as a welcome distraction from waiting for the bombs which never fell, although there was little cheer in the Slater household.

Dog-tired after a fourteen-hour shift, Thomas almost stumbled into the kitchen, throwing his work jacket over the back of a plain wooden chair and sitting down with a heavy sigh.

Ellen glanced at the kitchen clock on the wall, clucking sympathetically. 'You're late home again, love – and it bein' Christmas Eve as well. They're working you too hard at that dockyard.'

Thomas tried to smile, but failed. 'It's got to be done, Ellen. We have to keep our boys at sea.'

German U-boats and surface craft were taking an increasingly heavy toll of Allied shipping. Virtually every dockyard in Britain was working to capacity and beyond.

'Here, this'll buck yer up,' Granma said cheerily, pouring him a glass of pale, slightly murky liquid out of an unmarked wine bottle. 'Elderflower wine – don't taste like much but it's got a kick like a mule.'

The flushed grin on her face appeared to confirm this fact. Not having much choice, he accepted the glass as Granma thrust it into his hand.

'Where did this come from?' Thomas started to ask, then his eyes fell upon the large wicker hamper on the kitchen table for the first time. Curious, he pushed himself weakly from his chair and stepped across to inspect its contents. There were more bottles of home-made wine, along with a bottle of port, several pounds of apples, jars of home-made jam, cakes, biscuits, packets of cigarettes and carefully gift-wrapped presents.

Thomas turned on Ellen, suspicion in his eyes. 'What's all this, then?'

Ellen looked anxious. 'Now don't get angry, Thomas,' she told him gently. 'It's from the Hamiltons. Mary brought it over this afternoon.'

He was too tired to have any fight left in him. Thomas merely frowned, returning to his chair. 'Charity cases now, are we?' he muttered.

Ellen forced a smile. 'Come on, love – they only meant it kindly.' She took a packet of cigarettes from the hamper, extracting one and putting it in her mouth. 'I'm certainly glad of these, anyway,' she added, lighting up. 'My chest's really been playing up since I cut down. Besides, it'll be nice for Geoffrey and Billy to have a bit extra, what with Frank being so strapped.'

There was the sound of footsteps descending the stairs. Frank entered the kitchen, dressed in his brand-new Auxiliary Fire Service uniform. With building work practically non-existent, he'd joined up as much to fill his spare time as anything else.

'Evenin', Dad.' He glanced across at his mother. 'Did I hear someone taking my name in vain?'

Embarrassed, Ellen turned away. 'I am just saying it'll be nice to have Phyllis and the kids here for Christmas,' she lied. 'You going to fetch them now?'

Frank nodded. 'I was just on my way out. Should get them back in time for Mass tomorrow.' He headed towards the door.

'Frank,' Granma called out after him.

Frank turned.

'You won't forget, will yer?' Granma demanded.

Frank shook his head. 'No, I won't forget.' He walked out, leaving his mother staring at Granma curiously.

'What was that about?' she wanted to know.

Granma looked secretive, almost guilty. 'I told him to drive careful,' she said, lying through her teeth.

Ivy Collins was tacking a holly wreath to her front door as Frank stepped out onto the pavement. Turning, she smiled brightly. 'Heard you'd moved back in with your mum and dad,' she said chattily. She paused, eyeing him up and down flirtatiously. 'Like the uniform.'

'Thanks.' Frank grinned, a little self-consciously. 'Mind you, I ain't been near so much as a chimney fire so far.'

Ivy gave a little shudder, which made her full breasts jiggle provocatively. 'Still, rather you than me. I'd rather face guns than go in a fire. You must be awfully brave.'

She was coming on a bit strong, Frank thought, feeling embarrassed. He shrugged his shoulders. 'Yeah, well – we've all got to do our bit, ain't we?'

He started to move away, but it was obvious that Ivy didn't want to let him go. She stepped forward, grasping his arm. 'Did yer mum tell you we're all having dinner together tomorrow? I'm cooking a nice loin of pork. Bet you could do wiv some decent home cooking, what wiv your missus being away.'

Frank detached himself as discreetly as he could. 'Actually, I'm just going down to Ramsgate now to pick 'em all up,' he announced.

Ivy looked disappointed. She let go of his arm, turning to shout back inside her house to her husband. 'Here, Reg – why don't you get yerself a nice uniform?' she demanded.

Reg's disgruntled voice echoed out from the front parlour. 'I've got a bloomin' uniform,' he complained bitterly. 'What I deliver me milk in.'

Smiling from the exchange, and relieved to get away from Ivy, Frank made good his escape and headed for his lorry.

The sign over the door read: MORGAN BROTHERS – PIANO FRAMEMAKERS SINCE 1902. There was a big black Humber Hawk parked outside.

Frank stared at the warehouse building uncertainly for a

moment, finally pulling from his pocket the piece of paper which Granma had given him earlier to check the address. Satisfied he had the right place after all, he pushed on the old wooden door, which swung open with a loud creak of rusting hinges.

Inside the gloomy warehouse, poorly lit by a couple of dim gas mantles, only a single complete upright piano and two skeletal unfinished frames betrayed its former use. The place was now becoming a storehouse for more general goods. A considerable cache of Army petrol jerrycans took up most of one end of the building, whilst the adjoining wall was stacked with several crates of Navy rum, half a dozen large tea chests and four sacks of sugar.

'Who's there? Who is it?' a disembodied and rather nervous-sounding voice called out.

'It's me, Frank.'

Tom stepped out from the shadows, grinning with relief. 'Well shut that bleedin' door, quick,' he hissed. 'I ain't exactly in the business of advertising to the public.'

Frank did as he was told, closing the door behind him. Tom hurried over to join his brother, dropping down a heavy and old-fashioned gate-bolt. 'Gran gave yer me message, then?'

Frank nodded grimly. He was not pleased to see his brother, and he saw no point in pretending that he was. But Granma had begged him to keep the appointment, and he was honouring his promise to do so.

'What do you want, Tom?' he demanded tersely.

Tom seemed disappointed at his brother's brusque attitude, but he made an effort to rally himself. 'Well, what do you think?' he asked, waving his arms around the interior of the warehouse. 'Great, ain't it?' He smiled, pleased with himself. 'Had a real bit of luck. This geezer's brother had just died of flu, and both his sons were being called up – so I got it fer a song.'

Frank remained stony-faced. Tom's ideas of good luck

were somewhat different to his. 'What do you want?' he repeated.

The smile faded from Tom's face. He looked almost hurt. 'I wanted to show you this,' he said. 'I wanted to prove to you what I said – about going straight.'

Frank glanced cynically at the hoard of black-market goods. 'You call that going straight?'

Tom was part defiant, part indignant. 'I bought all this stuff, fair and square,' he protested. 'All right, so I didn't ask too many questions about where it came from – but I paid over good cash. The point is, I didn't thieve it, Frank. I'm done with all that. I got meself a place, I got some decent clothes and a new car. I'm a changed man, Frank – turned over a new leaf.'

He paused, extracting an identity card from his pocket and showing it to Frank with a rueful grin. 'Look – I've even got a new identity,' he boasted. 'Thomas O'Malley – that's me from now on.'

Frank remained unimpressed and unbelieving. 'You can't change what's inside you, Tom,' he muttered, heavily.

Tom stared at his brother's face for some time, searching for a sign of faith but finding none. Finally, he sighed hopelessly. 'I'll show you,' he vowed. 'I'll show you all.' He delved into the inside pocket of his jacket, pulling out a thick wad of banknotes. 'Meantime, I got money for Dad – to pay Mr Hamilton off wiv.'

Counting off a hundred pounds, he thrust it towards Frank. 'Here, this is just fer starters.'

Frank made no attempt to take the money. 'Dad won't take your money, you know that,' he pointed out, flatly.

Tom's eyes glinted craftily. 'Maybe not – but he'd take it from you, wouldn't he? You could tell him an old customer paid up a bill unexpected like – something like that.'

Frank shook his head slowly. There was a sad look on his face. 'You still don't get it, do you, Tom? More lies, more cheatin'. It just goes on.' He paused, nodding at the notes in

Tom's hand. 'Put your money away, Tom. You can't buy respect.'

His brother's shoulders slumped, all his normal swagger knocked out of him. Suddenly, he looked like a lost and lonely little boy.

'You haven't heard anything? About Moira, I mean?'

Frank shook his head. 'Bit late to start worrying, isn't it?' he said with a trace of bitterness. 'You leave her in an orphanage for half her life, let her roam the bloody streets in the freezin' cold.'

Guilt, even the stirrings of remorse, showed on Tom's face. 'You don't know what it was like, Frank. I was just a kid. They sent her mum in the workhouse. I was scared to death of being put in Borstal – even more scared to death of Dad.'

The story didn't ring true. Frank's lip curled in contempt. 'You know him better that that, Tom. He'd have stood by you, taken her in to the family. It was you – it was always you. Anything rather than ever own up to your own responsibilities.'

Frank turned away and began to walk towards the door. Tom stared after him, knowing there was nothing he could say.

19

Watched by the two ecstatically happy children, Dovey was putting the finishing touches to the Christmas tree as Rose bounded into the Albourne House drawing-room, dragging a young blonde-haired airman behind her.

'This is Toby Andrews,' she announced proudly to the whole room. 'He's a pilot.' She turned on Evelyn, still wrapping the last of the presents. 'Could you be an absolute dear, Auntie, and get him a drink while I get changed?'

Evelyn frowned slightly. 'Changed, dear? Are you going out again? Your mother and father will be here soon.'

Rose wasn't listening. Leaving Toby standing somewhat self-consciously in the middle of the room, she danced exuberantly over to Mary and tugged at her hand. 'Come on, you're coming too. I promised.'

Slightly bewildered but overcome by her cousin's enthusiasm, Mary allowed herself to be pulled to her feet. 'Rose, what on earth are you talking about?'

'We're all going to a dance at Toby's billet,' Rose gushed. 'There'll be champagne, a real jazz band and absolutely dozens of handsome young pilots.'

Mary smiled ruefully, looking down at the prominent bulge of her pregnancy. 'I'm hardly in a condition to be the belle of the ball,' she pointed out.

Rose dismissed the objection carelessly. 'Nonsense. You need cheering up with Harry not coming home for Christmas. Besides, it's your patriotic duty to keep up morale. Apart from a few WAAFs, they're absolutely desperate for girls.'

Mary giggled, patting her belly. 'They can't be that

desperate, surely?' she protested, but her resistance was already weakening.

'I've got just the dress,' Rose insisted. 'It'll hardly show. You'll look beautiful, I promise.'

Although she didn't believe it for a moment, Mary gave in. Rose was right, she told herself. She did need cheering up.

Granma had sadly underestimated the strength of the elder-flower wine and was slumped across the kitchen table, snoring loudly.

Thomas took the opportunity to say what had been on his mind all evening. 'I'm sorry, Ellen,' he muttered sheepishly.

His wife regarded him quizzically. 'Sorry for what?'

Thomas shrugged. 'This Christmas – having no money. You frettin' over Clifford. It's all my doing.'

There was a sad but loving smile on Ellen's face. She walked across to him, laying her arm around his shoulder. 'You really think I don't understand that's how you are, even after all these years?' she asked gently.

Thomas reached up, grasping her hand. The sound of the front door opening made them both start with surprise.

'Who can that be?' Ellen murmured. 'Frank ain't coming back until tomorrow.'

Despite his tiredness, Thomas dragged himself to his feet as Harry walked into the kitchen. All the worry seemed to drain out of his face instantly. He beamed with happiness. 'Son, it's good to see you.'

Harry clasped his father by the shoulders, hugging him briefly. He turned to his mother, opening his arms.

Ellen practically fell against him, pulling his head down on to her shoulder. 'Thought you wasn't getting any leave,' she said, happy that it wasn't so.

Harry nodded, smiling. 'That's what we all thought, too. The CO had a sudden change of heart.' His face became more serious. 'Could be a bit of a guilty conscience, if you ask me. I think we're on the move soon.'

Ellen's body went rigid, momentarily. She stepped back, looking up at her son with fear in her eyes. 'France?' she breathed.

Harry shrugged. 'They don't tell us anything.' He glanced over at Granma, still fast asleep. 'I see Gran's happy.'

'Your ma-in-law sent us some wine,' Thomas put in. He snatched up the half-empty bottle from the table. 'We got something to celebrate, now.'

It was good to see him happy again, Ellen thought. For his sake, and for Harry's, she pushed her fears to the back of her mind and put on a brave smile.

'Does Mary know?' she asked, as Thomas poured three fresh glasses.

Harry shook his head. 'I'll go on there tomorrow morning. Right now I'm going to celebrate Christmas with my family.'

He accepted the glass his father offered him, raising it in the air. 'Well, Merry Christmas to the Slaters,' he volunteered.

Granma stirred at the table, shaking herself awake. 'Merry Christmas,' she echoed drunkenly. 'I'll drink to that. Where's me ruddy glass?'

20

Mary had been expecting some dingy drill-hall, or a barracks building. She stared out of the side-window of Toby's car in amazement as they pulled up in the driveway of a huge and elegant mansion house.

'This is your billet?' she asked, stunned.

Toby grinned sheepishly. 'By default, I hasten to point out. The owners have swanned off to America and left the servants in charge. I guess they consider this is their contribution to the war effort.'

He jumped out of the car, walking round to the back door to help Mary out. Rose let herself out of the front, running round to join them. Sticking his elbows out with a chivalrous gesture, he allowed the two girls to take an arm each before leading them up the huge white steps at the front of the house.

The place was even more impressive on the inside, the front door opening on to a massive lobby with an inlaid mosaic floor. A wide, curving flight of marble stairs with an ornate brass balustrade led upstairs, from which the sounds of music and laughter drifted downstairs.

'Sounds like the lads have things pretty well in hand,' Toby muttered, grinning. Taking the two girls' coats, he ushered them towards the stairs.

On the first floor, he led them into a spacious ballroom with mirrored walls. Several liveried footmen scurried about dispensing champagne as a five-piece uniformed band played a jazzed up version of 'Smoke Gets In Your Eyes'. Rose squealed with delight at this, and at the sight of some three dozen young Air Force officers and sergeant pilots. The setting was fairly close to her personal view of Heaven.

Rose had been right about the women, or rather the lack of them, Mary thought. Only six or seven of the young men appeared to have permanent partners, and perhaps another dozen girls were seated in twos or threes at various tables. WAAF and FANY uniforms were much in evidence, although a few wore formal evening dress. Rose, resplendent in a flowing Schiaparelli dress, outshone them all. Mary felt dowdy by comparison, thinking that she looked fat rather than pregnant.

Toby ushered them both to an empty table, looking around for the nearest servant to order champagne. His eyes fell on a fellow officer, smooching on the dance floor with a girl in a WAAF uniform.

'Dixie – come over here and meet my friends,' he called out, waving. Leaning in towards Rose, his voice dropped to a conspiratorial whisper. 'Be nice to Dixie – his cousin's our CO.'

The young man in question stopped dancing, looked over and smiled as he recognized Toby. Tapping his dancing partner on the arm, he gestured over towards them.

The girl turned. With something of a shock, Mary realized that it was Kaye, and that Dixie was already beginning to lead her towards the table.

Kaye forced a polite smile as she came face to face with Mary. 'Well, small world,' she murmured. 'Fancy meeting you here. Painting the town, are we? Auntie Ivy told me Harry couldn't get leave.'

Mary bristled slightly at the implied rebuke. 'You think I should go into purdah?'

Rose was regarding them both with a puzzled frown. 'You two know each other?' she inquired.

It was obviously incumbent on her to make the introductions, Mary thought. 'Oh, Rose – this is . . .' she began hesitantly, choking herself off. She had been about to say 'This is Harry's old girlfriend', but it didn't seem right, somehow. 'This is Kaye, a friend of Harry's,' she blurted out finally.

Toby grinned happily. 'Well, that's a bit of luck,' he said brightly. 'If you two know each other, I can leave you to have a little chat.' He turned to Dixie. 'Be an absolute sport and take Rose for a twirl on the floor for me, will you? I really ought to go and socialize for a few minutes.'

Dixie eyed Rose with undisguised admiration. 'Rather,' he said eagerly. He took her arm, leading her out on to the floor. Pausing only to snatch two glasses of champagne from a passing servant, Toby set them down on the table, flashed Mary and Kaye one last smile and shot off.

The two women eyed each other over the rims of their glasses in stony silence for a long time. Finally, Kaye's face softened. 'Well, this is all a bit embarrassing for both of us,' she said quietly. 'But we do seem to be stuck with each other for a while, at least. We might as well try to be friendly.'

Mary nodded. 'Yes, you're right.' She gave Kaye an apologetic smile. 'And I'm not embarrassed, really.'

The silence was shorter this time, and less hostile. 'So, how was Harry the last time you saw him?' Kaye asked eventually. 'I don't see too much of his family these days to ask.'

Mary felt a wave of sympathy for her. It was bad enough waiting for letters. To have all news just cut off must be terrible. 'He's fine, just fine,' she told Kaye. 'Still complaining about all the square-bashing, but he tries to stay cheerful.' She read the unspoken question in Kaye's eyes, and answered it. 'Still no news of posting, though.'

The conversation was terminated by the return of Dixie, minus Rose and grinning ruefully. 'Just my luck,' he complained, jokingly. 'I get to dance with the most attractive girl in the place and it's an "excuse me".' Suddenly aware that he had made a faux pas, he smiled down at Kaye apologetically. 'Actually I meant the second most attractive girl in the place,' he corrected hastily. 'Shall we take up where we left off?'

Kaye accepted the offer gratefully. 'See you later, perhaps,' she said to Mary, rising from the table and taking Dixie's proffered arm. He swept her off into the middle of the floor as the band launched into a spirited rendition of 'St Louis Blues'.

Left alone, Mary watched the dancers idly for several minutes, sipping at her champagne and feeling rather left out of things. Rose was in her element, she noticed with a twinge of envy, being transferred from one young officer to another in a living version of Pass the Parcel. A footman stepped over to her table, refilling Mary's glass to the brim. Other than that, no one seemed to pay her much attention.

Toby returned eventually, breathless and apologetic, carrying a freshly opened bottle of champagne. 'Sorry I was so long,' he said, filling Mary's glass again. 'Got into a long and boring session of Hitler jokes. You know the sort of thing: Adolf's broken his leg – he tripped over a Pole in the corridor.'

Mary smiled politely, even though she'd heard it before. Toby lapsed into an awkward silence, following her gaze out on to the dance floor. Rose seemed to have settled down with a regular partner now. The band was playing a foxtrot, but they were moving slowly and dancing extremely close.

'Well, it looks as though your cousin is having a good time,' he muttered finally, putting on a brave smile.

Mary smiled gently, almost apologetically. 'She always does, I'm afraid. You seem to have lost your chance there.'

Toby was suddenly acutely and embarrassingly aware that he was also Mary's escort for the evening. 'Look, what must you think of me? I haven't asked you to dance.' His eyes flickered uncertainly over her belly. 'You *are* all right to dance, aren't you?'

Mary giggled, the champagne starting to get to her. 'I'm not a Dresden shepherdess, you know.'

Toby grinned back. 'Just as well. You'd be the enemy if you were.'

It wasn't much of a joke, but Mary laughed anyway. She pushed herself up out of her chair, allowing Toby to lead her on to the floor.

It felt good, Mary thought. Like coming alive again after laying in a sick-bed for months. She tried to think of the last time she had felt a young man's arms around her, then, sensing the rhythmic pulse of music coursing through her body, she surrendered herself to the almost-forgotten pleasure, encouraging Toby into a faster pace.

Rose and her beau drifted past, both drunk on champagne and music. 'Glad you came?' Rose called out. She was gone again before Mary could answer, but her happy face said everything.

The foxtrot came to an end. A rattle of snare drums announced a change of pace. Led by the trumpet player, the band launched into a lively jitterbug number. Several of the more adventurous couples began jiving.

Mary looked at them in astonishment. 'What's that?' she asked Toby, never having seen such wild and uninhibited dancing before.

Toby grinned. 'Great, isn't it? All the rage in America, so I'm told.'

Mary's eyes glittered. 'Can you do it?'

'Sure.' Detaching himself from her, Toby demonstrated a few steps, finally extending his hand. 'Want to try?'

Mary accepted the offer eagerly. She began, awkwardly, to try and match his unfamiliar steps, her movements quickly becoming more fluid and less self-conscious as the infectious beat of the music took over her body.

She beamed joyously, shouting breathlessly at Toby over the insistent pulse of the music, 'This is terrific. Can you show me how to do some of the twirly bits?'

Toby nodded, grinning. He lifted her hand, guiding her into a spin. Mary's eyes sparkled as she completed the manoeuvre. 'I haven't had so much fun for ages,' she called out, repeating it almost at once. A tiny spasm of cramp-like pain tore at her abdomen, but she ignored it.

The band seemed to be turning up the tempo even more. Caught up in the sheer exhilaration of it all, Mary adapted to it, panting for breath and giggling at the same time. The pain struck again – sharper this time. She faltered, momentarily, a slight grimace contorting her lips.

A look of sudden concern crossed Toby's face. 'Are you all right?'

Mary clenched her stomach muscles against the pain, smiling bravely. 'It's nothing – I'll be all right.' She attempted to pick up the rhythm again, but her belly suddenly seemed to knot up. She came to an abrupt halt, letting out a little cry as the pain really took hold.

'Look, maybe you'd better sit down and have a drink,' Toby suggested. He wrapped his arm around Mary's shoulder, leading her through the cluster of dancing couples.

It was agony even to walk now. The first premonitions of fear shuddered through Mary's mind as she hobbled towards the table, leaning against Toby for support.

Toby was feeling out of his depth and panicky as he finally got Mary back to the table and lowered her onto a chair. Helplessly, he turned to stare out into the throng of dancers, calling out Rose's name. Oblivious to everything except the man of the moment and the music, she danced on, ignoring him.

In mounting desperation, Toby saw Kaye and waved at her frantically. She hurried over. 'What's wrong?' she asked, seeing the worry on his face.

Toby nodded down to Mary, who was now contorted into a foetal ball in her chair, clutching at her belly and whimpering. 'She started having these pains,' he murmured weakly.

Kaye flashed him a contemptuous glance. 'You bloody fool,' she said angrily. She crouched by Mary's side, grasping her shoulders. 'Where are the pains, Mary?'

Grateful to have the attention of another woman – any woman – Mary spoke through gritted teeth. 'It feels like the curse,' she grated out. She looked up into Kaye's eyes, fear showing on her face. 'What is it? What's happening to me?'

It took a great deal of effort, but Kay managed to fix a

comforting smile on her face. 'Don't worry, it's all right,' she said, with a lot more assurance than she really felt. She glanced up at Toby, hissing urgently. 'Go and get Rose — now!'

Looking bewildered, Toby did as he was told. Moments later, he was back with Rose, too tipsy to fully appreciate the true gravity of the situation.

She had little choice, Kaye thought, taking charge. 'We have to get her to a doctor, right away,' she snapped. 'Are either of you fit to drive?'

Toby looked flustered. He glanced at his watch. 'It's after one in the morning,' he pointed out. 'Where are we going to find a doctor at this time of night?'

Rose giggled drunkenly. 'I'm an ambulance driver.'

Kaye whirled on her, slapping her across the face. 'Sober up, you silly little bitch,' she spat out. 'Don't you realize what's happening here?'

The blow stung, bringing tears to Rose's eyes. However, it did the trick. Her face blanched as she was jerked back to reality. 'We'll get her home. Daddy's a doctor, he'll know what to do.'

An icy calmness descended on Kaye as she realized, suddenly, what she had to do. Rose was a brainless little kid, hopelessly drunk. Toby was just a man.

'I'm coming with you,' she announced firmly. Co-opting Toby's help, she started to lift Mary out of her chair.

21

Everyone was gathered, grim-faced, at the foot of the stairs as Edward came down, treading softly. Evelyn spoke for them all.

'How is she?'

Edward's expression betrayed little. 'More comfortable now. I've given her something to make her sleep.'

'Have the pains stopped?' Rose wanted to know.

Her father shook his head, sadly. 'I'm afraid not. The baby's on its way, and there's nothing I can do to stop it.'

Evelyn let out a little sob. Arthur took her hand, squeezing it. It was too early, and they both knew it.

'Has the baby got a chance, then?' Kaye asked.

Edward sighed. His mouth framed the word 'perhaps'. His eyes said 'no'. He moved towards Evelyn. 'I think you should let me give you something too. You need some rest.' He glanced aside at Arthur, who nodded. Taking Evelyn gently by the shoulders, Edward led her away back up the stairs.

Arthur turned to Kaye and Toby. 'I can't thank you enough for what you did. You've both been very kind.'

Toby blushed gallantly. 'I only drove the car, sir,' he pointed out. 'It's Kaye you should be thanking. She was marvellous, took control of us all.'

It was an innocent enough statement, but Rose chose to take it as a personal rebuke. Still wobbly from alcohol, she was in a delicate mental state, poised on a knife-edge. Her desperate concern for Mary was made almost unbearable by an underlying sense of guilt at having taken her to the dance. She could still almost feel the sting of Kaye's slap, and the contempt in her voice as she delivered it. And now Toby – *her* Toby – was fawning over the woman, singing her praises.

Something snapped inside her. 'Thank her?' she blurted out, her voice taking on an hysterical edge. 'Don't you know who she is, Uncle Arthur? Don't you realize she's the one person who'd be glad if Mary lost the baby?'

Arthur stared at her, shocked. 'Rose, that's a terrible thing to say.' He glanced towards Kaye, a look of abject apology on his face. 'I'm so sorry, Miss Bentley. Please try to understand – we're all a little overwrought.'

Toby turned on Rose with a mixture of pity and scorn. 'I thought you were so pretty and sophisticated,' he muttered coldly. 'But you're just an over-dressed and over-indulged little brat.' He turned back to Kaye, his tone at once solicitous. 'Come on, I'll get you home,' he said gently, wrapping his arm around her shoulder.

He began to walk her towards the door as Rose burst into tears and ran up the stairs to her bedroom, slamming the door behind her.

Mrs Dovey came out of the kitchen in her dressing-gown, bearing two steaming mugs of coffee and some mince pies on a tray. 'I made these for Mary's friends,' she announced. She looked round uncertainly for Toby and Kaye, glancing out into the hallway as the front door closed with a faint snick, announcing their departure.

Arthur smiled at her gratefully. 'That was very good of you,' he murmured, taking one of the cups for himself. 'Seems a pity to waste them.' He nodded towards the drawing-room. 'Perhaps you'd like to join me,' he invited, as an afterthought.

Surprised, even a trifle apprehensive, Mrs Dovey followed him, feeling a strange sense of *wrongness* about the situation. Clearly, Captain Hamilton felt the need for company, but it was more than that, she sensed, almost clairvoyantly. He and her husband had always shared a special bond, born from their joint experiences in the First World War. Yet her place in the household had always been subservient, fixed. The Hamiltons were caring, sensitive employers, sure enough

– but employers nevertheless. Fine as it might be, the line between servant and master had always been clearly visible.

Now, Mrs Dovey thought, that line seemed oddly blurred – and it was not just the needs of the moment. This war was already having a strange effect on people, their attitudes, even their circumstances. There was change in the air, the social structure of the entire nation was starting to dissolve. In the forces, they were already talking about conscripting officers from the ranks. In civilian life, professional men were taking up menial tasks in the voluntary services. Even Evelyn Hamilton, the aloof and detached mistress of the household, was playing foster-mother to a couple of back-street children.

Arthur led the way into the drawing-room, putting his cup down on the coffee table. He moved to the fireplace, poking the faintly glowing embers back to life and tossing on a couple more logs. Finally, as a few tentative little flames licked up, he grunted with satisfaction and headed for the nearest easy chair to try and relax.

It was not to be. The silent house suddenly echoed to the sound of thundering footsteps on the stairs, and bright, giggly voices.

Janet and Philip burst into the drawing room, clutching the bulging stockings which Dovey had filled earlier. They were both wide awake, their eyes alight with happiness and a sense of wonder.

'He's been, Uncle Arthur, Father Christmas has been,' Janet screamed ecstatically, the words tumbling out of her mouth in her excitement.

'We stayed awake all night – but we still didn't see him,' Philip announced more solemnly, completely overawed in the presence of magic.

Mrs Dovey bustled towards the children like a mother hen, solicitous both for them and for Arthur. 'Now come along, you two. You belong back in bed,' she told them. 'It's still the middle of the night.'

Janet's face fell. She looked towards Arthur, her eyes moistening. 'Oh please, Uncle Arthur – can't we open our presents?' she pleaded.

'Father Christmas never came at our house,' Philip put in. He, too, looked as though he was about to start crying.

Mrs Dovey swept her arms around the pair of them, preparing to scoop them towards the door.

'Wait,' Arthur called out. He climbed slowly to his feet, regarding the two children with gentle affection. The smile on his face masked the sadness in his eyes. 'Actually, I think opening presents might be an excellent idea,' he said thoughtfully.

He crossed to the fireplace, taking a spill from the mantle and lighting it. Moving to the Christmas tree, he began to light its candles, smiling indulgently at Mrs Dovey. 'I never used to be able to sleep on Christmas Eve, Mrs Dovey. Could you?'

He returned to his chair to watch the joyous children start unwrapping their presents, taking comfort from being allowed to share their happiness.

Toby drove slowly and carefully, straining his eyes to pick out the contours of the road in the dim glow of the blacked-out headlamps. There was no longer any rush, and he was aware that he had not yet fully sobered up. Kaye sat beside him, gazing blankly out through the windscreen without really seeing anything. She had not said a word since they had left the Hamiltons' house, and she felt she had little in common with Toby to start any sort of conversation.

Rose's outburst had obviously upset her deeply, Toby thought, misinterpreting her silence. He felt the need to offer some sort of comfort.

'I meant what I said back there,' he blurted out at last. 'About you taking control and all that. You really were magnificent.'

Kaye laughed, a trifle bitterly. 'I seem to have spoiled your chances with young Rose, though.'

'Don't even think about it,' Toby grunted dismissively. 'I did that myself – and I'm glad about it. That was a sick, vicious thing to say to you.'

Kaye shrugged. 'Oh, I don't really blame her – any of them,' she murmured. 'They can't help seeing me as a threat. The jilted girl-friend, just waiting to get her claws back into her man.'

Toby hadn't understood quite what had been going on before. Now it all started to make sense. 'You knew Mary's husband – before her?'

Kaye nodded. 'Harry was the only boyfriend I ever had. When he ran off to marry her, I thought she'd fallen for the baby just to trap him. Anything rather than accept it was his choice. But he already seems to love it, love her.'

She seemed willing, even eager to talk, Toby thought. He'd been worried in case she thought he was prying. 'And what about you?' he asked gently. 'Do you still love him?'

Kaye shrugged again. 'I don't know,' she admitted honestly. 'At first I thought I was going to die of a broken heart, but I didn't. It was funny, but just being in her house seemed to put it all more into perspective, in a way.'

She glanced sideways, seeing that Toby didn't really understand what she was talking about. 'He was always on about changing the world, changing society,' Kaye went on. 'How everyone was entitled to the basic decencies of life. I'm not sure if you'd understand, but it wasn't just money, but about the things people like the Hamiltons take for granted. Good schools, a nice house, pictures in the hallway instead of an old tin bath.' She paused, sighing. 'I suppose I finally realized what Harry wanted. I'd be tempted myself.'

'I suppose you class me with the Hamiltons as well?' Toby said. 'You must despise us.'

'Of course not.' The denial was accompanied by a smile of genuine warmth. 'I'm talking about things, not people. Take

Mary's dad, for instance. He seems a really nice bloke. Bet he never slapped her around.'

'Did yours hit you?' Toby asked, reading between the lines.

Another bitter laugh. 'Yeah, that's how I first met Harry, when we were kids. I was always running away from home and going to my auntie's.'

Toby was silent for a while, taking it all in. 'You know, I've never met a girl like you before,' he said eventually.

Kaye gave him a thin smile. 'What – working class?'

It was Toby's turn to shake his head in denial. 'That's not what I meant at all. You're just so honest, so down-to-earth and in control of yourself. So *real*, I suppose.'

'I guess I'll take that as a compliment,' Kaye said, laughing.

Toby looked slightly hurt. 'Now you're mocking me,' he accused. He was thoughtful for a moment. 'Look, what are you doing tomorrow?'

'Today, you mean?' Kaye corrected, smiling. 'I'm back on shift in just over an hour. Why?'

Toby's face was serious. 'I wondered if you might join me for Christmas dinner. After you finish, of course.'

A look of apology formed on Kaye's face, masking the regret beneath. 'I promised I'd go to my uncle and auntie's,' she told him.

Toby looked disappointed. 'Well – perhaps some other time then, eh?'

Kaye regarded him quizzically, not sure whether he was actually trying to make a serious date or just going through the motions. Playing safe, she coppered her bets. 'We'll see,' she muttered noncommittally.

They were just coming up to a crossroads. Toby suddenly stamped on the brakes as a pair of shadowy figures loomed into view, standing in the middle of the road looking lost and hopeless. The car skidded to a halt on the frosty surface, Toby gasping with relief. 'Christ, I nearly hit them.'

Kaye regarded the pathetic-looking couple with concern.

The woman, shabbily dressed in a totally unseasonable frock and thin cardigan, looked pinched with cold. The man, more warmly clad in an Army greatcoat, looked merely desperate. He shuffled over to the side of the car, tapping pitifully on the side window. Warily, Toby wound it down a couple of inches.

'We're looking for Albourne House,' the man said, in a broad cockney accent.

Toby thought for a while, finally shaking his head. The name meant nothing to him. 'Sorry, but I've never head of it.'

Nodding miserably, the man returned to his wife. Picking up a heavy shopping bag, she began to trudge wearily along the road again. Slipping the car back into gear again, Toby started to move off.

'Poor buggers,' he muttered sympathetically. 'They must be freezing to death. Wonder what they're doing out here at this time of night in the middle of nowhere?'

22

Worn out by lack of sleep and playing with their presents, the children had finally been persuaded back to bed. Mrs Dovey had also retired to seize a few hours' rest, at Arthur's behest. Alone, he sat staring into the embers of the fire, smoking his fifth cigarette of the night without enjoyment.

The drawing-room door sighed open. Edward entered, surprised to see Arthur sitting there.

'I thought everyone had gone to bed,' he said quietly. 'I was just checking on Mary.'

A spark of hope flashed in Arthur's eyes. 'How is she?' he asked, almost pleading for a positive answer.

Edward couldn't give it. He regarded Arthur gravely. 'It won't be long now,' he murmured. 'We'll know for sure, then.'

Arthur rose to his feet, bracing himself against the truth. 'Realistically, Edward – what are the chances?'

'Maybe one in ten for the baby,' Edward said honestly. His candour was out of respect, his sympathy from blood ties. 'But there's every indication that Mary will be all right.'

Arthur nodded, taking some comfort from his brother-in-law's professional opinion. 'Thank you,' he murmured. He fell silent for a while, eyeing Edward thoughtfully. There was something which had been on his mind for days now, and he had wondered when and how, if at all, to broach it. Now, feeling especially close to the man, seemed as good a time as any.

'Look, there's something you ought to know,' he said at last. 'The police came to my office last week, asking questions.'

Edward raised one eyebrow fractionally. 'Questions?'

'About you, your politics, your friends. They already know about your membership of the British Union of Fascists, I suppose you realize that.'

Edward nodded knowingly. 'I wondered how soon they'd get round to the witch-hunt,' he murmured with a trace of humour. 'So what did you tell them?'

Arthur shrugged. 'Nothing, only that you're a patriot, a respected surgeon. That you are a family member and I know nothing of your private life.'

The doorbell rang, cutting off any reply Edward might have made. Arthur started towards the door, but Edward re-strained him. 'Relax, Arthur,' he insisted. 'Let Dorothea answer it. She's the only one in this house who's had a full night's sleep.' He crossed the room and picked up the whisky decanter. 'Drink? Doctor's orders.'

The bell rang again. Dorothea's irate voice screamed down from the top of the stairs. 'Can somebody please tell me the point of having servants when they won't even answer the door?' Receiving no answer, she began to storm down the stairs towards the hallway, muttering under her breath.

Reaching the front door, she wrenched it open, glaring out malevolently. 'Don't you know it's Christmas morning?' she demanded haughtily, before the visitors were even identified.

Woken by her sister's ranting, Evelyn called from the top of the stairs, 'Who is it?'

Dorothea inspected the couple standing on the porch for the first time, wrinkling her nose in faint disgust. At first she assumed them to be a pair of gypsies, although the absence of white heather bunches and the man's Army greatcoat were a bit of a puzzle.

'I haven't the faintest idea, but they look none too sa-voury,' she called back to Evelyn. 'Go back to bed, darling – I'll get rid of them.'

Facing the couple again, she put on her most imperious expression. 'Didn't you see the sign? It's large enough.'

The woman nodded faintly, wrapping her arms around her

shoulders against the bitter cold. 'Yer – it's Albourne House, innit?'

Dorothea let out an exaggerated sigh of exasperation, rolling her eyes in a gesture of disdain. 'Not that sign. I meant the one which reads "No Hawkers".' She began to close the door in their faces.

The man stepped forward, sticking his booted foot in the jamb. There was anger in his eyes. 'Not so fast, you snooty cow,' he snarled. 'We've come to see our kids.'

Faced with this sudden show of aggression, Dorothea blanched, stepping back into the comparative safety of the hallway with a little shudder. She called nervously back up to her sister. 'Evelyn, dear – I think you ought to come down here after all.'

Evelyn came running down the stairs, Arthur emerged from the drawing-room to join her and Dorothea retreated back upstairs like an animal licking its wounds as they both faced their visitors.

'We just wanted to see our kids,' Elsie Miller told them. 'Ronnie's off to France in five days.'

Evelyn looked shell-shocked. The unexpected visit was about the last thing she needed, or could cope with, right now. For her sake, Arthur summoned up inner reserves and took charge. 'Go and wake Mrs Dovey to fetch the children down,' he urged, pushing her gently back towards the stairs. He turned back to face the Millers with a forced smile of welcome on his face.

'So – you're Janet and Philip's parents? Come in, both of you. You must be frozen.'

He closed the door behind them as they stepped over the threshold. Taking Ron's coat, he was about to escort them through to the drawing-room when Dorothea reappeared at the top of the stairs, her voice panicky. 'Arthur – fetch Edward, will you? I think something's happening to Mary.'

Arthur's heart sank. Desperately worried for his daughter, but conscious of his obligations as a host, he had no choice but to show the Millers through into the drawing-room as Edward rushed past on his way to Mary's bedroom.

Ron and Elsie moved over to the fireplace, standing there awkwardly and obviously feeling out of place in such elegant surroundings. There was a long, terrible silence.

'So, you're happy in the Army?' Arthur asked Ron finally, knowing that he was obliged to make some sort of conversation.

Ron shrugged. 'It's a job. I had nine years wivout.'

That seemed to be that. Arthur was still racking his brains for something else to say as Mrs Dovey appeared in the drawing room doorway, pushing Janet and Philip ahead of her.

'Ah, here are the children,' Arthur announced, with some degree of relief.

Ron and Elsie's look of joy was not matched by the two children, who stood hesitantly in the doorway, staring at their parents as though they were strangers.

'Come on, where's all the manners you've learnt,' Mrs Dovey chided them gently. 'Say hello to your mum and dad.'

Philip pressed himself against her, burying his face in her skirt and starting to cry. Janet took one tentative step forward, eyeing her mother warily. 'Hello,' she said, in a quiet, almost cold voice.

It was an awful, awkward moment, with Mrs Dovey finally forcing herself to the rescue. 'I think they're a bit overcome to see you,' she muttered apologetically. 'You'll have to give them a couple of moments to get over the shock.'

Arthur moved towards the door, grateful for an excuse to escape. 'Well, I'll leave you all alone for a while,' he said to the Millers. 'You'll both stay to lunch, of course.'

In the doorway, Mrs Dovey blocked his path. There was a look of warning in her eyes. 'Don't go upstairs,' she whispered to him. 'Mr Edward said not to. You come on in the kitchen with me and Dovey, and I'll make us all a nice cup of tea.'

*

There was no festive cheer about Christmas lunch. Crackers remained unpulled, glasses of wine untouched. The death of the baby hung over the table like a curse, with only Edward's confident prediction that there had been no complications and Mary was going to be all right to lighten the gloom.

No one had much of an appetite except for Ron and Elsie Miller, who were both tucking into their roast dinners with relish. There had been little over-the-table conversation, other than polite comments about the food. Only Dorothea, who had returned to her normal overbearing self, prattled on, seemingly oblivious to everyone's anguish.

She smirked with amusement as Ron picked a goose bone up from his plate between his fingers and began to gnaw it.

'Of course, I suppose one gets out of the habit of using cutlery when one's huddling down in trenches with bullets flying all over the place,' she observed.

Janet started to giggle nervously, quietening abruptly as Rose kicked her under the table. Ron glared briefly at Dorothea, dropping the bone and wiping his fingers on his napkin.

'Well, as you see – the children have settled in nicely,' Arthur put in suddenly, nipping any potential trouble in the bud. 'You mustn't worry about them. We enjoy having them both.'

'Young Philip has almost learned to read and write,' Dorothea gushed, as though she was personally responsible. 'It really is quite amazing, when you consider . . .'

Arthur cut her off hurriedly, fearing she was about to say something totally outrageous.

'Yes, he's a bright little chap,' he put in. He smiled at Elsie. 'His teacher's very pleased with his progress.'

The interruption failed to shut Dorothea up. 'It just goes to show,' she went on. 'You get children out of the slums and give them a little care and attention and they can do just as well as normal youngsters.'

'Really, Mummy,' Rose hissed warningly, but it was too late.

There was a sudden, heavy silence, broken only by the sound of Ron's knife and fork being dropped to his plate. His face registered incredulity rather than rage. He began to push himself to his feet.

Edward leaned across the table, trying to minimize the damage. 'Look, Mr Miller – I'm sure my wife didn't mean . . .'

Ron was on his feet now. He stared at Edward coldly. 'I know exactly what she meant,' he hissed. He turned to his wife. 'Come on, love – we're leaving, right now.'

Elsie looked up, flustered. 'We can't just leave in the middle of dinner,' she protested, helplessly.

Ron ignored her. He looked at Janet. 'Go and pack your things,' he told her sternly. 'You too, Philip.'

Both children stared at their father in confusion for a moment, then started to cry.

Sitting next to them, Dovey rose slowly to his feet, looking quite choked with emotion. He stared at Dorothea with an expression of undiluted hate. 'You evil bloody bitch,' he spat out. 'You've really gone and done it this time, haven't you?'

Dorothea shivered with shock. She turned towards her husband for support, but none was forthcoming.

The sound of the front doorbell shrilled through the silence like an alarm. Rose jumped to her feet, thankful for a chance to escape the stifling, poisonous atmosphere in the room. 'I'll go.'

She ran to the door, pulling it open. Harry's presence hit her like a thunderbolt, draining the colour from her face.

He grinned at her. 'Sorry I'm a bit late – Christmas trains,' he explained cheerily. 'Think your auntie and uncle can find a spare place at the dinner table?'

23

Still numb with shock, Harry stared through his tears at the small, oblong mound of freshly turned earth in the top right-hand corner of the lawn.

'We'll have Dovey plant a tree,' Evelyn murmured softly. 'I thought a holly would be nice, then there'll be berries every Christmas.'

Arthur clapped a comforting hand on Harry's shoulder. 'Well, at least Mary's going to be all right. That's the main thing.'

Harry nodded, dumbly, although his mind screamed out, Is it?

'Can I see her?' he asked, at last.

Arthur shook his head sadly. 'None of us can. Edward expressly forbids it. The one thing she needs more than anything else in the world is sleep, and rest.'

He pulled Harry gently away from the grave, turning him back towards the house. 'You've got a lifetime to have other children,' Arthur went on. 'We lost two between Mary and William. That's if . . .' His voice tailed off uncertainly.

'If what?' Harry asked, huskily.

Arthur sighed. 'If you love her enough,' he finished off. 'Maybe this is an opportunity for you both to look at things objectively, find out how you really feel.'

The words were supposed to be consoling. Instead, they had the opposite effect. Harry stopped dead in his tracks, turning to confront Arthur directly, a look of disbelief on his face. 'So it's a good thing – is that what you're saying?'

Arthur struggled to cover his error of judgement. 'That's not what I meant. But you have to understand, Harry – our first concern has to be for our daughter's well-being.'

Bitterness blazed in Harry's eyes, a surge of negative, frustrated emotions battering against the floodgates of his self-control. 'Then why can't *you* people understand?' he shot back. 'For God's sake – I lost my son today.'

'I know – and we're sorry,' Evelyn put in, gently, but Harry was no longer really hearing clearly.

The floodgates burst, great waves of irrational, bitter anger washing over every other emotion. 'Are you?' he said, his voice rising almost to a shout. 'Are you really sorry – or are you secretly relieved? The dirty slate's wiped clean again, a little social stigma on the family's been removed. Your precious daughter has a second chance to make up for her mistake, put everything right again.'

Arthur tried to calm him. 'Come on, Harry – we can understand that you're upset and you're not thinking clearly,' he reasoned. 'But you don't know what you're saying.'

Harry refused to be pacified. He detached himself from the pair of them, backing towards the house. 'Don't I?' he went on. 'Do you think I don't realize that you never wanted me in this family? Mary's too good for me – isn't that what you really think? You can't accept me and you're never going to.'

Under attack, Evelyn bristled with defiance. 'That's utter nonsense,' she snapped. 'We've done everything we could to make you feel a part of the family. For God's sake, my husband even paid up when your stupid brother jumped his bail.' She regretted the words even as they left her lips, but it was too late.

Harry's face seemed to clear suddenly, as though some great and final truth had just been revealed to him.

'Yes, you would bring that up, wouldn't you?' he said, almost calmly. 'Another thing to hold against me. Something else to use to turn Mary against me.'

He turned his back on them abruptly, and began striding towards the front of the house, where Dovey was loading the last of the Miller children's meagre possessions into the Rover.

'Where are you going?' Arthur called after him.

Harry spoke over his shoulder, not looking back. 'I'm going to be with my family. I'll get a lift into Ashford with the Millers. That'll be another unwanted visitor you're rid of today.'

24

The house was strangely silent as Thomas, Ellen, Frank, Phyllis, Geoffrey and Billy returned from church service.

'Look's like Mum must be taking a little nap,' Thomas observed, pushing open the front door. 'We can all relax before Christmas dinner.'

He was wrong on both counts. As the door lock clicked shut, a crash of piano chords leading into 'Teddy Bear's Picnic' shattered the silence. Granma's thin, reedy voice sang out from the parlour. 'If you go down to the woods today, you're sure of a big surprise . . .'

Geoffrey's eyes opened wide with excitement. 'Blimey, Grandad, it sounds as though Santa Claus has brought you a piano,' he said to Thomas.

Frank nudged his son hastily, shutting him up. He knew exactly who Santa Claus was. Foreseeing trouble and trying to forestall it, he clutched at his father's arm. 'Dad – please! Don't go off the deep end.'

Thomas ignored him, striding into the parlour. His face darkened as he saw Tom, seated at the piano from his warehouse, continuing to play as Granma launched herself into the second verse of the song. He played it through before stopping, climbing slowly to his feet to confront his father.

'And before you say a word, I had enough trouble getting it here so I ain't taking it back,' he muttered firmly. 'Besides, it's fer Granma.'

On top of the piano were a pile of brightly wrapped presents, a crate of Navy rum, a box of crackers and more fruit than Ellen had seen in a month. Tom picked up a small, plain brown-paper parcel, holding it out towards his mother. 'And this is for you and Mum.'

Thomas glared at him. 'You think we want your bloody presents?' he demanded, angrily. 'I told yer – I don't want nothing of yer, nothing! Don't you understand that?'

Granma turned on him scornfully. 'You speak for yerself, Thomas Slater. I've dreamed all me bleedin' life about having a pianna. What's more, it's Christmas – the season of bleed-in' goodwill and I want as much of me family around me as I can get. So does Ellen.'

Tom thrust the parcel into Ellen's hands. 'Anyway, this isn't a present,' he said quietly to his father. 'It's from Clifford.'

Thomas was temporarily speechless. With a little cry, Ellen began to tear at the wrapping paper, pulling out several other small, gift-wrapped packages and a folded letter. With trembling fingers, she unfolded it and started to read out loud.

HMS HAWK.
Dear Mum and Dad.

You won't get this 'til after we've sailed, as I know Dad might think you ought to go to the police. I'm sorry I just went away like that, but it seemed for the best. I didn't want to go to prison, but I could never bring Tom into it. I know he was involved, but he's my brother and I wouldn't be able to forgive myself. I hope you both forgive me now. I'm in the Navy and to prove it I'm enclosing a photo. Hope you like the presents.

Love from Clifford.

She looked up at Thomas, tears of joy in her eyes. 'Oh Thomas – he's all right. I'm so happy.' She fumbled through the parcels, finally finding the promised snapshot and staring at it proudly. 'Look how fine he looks in his uniform,' she went on, holding it out for his inspection.

Unsmiling, but deeply moved, Thomas took the photo from her fingers and studied it. A faint glow began to spread across his face. 'Well, maybe the Navy'll be the makin' of

him,' he muttered, finally, passing the photo back almost reluctantly. He regarded Ellen's happy, smiling face for a few
seconds, then glared at Tom. 'You had to find a way, didn't
yer? You had to find a bloody way.'

'Now, Thomas,' Ellen chided him, with unusual forceful-
ness. 'He came here to make peace, and God knows there's
little enough of that.'

Tom stepped across to his mother, hugging her. 'It's all
right, Mum. I've done what I came to do.' He paused,
sniffing in the air as the unmistakable smell of roast pork
drifted up the hallway. 'Anyway, it looks like your Christmas
dinner has arrived.'

He kissed Granma, moving towards the door as Ivy came
in, proudly bearing the meat in a roasting tray. She was followed by Reg and Kaye, carrying golden-brown potatoes and
steaming vegetables respectively.

Ivy looked surprised to see Tom. He winked at her, grinning. 'It's all right, Ive – I won't be after your crackling today.
I'm just off.' He tapped the side of his nose suggestively. 'And
you ain't seen me – right?'

Ellen saw him to the front door, and stood watching as he
walked down the street and turned the corner. Still smiling
happily, she bustled back into the kitchen to help with the
serving up.

'I don't know how we're going to fit everyone around the
kitchen table,' she fussed. 'It's going to be a terrible squeeze.'

'We'll manage, ducks,' Granma cackled, licking her wrinkled lips with relish. She scuttled back to the parlour for a
few seconds, returning with a bottle of Tom's rum and a
handful of crackers. 'Right, let's have a party then, shall we?'

Dinner was long since over, the last cracker pulled. Ellen,
Phyllis and Ivy were in the kitchen finishing off the clearing
up whilst Frank and the two boys chased fruitlessly around in
the windless back garden, trying to fly the small box-kite
which Tom had brought for Billy. Granma had retired to her

bedroom with a bottle of rum and both Thomas and Reg were fast asleep in the parlour, snoring their heads off while Kaye tried to read a book.

It was not a pretty sound – or sight. Kaye put up with it for as long as she could, finally climbing to her feet and walking out into the hallway. 'I'm just going to fetch my coat from next door and I'm going for a walk,' she called to Ivy in the kitchen. Without waiting for an answer, she let herself out of the front door.

'Hello, Kaye,' Harry said, with a funny little catch in his voice. He was standing in the street, smoking a cigarette and staring at the house with the look of a man locked out of Paradise.

Kaye rallied from her shock quickly. 'Blimey, Harry, you gave me a turn. How long have you been out here?'

Harry shrugged. 'Not long. I want to go in, but I don't want to spoil their Christmas.'

Kaye stared at his careworn, hopeless face. It said everything.

'She lost the baby?' she whispered, her heart surging with pity.

Harry nodded miserably. 'And they won't even let me see her.'

Kaye managed a sad, sympathetic smile. 'Need a shoulder to cry on?'

Harry nodded again. 'I know it's a liberty, you of all people.'

Kaye shook her head, dismissing his fears. 'Don't be silly, Harry. What are friends for?' She stepped into the street, taking his hand. 'Come in next door, it's nice and quiet. Everyone's in yer mum and dad's.'

Unprotesting, Harry let Kaye lead him into the house and through to the parlour. She pushed him gently down onto the settee, sitting beside him, still holding his hand.

'Want a cup of tea?' she asked.

Harry shook his head. 'No, thanks.' He was silent for a

while, staring down at the floor. Suddenly, he looked up, his face curious. 'How did you know? About the baby?'

Kaye sighed. 'I helped bring her home after the pains started. Last night, from the dance.'

The information seemed to seep into Harry's brain slowly, like percolating coffee. His expression hardened from puzzlement to incredulity. 'Dance?' he repeated, dully, at last. 'She was out *dancing*?'

Kaye felt like biting off her tongue. 'She'd only come along to keep her cousin Rose company,' she lied quickly, wanting to minimize his pain.

Harry shook his head, unconvinced. 'No, that's how much she really cared, Kaye. I should have seen it all along. First thing she thought about when we got married was getting her job back. I saw the look on her face when Mum gave her some baby clothes she'd knitted. To her, the baby was just something that got in the way of living.' He broke off, starting to weep uncontrollably. 'I'm just so sorry – so sorry about everything.'

Kaye slipped her arm around his shoulder, comforting him like a child. 'You know, I haven't seen you cry since you was ten,' she murmured gently. 'You look just the same.'

Harry turned towards her, his eyes brimming. 'I cried before the wedding,' he told her.

Kaye nodded. 'I did, too,' she said simply. She kissed him comfortingly upon the cheek, her lips sliding through his tears as he turned his head until their mouths met.

They were making love before either of them fully realized what was happening.

The kite was not going to fly, Frank realized. Fed up with trying, he smiled at his two sons apologetically. 'I think it's about time we gave up,' he suggested. 'Wait for a windier day.'

'One last try – please, Dad,' Billy begged. He thrust the

137

kite into his father's hands, letting out several feet of string and preparing to dash the length of the back garden.

The kite jerked into the air, rose to the end of its string and then nosedived earthwards again, plunging down into the tunnel of the Anderson shelter.

'I'll get it,' Geoffrey announced. He ran to the shelter entrance, scrambling down the boarded earth steps to retrieve the kite. He stopped, suddenly, in his tracks. 'Blimey!' he said loudly, staring into the recesses of the shelter with a stunned look on his face. He turned to his father. 'Here, Dad – you'd better come over here, quick.'

Mystified, Frank came running over, reaching the top of the steps and following his son's line of vision into the gloomy interior of the shelter.

Geoffrey turned to face his father, his face pale. 'Is she dead?' he asked, in a shaken voice.

The question echoed Frank's own, initial fears. Then the huddled bundle of rags and newspapers moved slightly, and a baby's crying broke the stunned silence.

Moira awoke with a start, instinctively clutching Shirley more tightly against her body. She stared up at Geoffrey and Frank with the pitiful look of a trapped animal, shivering with cold and fear.

'My God,' Frank breathed. He pulled Geoffrey back up the steps, moving him out of the way. The boy moved back towards the house in the wake of Billy, who had also taken a quick peek and was now running full-pelt towards the kitchen door, screaming excitedly at the top of his voice, 'Gran, Gran – we found a girl and a baby hidin' in your shelter.'

Moira scrambled to the very back wall of the shelter, cowering there as Frank climbed down towards her, holding out his arms.

'It's all right, love – no one's going to hurt you,' Frank murmured, soothingly. He bent over her, helping her to her feet. Peeling off his jacket, he wrapped it around her shoulders, pushing her back towards the steps.

The kitchen door was already open as they reached it, Ellen and Phyllis standing there with bemused, apprehensive looks on their faces. Woken from his doze by Billy's commotion, Thomas was on his way along the hall, followed by Granma who had come back downstairs to see what all the excitement was about.

Frank bundled Moira into the kitchen, pushing her down on to a chair. 'Someone make her a hot cup of tea,' he ordered. 'She's half-frozen to death.'

Phyllis regarded Moira's filth-encrusted body and matted hair with a shiver of distaste. 'Christ, Frank, she's crawling,' she complained.

'Well, she can have a bath, can't she?' Frank snapped back, irritably. He ran to the cupboard, finding a left-over mince pie. He thrust it into Moira's hands and hovered over her solicitously as she tucked into it ravenously.

'What the 'ell was she doing there?' Thomas asked, totally flummoxed. He eyed Frank suspiciously. 'You're acting like you know her. Who is she?'

There was no easy way to break it. 'She's your granddaughter,' Frank said quietly. 'She's Tom's kid.'

The ensuing silence was broken only by a chorus of indrawn breaths. It was Granma who spoke first. 'Well, stop gawpin', the lot of you,' she muttered. 'She's not a bleedin' freak show.' She pushed Frank out of the way, standing over Moira like a mother hen. 'Tom? Yer Tom's?'

Moira regarded them all sullenly. 'He never told yer?'

'No, he bleedin' didn't,' Thomas exploded in sudden fury. 'I'd have made him do the decent thing if he had.' He turned on Frank, his eyes blazing. 'If you know where he is, you'd better go and fetch him. I ain't too old yet to give him the tanning of his life.'

'No.' Moira's voice rose in a scream. 'I told Frank – I don't want nuffink to do wiv him.' She rose to her feet, eyeing the back door nervously. 'I don't know why I came here, I'm sorry. I was desperate, I just didn't know what to do. I wanna go.'

Granma wrapped her arms around the girl's shoulders. 'Don't be soft,' she said gently. 'You ain't going nowhere, except up to a nice warm bed in my room.'

Ellen had so far been totally dumbstruck. Now, finding her voice at last, she could only manage a faint protest. 'But she's filthy, she needs a bath.'

'She can have a bath termorrer,' Granma said, firmly, in a tone that no one was going to argue with.

25

Tom jumped up from his table in the lounge bar of the Dog and Duck as Granma's head appeared round the door, peering around uncertainly. 'Over here, Gran.'

She hobbled over, sitting herself down. There was a glass of rum already on the table, waiting for her.

'Thanks for coming, Gran,' Tom said, meaning it. 'You're my only contact now. Harry's gone, Frank won't speak to me and Dad's threatened to take his belt to me if he ever claps eyes on me again.' He paused, allowing Granma to take a sip of her rum. 'So, how's Moira and the baby? How's Mum? Everybody getting on all right?'

Granma shrugged, giving him a thin, wry smile. 'Two women, one kitchen,' she muttered. 'Bound to be a few problems. But we're coping.'

She didn't seem her normal, cheery self, Tom thought. She looked tired.

'You feeling all right?' he asked, with genuine concern.

Granma nodded. 'Just need a good night's kip, that's all. That nipper of yours has fair worn me out with all her scratching and screaming all night.'

A worried frown furrowed Tom's forehead. 'What's up – is she ill?'

Granma shook her head, dismissing his fears. 'She's got the chickenpox, that's all.'

Tom's hand flashed to his pocket, coming out grasping a fistful of notes. 'She'll need a doctor. I'll give you the money.'

'She don't need no bloody doctor,' Granma muttered scornfully, dismissing the entire medical profession. 'A few spots, that's all.'

Tom was still proffering the cash. 'All right, then. Use it to buy our Moira something nice – present from her dad.'

Granma fixed him with a patronizing, faintly sad smile. 'She don't want presents, you great fool. She wants a dad she can depend on.'

It was Tom's turn to look sad. 'Yeah – well, that ain't too easy, is it?' he said morosely. 'I ain't allowed near the house, I can't afford to go any one place too regularly and I can't stay anywhere for too long at a time.'

'You made yer own bed, Tom,' Granma reminded him.

He nodded, letting out a sigh. 'Yeah, I know.' He was silent for a while, finally thrusting the money into Granma's hands, folding her fingers over it. 'Well, take the money anyway. Things must be pretty tight with two extra mouths to feed. You can find some way of sneaking it into Mum's housekeeping, can't you?

Granma looked uncertain, finally giving a little shrug. 'Well, all right – if you're sure. I'll get two bottles for a start – calamine for Shirley, rum for me. That way we might both get a decent night's sleep.' She hesitated before tucking the cash away in her purse. 'You sure you can afford this?'

Tom let out a hollow laugh. 'Might as well be put to good use while I've got it. Won't be for much longer, the way things are looking.'

Granma's eyes narrowed. 'You in trouble again?' she asked him.

Tom shook his head. 'Not that sort of trouble. Had a visitor at me warehouse, didn't I? Government geezer, from the Ministry of Aircraft Production.'

Granma was intrigued. 'What did 'e want?'

'Seems the place I paid good money for is too big for my needs,' he muttered, somewhat bitterly. 'So they're going to take it away from me, turn it into an assembly plant. Requisition, they call it. Old-fashioned bloody thievin', in my book.'

Granma regarded him sympathetically. 'So what yer gonna do?'

Tom shrugged. 'What can I do? Going to have to do a runner, ain't I? Just when I thought I had something going for me, something I could build on for Moira and Shirley.' Something between a laugh and a sob escaped his throat. His eyes held a deep sadness. 'I've really had enough of runnin', Gran.'

'Then don't,' Granma told him flatly. 'Dig your heels in. They want to set up a factory, then they're going to need someone to manage it, ain't they? It's your place. The least they're gonna do is give you the job, if you ask for it.'

It all sounded too easy, Tom thought, snorting. 'I don't know nothing about aircraft parts,' he pointed out.

Granma was ready for the objection. 'Being ignorant's never stood in your way before. Put yourself forward.'

Tom's eyes held a mixture of hope, and doubt. 'But the cops are still looking for me, and I got a false ID.'

Granma grinned knowingly. 'So you'd be working for the Government, wouldn't yer? That's the last place the cops are going to come snoopin' around.'

Tom dared to think about it seriously for the first time. 'Blimey, Gran – do you honestly reckon I could get away with it?' he breathed.

She grinned at him. 'With your bleeding cheek? Chance don't even come into it.'

'You're a champion, Gran,' Tom said. 'You deserve another drink.' He got up, walking over to the bar.

When he returned, Granma was looking around the pub approvingly. Freshly decorated, it had a definite air of respectability about it. The bar counter and every table were dry and polished and there was even carpet on the floor.

'Always was a nice boozer, this,' Granma observed, a wistful smile creeping over her face. 'I used to sing here sometimes, in the old days. Wouldn't mind going back to it, either. I was thinking of joining ENSA, doing me bit for the war effort.'

'What, "Every Night Something Awful",' Tom mocked

145

gently. 'Fancy being sent off to the front to entertain the troops then, do yer, Gran?'

She took the sarcasm in good part, grinning at him. 'Nah, you daft bugger. But I heard they was recruiting for people to go round the factories and such, cheering up the workers. Wouldn't mind a bit of that.'

Tom lifted his glass to her. 'Good for you then, Gran,' he said, smiling. 'You'll knock 'em in the aisles again.'

26

Dorothea was bored, and had been knocking back the gin all evening. It was a dangerous mixture. She sat in the drawing-room of Albourne House with Arthur and Edward, brooding about the continuing collapse of her social life.

Outside, in the hallway, Mrs Dovey banged on the gong to announce that dinner was served. Arthur climbed to his feet, heading for the dining-room.

Dorothea drained her glass, holding it out for a top-up. 'Pour me another gin, will you, darling?' she purred to Edward.

He flashed her a look of quiet exasperation. 'We'll be late for dinner,' he pointed out.

Dorothea rolled her eyes. 'Well, that's hardly a treasonable offence, even in your book,' she said sarcastically.

Edward sighed, recognizing her mood, 'What the hell's wrong with you, Dorothea?' he demanded wearily. 'You've been like this all day.'

She sniffed haughtily. 'Nothing. Nothing whatsoever. I'm just thrilled and delighted at the prospect of yet another evening *en famille*.'

She was still waving her empty gin glass in the air. Sighing, Edward refilled it, returning the decanter to the sideboard. 'Look, it's hardly my fault if you find your own family dull,' he muttered, defensively.

Dorothea glared at him, her mood hardening from mere petulance into out-and-out bitchiness. 'Really?' she demanded, with heavy irony. 'Then whose fault is it that we don't have much other choice these days? No one has invited us out for nearly two months now. Anyone I telephone just happens to be busy. People cross the street to avoid us in case some snotty little plainclothes policeman is going to follow them all the way home asking questions about their political affiliations. Face it, Edward – you've turned us into a pair of social outcasts.'

The drawing-room door opened. Mrs Dovey peered into the room. 'Excuse me, but dinner's on the table,' she informed them politely.

Dorothea flashed the woman a dismissive glance. 'Can't you knock?' she snapped.

'I did, several times,' Mrs Dovey said pointedly, bristling at her attitude. 'I also rang the dinner gong, some minutes ago.'

Dorothea slurped down the rest of her gin. 'Oh, well – in that case we'd better rush to the table, hadn't we?' she said cattily. 'Can't keep the servants waiting. No doubt you also have some riveting topic of conversation to enjoy over dinner as well. Another account of the state of Mr Dovey's lungs, perhaps?'

Mrs Dovey's face was a cold, grim mask. 'My husband was gassed fighting for his country,' she said, icily. 'He deserves some respect.'

Edward jumped in hurriedly, trying to make peace. 'Of course, Mrs Dovey – I'm quite sure my wife didn't mean . . .'

Dorothea would not be apologized for. 'Don't tell me what I mean, Edward,' she snapped curtly. 'You haven't seen him in the vegetable patch, hawking and spitting for victory. It's a wonder we haven't all come down with TB.'

It was the straw which broke the camel's back. Mrs Dovey drew in a long, deep breath, her body quivering with pent-up hate and rage. Exhaling again with a deep sigh, she began to unpick her apron strings.

'That's it,' she hissed. 'I've had enough of your remarks.'

Dorothea's lips curled in a sneer. 'My God. The staff are turning bolshie.'

Mrs Dovey threw her apron to the floor. She turned on Dorothea, her eyes blazing. 'Don't you sneer at me, just 'cause you're clever with words,' she raged. 'You're no better than me and you've got less manners, for all your breeding.'

It was too late to save the day, Edward realized, with a sinking feeling. He could only flash Arthur and Evelyn a helpless, hopeless glance as they entered the drawing-room, wondering what was holding up their dinner guests.

Mrs Dovey was in full spate now, the last barrier of social convention in ruins.

'My Dovey ruined his health fighting for the likes of you,' she spat at Dorothea. 'He may not have much learning but at least he knows how to treat another human being, which is more than you do.'

Evelyn couldn't quite take in what was going on. 'Is something wrong, Mrs Dovey?' she inquired innocently. 'The rissoles are going cold.' Her eyes fell on the discarded apron on the floor, and she began to fall in. 'Oh dear, has my sister upset you?'

'For the last time, as it happens,' Mrs Dovey answered her, coldly polite. 'I've taken all I'm prepared to take. I'm off.' With a final contemptuous glance at Dorothea, she stormed from the room.

Seemingly unaffected by it all, Dorothea finished her gin and poured herself another. 'Well, well,' she observed, loudly to herself. 'Cold rissoles. The perfect end to a perfect day.'

It took every ounce of self-control that Evelyn possessed to refrain from hitting her. Instead, she turned on her heel without a word and rushed in pursuit of Mrs Dovey.

She was in the kitchen, busily gathering her few personal things together. She looked up as Evelyn entered, almost apologetic. 'I'm sorry, Mrs Hamilton – but this time she went too far. We're both leaving, and there's nothing you can say to make me change my mind.'

Evelyn was totally flustered. 'But you can't just leave. I mean, where will you go?'

The woman shrugged. 'My sister's been wanting us to go

back home for some time. She's on her own now, and she needs me.'

'But I need you, too,' Evelyn said, almost pleading.

It fell on deaf ears. 'I'm sorry,' Mrs Dovey repeated. 'But you've got your family, and I've got mine. It's for the best.'

Somehow, Evelyn doubted this, but there was obviously nothing she could do.

'Well,' Arthur muttered, heavily. 'This has all come as a bit of a shock, as you might guess.'

Dovey nodded, sipping at the glass of brandy which Arthur had poured for him. 'I'm sorry about that, sir.'

The two men stood in Arthur's study, facing each other squarely, not equals, not quite friends, yet somehow bonded by something else, something stronger.

'We go back a long way, Dovey,' Arthur murmured, distantly. 'And here we are at war again.' He paused, holding himself in check against a rising emotional tide. 'I suppose there's nothing I could possibly say to change things?'

Dovey shook his head, looking genuinely sorry. 'You know how it is, sir. Mrs Dovey's very loyal.' He finished off his drink.

Arthur nodded understandingly. 'Yes, of course.' He took the empty glass from Dovey's hand. 'You'll keep in touch, I hope?'

'Of course.' Dovey nodded, beginning to turn towards the door.

Arthur felt a deep sadness welling up inside him again. He turned towards his desk, putting down the glass. 'Well, thank you – for everything,' he muttered, over his shoulder.

Unwilling to actually see the man go, he busied himself tidying the surface of his desk until he heard the faint sigh of the study door closing.

27

Ellen looked up with a start as the front door opened and Tom stuck his head into the hallway, peering about nervously. 'Is the coast clear?'

Concern clouded his mother's face. 'What are you doing here?' she asked, anxiously. 'Your father will be home any minute now. There'll be hell to pay if he finds you here.'

Tom nodded, also looking worried. 'I know, but I had to come. I've been worried sick about the little 'un.'

Ellen's eyebrows raised, fractionally. 'Don't tell me you're growing up at last?'

Tom looked sheepish. 'Where's Moira? Where's Shirley?'

The first part of the question was answered as Moira stepped out from the parlour. She glared at her father. 'She's up in Granma's room, both of 'em fast asleep,' she muttered. 'And she don't want to see you any more than I do.'

The hostility hurt. Rallying himself, Tom managed a thin smile. 'Hello, love,' he murmured gently. He delved into his pocket, pulling out a medicine bottle. 'Look, I've brought some more calamine lotion.'

Moira was unmoved. 'Don't need any more. We got plenty.' She turned her back on him, heading towards the stairs.

Tom clutched at her arm, but she shook it off. 'Look, she's just had the chickenpox, but she's all right. Now just leave us alone and go, will yer?' She marched up the stairs without another word.

Ellen saw the pain of rejection in her son's eyes, but there was nothing she could do. 'Come on, Tom – it really is better if you leave now,' she murmured, pushing him gently towards the front door. 'Yer dad's not at his sunniest right now, with what little news has been coming back from France.'

Tom nodded miserably. 'Perhaps you're right, Mum.' He was about to open the front door when a bloodcurdling scream from Moira shrilled down the stairs, making them both stop dead in their tracks.

Unfreezing, Tom was up the stairs like a shot, his reflexes honed by a lifetime of getting away from trouble. With Ellen on his heels, he ran into Granma's bedroom.

Granma was sitting up in bed, one eye bloodshot and swollen and the entire side of her face livid and blotched with huge, ugly red blisters. Moira was staring at her in horror, as though she was something straight out of an Edgar Allan Poe novel.

'I just went to wake her up, and she was like that,' she told Ellen, her voice shaking slightly. 'It's horrible – what's wrong wiv 'er?'

The immediate panic over, Ellen assessed the situation at a glance. 'Looks like she's got shingles,' she observed calmly. She bent over Granma, easing her back down on to the pillows. 'Come on, Gran – lay back and take it easy.'

Granma groaned. 'Ooh, me head hurts,' she complained. 'And I've got little men wiv pick-axes working on me eyeballs.'

'How d'you feel in yourself, Gran?' Tom asked her, solicitous.

Granma pulled a face. 'Bloody horrible, like something the cat sicked up,' she said, expressively.

Tom glanced at his mother. 'D'you reckon we ought to call a doctor?'

Ellen gave him a patronizing smile. 'Don't be daft. It's only shingles,' she said, not seeming too worried.

Granma glared up at her. 'What do you mean – only?' she demanded indignantly.

Ellen ignored her, crossing to the window to pull the blackout curtains. 'This'll make your eyes feel better, anyway,' she murmured, suddenly giving a little start of alarm as she looked out through the window. She turned back to Tom, quickly. 'Here's your dad home. You'd better scarper.'

Tom glanced briefly at Granma. 'You're sure she's going to be all right?' he asked his mother.

Ellen nodded impatiently. 'She'll be fine. Now go.' she urged.

Tom did as he was told, legging it down the stairs and running out the back door at the very second his father came in the front.

Thomas stood, rock-still and zombie-like, just inside the hallway, still facing the door. He hadn't even bothered to take off his work jacket. At first, Ellen thought he had been in the pub after work, quickly dismissing the thought as fanciful.

It was only at the sound of her footsteps descending the stairs that Thomas turned, slowly, to face her. He looked pale, his expression more grim than Ellen could remember in many years.

Attack seemed suddenly the best form of defence. 'Look, Thomas – if you're angry because Tom was here, I've got more important things to worry about,' she told him. 'Your mother's poorly, and she's going to need a bit of nursing and fussing over for the next few weeks.'

There was no response, even at the sound of Tom's name. Thomas continued to stand there like a broken puppet, his expression unchanging.

Suddenly, Ellen felt a coldness in the pit of her belly. She remembered now the last time she had seen that look on his face – the night his father had died. A lump rose in her throat, threatening to choke her.

'Tell me?' she managed to say, in a tight and strangled little voice.

He could not speak. Instead, he pulled the folded newspaper from under his arm, thrusting it out towards her.

The headline screamed off the front page: HMS HAWK SUNK AT NARVIK.

Ellen's voice rose in a scream of denial. 'NO! Not my baby.' She tore at the newspaper in a frenzy, ripping back the pages one by one. 'There'll be a list of survivors,' she said, finding a spark of hope. 'They always print a list of survivors.'

Thomas spoke for the first time. 'Clifford's not on it,' he muttered quietly. 'I've already looked.'

Ellen stared at him with misty eyes, although the tears had not yet started to flow. The pain of grief was still a few seconds away, kept at bay by shock. 'Narvik?' she murmured in a dull, faraway voice. 'I don't even know where that is.'

'Norway,' Thomas said flatly. 'It's off the coast of Norway.'

He gave up then, surrendered himself to the heavy, terrible burden he had taken upon himself for Ellen's sake. Thomas began to sob – great, racking spasms of grief which shook his whole body.

Ellen threw herself at him, wrapping her arms around his shoulders and hugging him with all her strength. She began to pat his back, making little soothing noises in her throat as though she were comforting a child.

28

Granma stared morosely out over Ramsgate sea front, determined to be miserable. The shingles scars were still causing her considerable discomfort, and she was missing the consolation of familiar surroundings, even Moira and the baby.

'Bloody daft, if you ask me,' she muttered to Frank, as they sat on the promenade wall. 'Who comes on holiday to the seaside in bleedin' May?'

Frank was watching his wife and two sons paddling in the sea. He turned back to Granma with an indulgent smile. 'It'll be June in three days' time,' he pointed out to her. 'And anyway, this isn't exactly a holiday, it's convalescence. You've been poorly.' He glanced back at Geoffrey and Billy again. 'Besides, it's nice for me to be able to spend a bit of time as a proper family again.'

Granma couldn't argue with that. Instead, she aired her personal objections. 'I bloody hate the seaside,' she said venomously. 'I died in Margate in 1936. All the bloody punters wanted was fan dancers and monologues. Didn't appreciate a bit of class when they heard it.'

The two boys were running up the beach towards them now, Phyllis walking behind them. Frank's face glowed. He picked up Clifford's old leather football he'd brought from Nelson Street. 'How about a nice game of soccer on the beach?' he suggested to his sons.

Billy looked reasonably enthusiastic, Geoffrey less so. 'Don't really fancy football any more. I'd rather go sailing with Maurice.'

Frank looked astounded. 'You? Gone off football? I don't believe it.'

Geoffrey shrugged. 'Kid's game, innit?'

Frank grinned ruefully at Phyllis as she joined them, nodding at Geoffrey. 'He's growing up,' he observed.

His wife nodded. 'Yeah – too fast.'

Frank frowned slightly, a look of doubt, not quite suspicion, in his eyes. 'What's all this about sailing?' he asked. 'And who's this Maurice?'

Geoffrey's eyes seemed to come alight at the mention of the man's name. 'Mr Simpson, Dad. He's been all round the world,' he said excitedly. 'Durban, Sydney, Rio – even New York. That's what I'd like to do.'

Granma had been listening to the conversation with interest. 'How old is he, this Maurice?' she asked Geoffrey.

The boy shrugged. 'Pretty old. About fifty, I suppose.'

'Married, is he?' Granma wanted to know.

Geoffrey shook his head. 'Don't think so.'

'Then I'd watch your back, if I was you, ' Granma told him. 'They can be a bit funny sometimes, sailors.'

It was a joke, but there was no humour in her old eyes as she glanced up, flashing a message at Frank. The message was pretty clear: 'A little bit of checking up wouldn't come amiss.'

Ellen was on her knees on the kerb, cleaning the front step. She paused in her work as a shadow fell over her, glancing up in surprise. Seeing Tom, she climbed to her feet, managing a faint smile. 'Hello, stranger.'

Tom nodded towards the hallway. 'Dad in?'

Ellen shook her head. 'No, you're all right. He's at work, won't be back till late. Moira's out too, if that's who you've come to see. Going after some part-time job she saw advertised in a newspaper shop window. Waitressing in a tea-shop, or something.'

A quick flash of disappointment crossed Tom's face, then he grinned again. 'As it happens, I came to see you, brought you some good news,' he said. 'Any chance of a cuppa?'

'Long as you don't mind it without sugar. Can't get it for love nor money.' Ellen walked down the hallway towards the kitchen, Tom following her.

'You want some sugar? I'll get you some. Butter too, if you want it.'

Ellen put the kettle on, turning to face him. 'I want it honest, Tom,' she said, wearily.

His face was the picture of innocence. 'I paid good money for it, Mum – believe me.'

Ellen wasn't in a mood to argue. 'All right,' she agreed. 'Thousands wouldn't.' She paused, wondering why Tom seemed so cheerful. 'Things going OK for you then, are they?'

Tom nodded emphatically. 'Taking over this aircraft factory's the best thing I ever did. You know I've got seven girls working for me now? Mr Crabtree, this geezer from the Ministry of Aircraft, is already talking about expanding. He says I'm a man who can get things done, make things happen.'

'Cut a few corners, you mean,' Ellen said, almost smiling.

Tom gave her a crafty grin. 'Whatever it takes.' His face became serious for a moment. 'Tell you the truth, Mum – I'm thinking of ditching all the stuff on the side, going completely straight. There's one of the girls, Sandra. We've been out a couple of times and she really likes me, I can tell.'

Ellen was unconvinced. 'Likes the money you spend on her, you mean?'

Tom looked wounded. 'No, she's not like that, Mum,' he protested. 'She's a really nice girl – decent, know what I mean? I reckon she could make an honest man out of me, one day.'

Ellen took the news at face value, with a thin smile. 'That's the good news, is it?' she asked.

Tom shook his head again, beaming at her. 'No, better. Much better. It's about Clifford. Mum, he's alive.'

The colour drained from Ellen's face. She stared at Tom in shock, wanting to believe him but afraid to. 'Don't you be mucking me about, Tom – not about Clifford,' she said in a shaken voice.

Tom was mortified. 'Blimey, Mum – d'you think I'd lie about something like that?' He delved into his pocket, producing a telegram. 'Look, it says it right here.'

Ellen snatched the telegram from his fingers, eagerly scanning its terse message: *Thomas Franks – in hospital Norway*. She looked back at Tom, disappointment and confusion on her face. 'Who's Thomas Franks?'

Tom laughed nervously, his voice cracking with emotion. 'It's bleedin' Cliff, ain't it? That's the false name he used when he joined up.'

Ellen was still completely bewildered, but there was nothing ambiguous about the sparkle in Tom's eyes. Finally, she dared to believe him. 'Then it's true? He's alive, my Clifford?'

Tom nodded. 'Yes, Mum – he's alive.'

Tears of joy pricked out in Ellen's eyes. 'Oh, Tom, Tom,' she said, with a funny little sob. She fell against him, hugging him tightly for several moments. Finally, she detached herself, looking up into his eyes. 'He really is alive?' she asked again, as if confirmation would make it doubly so.

Tom grinned, nodding. 'Yes,' he said, firmly, finally.

A wave of euphoria swamped Ellen's emotions. It was only after a long time that other thoughts resurfaced. A trace of her earlier confusion returned to her face. 'But why did they send the telegram to you?' she wanted to know. 'I'm his mother – you'd have thought I'd be the first to know.'

'They had my address – at the pub,' Tom told her. 'That's what Cliff used, see, when he signed up.'

A hurt look passed across his mother's eyes. 'So your Dad was right? You were in on this right from the start?'

Her tone was accusatory. Tom went on the defensive. 'He

asked me to help him, that's all. It's what he wanted – he was desperate.'

Bitterness was creeping into Ellen's voice, as she remembered the days of numbing pain, the nights she had sat up crying. 'He was just a frightened child, and you took advantage of that.'

'No!' Tom's denial was vehement. 'I did it for him, Mum.'

'You did it for yourself, more like,' his mother observed, shaking her head sadly. 'Just like you do everything for yourself. All you ever think about is you, isn't it?'

Tom tried to calm her. 'Come on, Mum – please.'

Ellen backed away from him, retreating across the kitchen. She leaned against the sink, regarding him sullenly. 'You could have told us. You knew how we was hurting.'

That was unfair, Tom thought, struggling to justify himself. 'He was listed as "Missing Presumed Dead". Is *that* what you'd have wanted to hear?'

Ellen's voice rose, almost to a shout. 'Yes, I'd have wanted to know – can't you understand that? I was desperate to know anything.'

Tom's shoulders slumped. 'I'm sorry, Mum. I did what I thought was for the best.' He smiled, weakly. 'Anyway, he's all right, and he'll be coming home. That's the main thing, isn't it?'

There was no reply. Ellen had unfolded the telegram again and was rereading it.

'Well, I'll leave you to explain it all to Dad,' Tom muttered. 'He won't take it from me.' He slunk out of the house, his spirits completely crushed.

The studio was up a bare flight of stairs tucked between a hardware shop and a greengrocer's, with a small sign over the open doorway which read, simply: VICTOR D'ARCY – PHOTOGRAPHER. Portraits a Speciality.

Moira paused in the doorway, checking the address against

the note she had scribbled down. Then, picking up Shirley in her arms, she began to mount the stairs.

There was another door at the top. Moira pushed it open, stepping inside. There was a very small reception area-cum-office, with a sofa, a couple of filing cabinets and a small desk, leading through to a screened-off room which served as both studio and darkroom.

Victor put on his best professional smile as Moira entered. 'Come for a portrait of the baby, have you?' he inquired. He stepped over, feigning admiration for Shirley. 'Oh, she's a real pretty little thing – just like her mum. She'll make a beautiful picture.'

Moira's voice was hesitant, nervous. 'Actually, I came about the job in the shop window: Photographic Models Wanted.'

Victor's attitude changed abruptly, the smile disappearing from his face. 'All right, put the nipper down and stand still so I can take a look at you,' he said curtly.

Moira did as she was told, laying Shirley down on the sofa as Victor walked around, appraising her from head to toe.

First impressions were favourable. She had a good figure, Victor thought – fair amount up top without being blowsy. The face was pretty enough, although the girl would need a bit of make-up. The main thing was that she was fresh, wholesome-looking, and not like some of the tired old tarts and scrubbers he was used to working with.

He made up his mind on impulse. 'All right,' he said, with a nod. 'You'll do. I'll pay you five bob an hour for each session, and we can do two, maybe three sessions a week.' He paused, his eyes narrowing. 'You don't mind posing in a swimsuit, do you?'

Moira was overcome. Two shillings an hour was a reasonable wage for a working man – five bob was a fortune. She shook her head, her eyes glittering. 'That's all right – anything,' she said eagerly.

Momentarily, Victor regretted his rash generosity. The girl

would probably have settled for half a crown. He consoled himself by looking at the bright side instead. She was young, apparently innocent – and having the baby made her vulnerable.

Just how he liked 'em, he thought to himself, licking his lips.

29

Ramsgate harbour seemed unusually busy, Geoffrey thought. It seemed that every vessel, from fishing smacks and pleasure craft to small sloops and day boats, was being rigged up and readied. The bustle of activity was all the more surprising because it was not a particularly nice day.

The slight sense of mystery passed out of his mind as he spotted the 20-foot *Silver Seal*. 'That's it, that's Mr Simpson's boat,' he told his father excitedly, pointing it out.

Maurice Simpson looked up from filling the inboard fuel tank as the pair of them approached along the jetty. Normally, he would have given young Geoffrey a smile of welcome, but today his face was grim.

'No pleasure sailing today, I'm afraid,' he announced flatly. 'Bit of a flap on.'

Geoffrey took another look around the bustling harbour, and then to the decks of Maurice's boat. The man had already lashed spare cans of fuel and full water canisters to the prow rail – quite obviously far more than would be needed for a day trip.

'What's going on?' he asked, mystified. 'You're loading up as though you were putting to sea.'

Maurice nodded, curtly. 'I am – to France, provided I can find a crew. There doesn't seem to be a spare hand to be found in the entire town.'

Geoffrey's eyes glittered. 'Me and my dad could crew for you,' he blurted out, acknowledging Frank's presence for the first time.

Maurice smiled apologetically. 'Sorry, Geoffrey – it'd be far too dangerous,' he muttered.

'I ain't bloomin' afraid,' Geoffrey asserted firmly. He

turned to his father, anxious and desperate. 'We could go, couldn't we, Dad? You'd be all right, I'd look after you.'

Frank regarded his son with a mixture of dismay and horror. 'Don't be bloody daft, Geoffrey. Your mother'd kill me.'

Geoffrey's eyes blazed with defiant anger. Before Frank could stop him, he had jumped on to the boat's beck and sat down. 'Well I'm going,' he announced firmly. 'And if you want to drag me off kicking and screaming in front of all these people, that's up to you.'

Frank gritted his teeth, trying to control his anger. 'Don't bloody think I won't,' he threatened. His hand dropped to his belt, loosening the buckle. 'In fact, if you don't get up right now, I'll strap you in front of Mr Simpson. D'you fancy that?'

Geoffrey's defiant expression changed to one of scorn. 'You're scared, aren't you?' he said bitterly. 'You're afraid – that's why you're just in the Fire Service instead of going off to fight like Uncle Harry.'

The bitter words struck Frank like a blow in the face. Stunned, he stared dumbly at Geoffrey's scornful face, not knowing what to say.

Maurice stepped in, trying to make the peace. 'Do as your father tells you and get up at once,' he snapped at Geoffrey. He turned towards Frank. 'Don't be too hard on him, Mr Slater. He's not aware of what he's saying.'

Frank was silent for a long time. 'Would we do?' he asked Maurice finally. 'Could you take us?'

Maurice was caught on the hop. 'Well, Geoffrey's a fine sailor – a natural,' he muttered, uncertainly. 'But he's just a boy – I couldn't take responsibility.'

Frank's face was set and impassive. 'He's my son. He's my responsibility,' he said flatly. He looked back at Geoffrey. 'Give me fifteen minutes while you finish loading up. I'll have to leave a note for your mother.'

Frank walked away, feeling good despite his severe

reservations. Briefly, he had seen in his son's eyes something he hadn't known for a long time. It was the look of respect.

Geoffrey was happy now. He climbed to his feet, smiling at Maurice. 'So, where we going, then?'

The smile was not returned. 'Dunkirk,' Maurice told him.

Edward was in his study as Dorothea let herself into the house, loaded up with Harrods shopping bags. Her face fell as she set eyes on a scene of minor devastation. The entire study looked as though a cyclone had hit it. Furniture had been ripped and overturned, Edward's desk had been gutted and papers strewn all over the floor, and the rolled-back carpet even revealed where floorboards had been prised up.

'What happened here?' Dorothea asked, horrified.

Edward was busy throwing things into an overnight case. He looked up briefly to throw her a thin, rueful smile. 'Modern democracy paid me a visit,' he muttered, cryptically.

Dorothea flared up. 'They can't do things like that,' she blazed.

'I'm afraid they can – and more,' Edward contradicted her. 'To quote: Regulation 18B of the Emergency Powers Act – to provide for the custody on security grounds of persons against whom it is not practicable to bring criminal proceedings.'

Dorothea looked shaken. 'You mean that they could *arrest* you?'

'They prefer the word "detain", I believe,' Edward said. 'And it's not imprisonment, it's internment.'

'But not if they didn't find anything,' Dorothea protested. 'I burned all that fascist rubbish.'

Edward's eyes narrowed. 'Oh, so it *was* you. I did wonder. You might well have destroyed my only line of defence, Dorothea – do you realize that? If they'd seen I didn't have anything to hide, they would have probably left it at that. Now, of course, they'll be even more suspicious.'

'You mean they could be back?' she asked, aghast.

Edward shrugged, closing his case, 'If they do, then they won't find me,' he murmured, almost casually. He began to walk towards the door.

Dorothea ran after him, clutching at his arm. 'Where are you going?' she demanded.

'Somewhere on the south coast,' Edward told her. 'They've put out an emergency appeal for every doctor they can get.' He paused, sighing deeply. 'Reading between the lines, my dear – I think we have already lost the battle we should never have started in the first place.'

'Blooming long way round to the coast of France,' Geoffrey observed. He had already picked up enough tips on navigation from Maurice to know what he was talking about.

'They sent us this way to avoid the mines,' Maurice told him. 'We should be there just after nightfall.'

Geoffrey gulped. 'Blimey, I never even thought about mines,' he admitted. He looked over to his father on the tiller, looking distinctly green about the gills. 'How you feeling, Dad?'

Frank smiled bravely. 'Fine,' he lied. There was a distant rumble from over the horizon. 'Thunder?' Frank queried, looking at Maurice.

'More likely guns. The BEF in Belgium, I shouldn't wonder.'

Geoffrey grinned gleefully. 'Well, fancy being able to hear them from here.' He looked at Maurice, something like hero worship glowing in his eyes. 'You fought in the last war, didn't you, Mr Simpson?'

The man's face was grim. 'Yes,' he said tersely.

'Where were you?' Frank put in.

'France.' Maurice did not elaborate, and Frank didn't press him.

'I'm going to fight as soon as I'm old enough,' Geoffrey announced proudly.

Maurice whirled on him, suddenly angry. 'Don't be a bloody little fool,' he said scathingly. 'You keep out of it for as long as you can. Stay home. This is as near as you ever want to get, believe me.'

The light in Geoffrey's eyes went out. Subdued, and slightly embarrassed, he walked to the prow of the boat, staring out over the rails.

'Thanks,' Frank whispered.

Maurice shrugged, fishing in his pocket for his pipe and filling it. The guns rumbled again, breaking the ensuing silence.

'I'll castrate the bastard,' Phyllis shrieked. 'What does the bloody lunatic think he's doing? The boy's only fourteen, for God's sake.'

Deprived of her husband himself to vent her anger on, she turned on Granma, thrusting his note under her eyes. 'Is the entire Slater family light in the head, or what?'

Granma scanned the brief note quickly. *'Dear Phyllis, Don't worry about Geoffrey, he's with me. We've gone to France. He'll be quite safe, I'll take good care of him. Wish us luck, Frank.'*

'Well?' Phyllis demanded.

Granma shrugged philosophically. 'No use getting yerself in a tizz, Phyllis,' she pointed out. 'Screaming and ranting ain't going to bring 'em back. Anyway, Frank's not the sort to go rushing in to anything. He'll be all right.'

Phyllis was not appeased. 'I don't give a monkey's toss about bloody Frank,' she raged. 'Bloody useless sod even gets sick rowing on the Serpentine. It's Geoffrey I'm worried about. What if he gets killed?'

Granma pooh-poohed the idea with a scornful laugh. 'How's he gonna get killed?' she demanded. 'They ain't going near no fighting – they're in a boat.'

Shells were bursting everywhere – behind the beach, on the

shoreline and in the sea, between the flotilla of small boats gathered offshore.

The sea itself was alive, thick with thousands of British and French soldiers floundering waist- and chest-deep in the water, dropping their rifles into the sea as they scrambled desperately to find any craft which would take them out of hell. Hundreds of others, bobbing face-down in the water, would only find their home soil again if the tides were favourable.

Aboard the *Silver Seal*, its prow pointed out to the open sea, Geoffrey hung anxiously on the inboard motor controls as Maurice and his father fought to control the human tide of soldiers attempting to clamber up on to the decks.

'Get back, get back,' Maurice was screaming. 'I can only take twenty. You'll scupper us all.'

The warning had no effect. Panic and fear were the ruling forces of the day, completely overriding reason.

Bitterly reluctant, but knowing he had no other choice, Maurice resorted to brute force, for all their sakes. He began stamping on fingers clawing at the deck-boards, physically body-charging other boarders, knocking them back into the sea. Frank was equally busy, wielding a boat-hook to fend off half a dozen soldiers trying to scramble over the stern rail. Finally pushed back into the water, they began fighting amongst themselves for the best position to make a second attempt.

A shell burst in the water less than twenty feet away, rocking the boat violently and showering the decks with spray. Maurice turned to Geoffrey, yelling at the top of his voice. 'Get moving, Geoffrey – get us out of here.'

Geoffrey did as he was told, throttling up slowly. Over-laden and sitting perilously low in the water, the boat began to chug laboriously away from the beach towards the waiting fleet of larger transport vessels moored outside the range of the German big guns.

*

The last passenger scrambled over the stern rail, beginning to climb the cargo netting festooning the destroyer's sides. Taking the controls, Maurice backed the *Silver Seal* away into open water, clearing an approach channel for other small craft. He cut the engines, staring back through a pall of shell-smoke hanging over the water.

Frank joined him, following the direction of his gaze. 'Could we manage one last trip?' he asked, quietly.

Maurice half-turned towards him, his face drawn and tired-looking. 'The first match they see you. The second match – they line you up in their sights. The third match – they shoot you.' He paused, with a sad, distant smile. 'I went back twice in the last war. I reckon I've used up my luck ration.'

Geoffrey had overheard. 'Yes, but this is a new war,' he pointed out.

Maurice let out a bitterly ironic laugh. 'Clean slate, eh?'

Frank stared back towards the shore. The smoke had thinned, temporarily, enabling a clear view of the beach, thick with khaki-uniformed figures. 'My brother's out there somewhere,' he said, distantly. 'One last trip?'

'Come on, we can't go back with an empty boat,' Geoffrey put in.

Outvoted, Maurice sighed heavily. He pulled his pipe from his pocket again, filling and tamping it down slowly and methodically. Producing a box of matches, he extracted one and held it poised against the side of the box. Momentarily, a proud, defiant grin returned to his face. 'Third match,' he announced, striking it with a grand gesture and applying the flame to the bowl of his pipe. Taking a few puffs, he moved to the inboard controls and started the engine, bringing the boat around in a slow, arcing sweep towards the shore.

Above their heads, the droning of an aircraft engine suddenly changed in tone to a whine as it went into a steep dive.

'Stuka dive-domber,' Maurice yelled out in warning. 'Take cover.'

Geoffrey and Frank threw themselves to the decks, huddling against the side of the hull. The whine of the plane grew to a screaming roar, accompanied by the vicious chattering of machine-guns and the thud of bullets ripping into the deck planking. Then the Stuka was over their heads, its engine tone changing again as it flattened out and began to climb away once more.

Thrown across the deck by the impact of the bullets, Maurice's body lay over the rails, half-in and half-out of the boat. He was quite dead.

'Christ!' Frank breathed, climbing to his feet, suddenly feeling violently sick again. He moved to comfort Geoffrey, who had started to cry.

30

The entire town of Ramsgate looked as though it would never be normal again. Confusion reigned everywhere. Perhaps a hundred boats, large and small, held positions off the outer harbour, waiting for berthing spaces to unload. Every road up through the town was nose-to-tail traffic, predominantly army vehicles and makeshift ambulances. Policemen, both civilian and military, were much in evidence.

Pushing her way through the crowds, dodging through the streams of stretcher-bearers, Mary finally found her father, cordoned off with a couple of dozen other journalists behind a tape barrier like a pack of rabid animals.

'Have you found out where he is yet?' Mary asked, breathless.

Arthur nodded, managing a faint smile. 'That's about the only thing I *have* managed to find out. No one's very hot on Press privilege at the moment.' He paused, noting the anxiety on her face. 'All the minor casualties have been moved to Maidstone hospital,' he told her gently.

Mary's face fell. 'Maidstone?' she echoed, hopelessly. 'How am I going to get there? They've commandeered all the trains.'

Arthur lifted up the tape, stepping under it. 'Don't worry, I'll take you,' he offered. He put his arm around her shoulders, steering her away from the cordon. 'There's not much point in me being here, anyway. We're forbidden to talk to anyone and an official Army briefing's been promised for the last three hours.'

Another line of stretcher-bearers passed in front of them, stopping them in their tracks. Mary eyed them briefly, turning to her father. 'Well, you hardly need an official briefing to tell you what happened here,' she observed, heavily.

Her father frowned slightly. 'It may look like total confusion at the moment, but the top brass are hailing it as a triumph.'

Mary flashed him a curious glance. He sounded as if he almost believed it. 'Triumph? How can you call a mass retreat a triumph?'

Arthur lowered his voice to a whisper. 'Mary, this is no time for defeatist talk.'

Mary regarded her father with frank disbelief. 'Daddy – you saw the boats coming back. Did you see any triumph on those boys' faces?'

Doubt flickered across Arthur's face briefly. Then he was defensive, even slightly guilty. 'They'll have evacuated the worst first – the wounded, the shell-shocked. Anyway, at least we know that Harry's not badly hurt, that's the main thing.'

Still not quite convinced, Mary nodded. 'Yes, you're right,' she conceded. 'As soon as I see him I'll be all right.'

They were clear to move again now. Arthur slipped his arm through his daughter's. 'Come on, it's not far,' he said reassuringly. 'Lucky I left the car outside the town centre.'

'Well, self-inflicted wound, was it?'

Recognizing the voice, Harry's eyes flickered open. He dragged himself out of a morphine-induced sleep, the effects of the drug now almost worn off. Kaye was standing over the hospital bed, smiling down at him tenderly. It was the first smiling face Harry had seen in over a week, and the sheer warmth of it seemed to wash away the pain in his bandaged arm.

'Oh, Kaye, it's so good to see you,' he muttered weakly. 'How did you find me?'

She grinned. 'The uniform helps. Your mum told Ivy and Ivy told me. I had transport. Your mum and dad'll be down to see you as soon as they can.' Kaye paused, eyeing his wounded arm. 'So, apart from that, how are you?'

Harry managed a weak, rueful grin. 'I was lucky. Another inch higher and it would probably have shattered my elbow. I'm surprised you didn't hear the yell back in England.' The grin faded from his face, suddenly, as he remembered those last few hours on the beach at Dunkirk. 'You've got no idea what it was like over there, Kaye. Nobody has.'

Kaye put her finger to her lips, urging caution.

Harry nodded, grimly. 'Yes, I know. Say nothing that might give comfort to the enemy. Well, they can't stop the truth, Kaye – and as soon as I get out of here I'm going to tell it.'

Kaye changed the subject, abruptly. 'Does Mary know where you are?'

Unable to shrug his shoulders, Harry rolled his eyes. 'I asked for a telegram to be sent to her parents. It must be pretty chaotic trying to track people down.' He smiled up at her. 'Anyway, she's not here at the moment – you are. So how about a kiss?'

An uncertain look passed across Kaye's face. Interpreting it as rejection, Harry sighed, miserably. 'You regret it, don't you? What happened at Christmas?'

Kaye shook her head, awkwardly. 'No, of course not,' she muttered, but there was no conviction in her voice. There was a short, embarrassed silence, before she switched her smile on again. 'I would have written to you, but I didn't think the Jerries would be taking time off to forward letters to Allied soldiers.'

They were just making conversation now, and they both knew it.

'So, tell me about life with all your Brylcreem Boys,' Harry said, with forced brightness. 'All the Ralphs, and the Jeremys and the Ruperts.'

It was the perfect opportunity, but still Kaye baulked slightly at saying what had to be said. She steeled herself, holding her breath.

'Toby,' she murmured softly, after a while. 'His name's Toby.'

So there was a 'him', Harry thought fleetingly. No bullet could have struck home with more pain, or caused a greater wound. In a moment, with the mention of a mere name, a part of him had died. The sob that rose in his throat was stillborn, choked by a bitter laugh.

'Yes, of course,' he muttered, finally, distantly. 'It would have to be Toby.'

A nurse came towards them, looking somewhat flustered. She hovered nervously behind Kaye, not sure how to handle an extremely delicate situation.

'Look, I let you in because I thought you were his wife,' she whispered, finally, in Kaye's ear. 'Only . . .' Her voice tailed off as she looked awkwardly back over her shoulder towards the ward entrance. Mary stood just outside the double swing doors, peering in through the glass with a frown on her face.

'Please, let her come in,' Harry said.

The nurse looked dubious. 'Rules is very strict,' she muttered. 'Only one visitor at a time.'

Kaye smiled at her. 'It'll be all right. I'm leaving in a moment.' She looked back down at Harry as the nurse left to fetch Mary. 'I didn't ask for it to happen,' she murmured gently. 'But he needs me. They all need someone to hold on to. And you've got Mary.'

Harry nodded miserably. 'Yes, I've got Mary,' he agreed.

She was almost at the bedside. Harry forced himself to brighten, for her sake.

Kaye was already turning to leave as Mary reached them. 'Hello, Mary,' she said, polite but formal.

Mary acknowledged her with a curt nod. 'Official duties?' she inquired with a hint of sarcasm. 'Welcoming home the wounded?'

Kaye let it wash over her. 'I came to give Harry a message from his mum and dad,' she said. It was only half a lie. She flashed Harry a last quick smile. 'Well, I'll leave you two alone,' she announced, departing.

Mary waited until she had left the ward. Finally, she bent over Harry's bed, embracing him as best she could. Straightening up, she pulled over a chair and sat down beside him, clutching his hand. 'I was beginning to think I'd lost you,' she murmured.

Harry forced a grin. 'I swam the Channel, with one arm,' he joked.

Mary tried to smile, but there was a nagging worry eating away at her thoughts. 'When I came in and saw Kaye by your bed . . .' she started.

'Yes?' Harry prompted.

It came out in a rush – not a question, not quite an accusation. 'Is there still something? Between you and her?'

Harry shook his head wearily. 'That's all in the past, I promise. I've got you, she's got herself some dashing young RAF pilot. The war seems to have sorted out our priorities for us.'

Mary looked at his wounded arm pityingly. 'Was it bad?' she asked.

Harry's face became serious. 'Not for me, it wasn't. Just a flesh wound. The bullet ricocheted off the bone. After that, it took most of another poor bastard's face off.'

Mary shuddered. 'Please, Harry, you don't want to talk about things like that now.'

He stared up at her, his face grim and earnest. 'But I do, Mary. I do want to talk about it. I want to tell you, and I want you to tell your father – and I want him to put it in his newspaper and tell everyone else. People need to know, Mary – about what hell and chaos it was out there, and what kind of a bloody war this is going to be.'

'Not now,' she urged him. 'You're back, and you're alive – and that's all that really matters.'

Harry wasn't listening to her. He was back on the beach at Dunkirk. 'Do you know the bloody officers were the first to run?' he demanded angrily. 'Like frightened bloody rabbits. Getting off that beach was just a case of every man for himself – forget discipline, forget honour. I saw some of our own lads shooting French soldiers so they could get space on the boats. I don't think I've ever felt so ashamed in my life.'

He was getting too worked up, Mary thought. She stroked his brow, soothingly. 'You should rest now, try to get some sleep.'

Harry regarded her with a sad, disappointed expression. 'You don't understand, do you? I don't want to sleep, Mary. I want to remember. I don't ever want to forget.'

Mary sighed. 'Things will look different when you're feeling better, I'm sure.'

Harry shook his head. 'No, they won't,' he muttered firmly. 'I've already made up my mind, Mary. I'm not going back.'

She stared at him blankly, failing to understand. 'What are you saying?'

Harry's face was adamant. 'When my arm heals, the regiment will call me back to barracks, and I won't go. Simple as that!'

Mary looked aghast. 'But they'll throw you in gaol, maybe worse.'

Harry seemed unconcerned. 'Let them,' he muttered. 'I'm just not going back to get myself killed while the officer class works out what its battle plans are.'

Mary struggled to come to terms with this bombshell, to find some way out of a seemingly impossible situation. 'I suppose you could always declare yourself a conscientious objector,' she murmured finally.

Harry nodded. 'Yeah. I've thought about that, too,' he said calmly.

31

Frank had hardly been expecting a hero's welcome, but the sheer vituperation of Phyllis's response stunned him. Her immediate greeting was a full-blooded slap across the face which rattled his eyeballs in their sockets.

'You bastard,' she spat at him. 'You're not fit to be a father.'

Frank ducked back, in case the slap had a twin brother lurking about somewhere. 'I brought him back safe, didn't I?' he muttered sullenly.

Phyllis glared at him. The blow had vented some of her fury, but none of her anger. 'What were you thinking of, damn you? You could have got our Geoffrey killed.'

Granma intervened, more for Geoffrey's sake than to protect her grandson. 'If you're that concerned about your boys, Phyllis – just look at them both,' she pointed out.

Geoffrey was still pale and shaken from Maurice's death. Now, witnessing the violent exchange between his mother and father, he looked as though he was about to withdraw into traumatic shock. Billy, upset by his mother's crying for two whole days, just looked bewildered.

Granma slipped her arm around Geoffrey's shoulders, pulling him aside. 'You've got to understand yer mum's upset,' she told him gently. She pulled at his ear affectionately, a rueful grin spreading across her face. 'We both thought we might have lost you, you little bugger.'

Phyllis seemed to put her priorities in order, finally. She turned away from Frank with a gesture of scorn, taking in a slow, deep breath and holding it as maternal concern overrode her anger. Calmer, she prised Geoffrey away from Granma and hugged him silently against her breast for a long time.

He pulled himself away, finally, finding his voice at last. 'It ain't fair to go on at Dad like that, Mum,' he complained. 'We saved lives – scores of lives. You should be proud of him. I am.'

Phyllis sighed as the last of her anger washed away and only a residual bitterness remained. She looked at her son's smoke- and tear-streaked face, his damp and salt-encrusted hair and clothing. 'You need a good hot bath,' she told him. She glanced over to Granma. 'Take Billy, will you, Gran? Frank and I have to talk this thing out.'

Granma nodded. She gathered the two boys together, preparing to shepherd them away. 'Don't be too hard on him,' she muttered to Phyllis. 'They're both back safe, and that's the only thing that matters for now.'

Phyllis waited until they were all out of the way before turning back to her husband. 'What *happened*, you selfish swine?' she demanded.

Frank had organized his defence a little more by now. 'You must have heard it on the bleedin' radio. They needed every scrap of help they could get over there. I was just doing my bit.'

He looked more like a scolded little boy than his own son, Phyllis thought. Even her bitterness was gone now, leaving only a sense of resignation.

'Look, that even I can understand,' she said wearily. 'But how could you involve Geoffrey? Where the hell was your sense of responsibility?'

'He's fourteen, almost a young man,' Frank pointed out. 'He had a right to make his own choice, do something for his country if he wanted to.'

It was no good, Phyllis realized. Frank appeared incapable of understanding her point of view just as she could not sympathize with his. Suddenly, the situation seemed to encapsulate all the lack of understanding and communication which had blighted their marriage for years.

She sighed heavily. 'This has been the last straw, Frank –

you realize that?' She paused before going on. 'I've come to a decision. I'm taking the boys up to Wales to stay with my mum. This war may make me a widow, but I'm not losing my sons.'

Frank looked totally stunned. 'Aw, come on, Phyllis, there's no need to overreact,' he protested weakly. 'This'll all blow over when you've had a chance to calm down.' He broke off, his tone changing to a plea. 'Look, love – come back to Gillingham, we'll all be together again.'

Phyllis faced him squarely. 'I have calmed down,' she said flatly. 'And I've made up my mind.' Momentarily, a flash of humour surfaced, and she gave a wry smile. 'Anyway, if I came back it'd be a toss-up who'd kill 'em first – you or Hitler.'

She was adamant, Frank could see. 'Why?' he asked, miserably.

Phyllis shrugged. 'Because I don't trust you anymore. And because I've finally had to face up to the truth.'

Frank regarded her piercingly, a glimmer of understanding in his eyes. 'This isn't really to do with me and Geoffrey, is it?'

Phyllis was silent. It was answer enough.

Reason had failed, pleading had no effect. With his back to the wall, Frank could only resort to threat.

'He won't go with you, surely you must realize that? Geoffrey will want to stay with me – and I'll fight you tooth and nail to make sure that he does.'

It was as though a gauntlet had been thrown down between them. They faced each other warily, like adversaries. Finally, it was Phyllis who capitulated with a resigned nod, conceding the point. 'Yes, you're probably right.' She shrugged. 'Well, I suppose you can both play war heroes together for a while. You'll be moved out of Kent soon enough when Hitler's mob sets sail.'

There was silence between them, each realizing that there was little else to be said.

'Well, I might as well go and start packing,' Phyllis announced finally. 'I'll tell Gran and Geoffrey you'll be taking them back in the morning.'

Against a backcloth of draped silk cloth, Moira sat perched on the top of a bar stool, her body arched to accentuate the swell of her breasts beneath a thin, almost transparent plain cotton dress.

Grinning with satisfaction, Victor fired off another shot and removed the plate, slipping it away into a darkened drawer before reloading the tripod-mounted camera.

'Now, let's have a nice sexy one,' he suggested. 'Purse your lips as though you were blowing someone a kiss.'

Moira did as she was told, pursing her painted, glossy lips into a suggestive pout.

'Wonderful,' Victor enthused. He took the shot, moving the camera across the studio floor slightly for a different angle. 'Now, pull your dress right up past your knees and we'll show 'em a nice bit of leg.'

Moira hesitated only briefly, finally grinning. It was all just a bit of fun, after all. A bit saucy and suggestive perhaps, but innocent enough.

It was a good end to a good session, Victor congratulated himself. Moira was coming along really well, and had already learned to relax in front of the camera. More importantly, she was beginning to trust him, and rapidly becoming more and more susceptible to his suggestions. A little bit of praise wouldn't come amiss at this point, he thought to himself.

'You really are a superb model, Moira,' he told the girl. 'One of the best I've ever had. A real Forces sweetheart, you're going to be.'

Moira blushed slightly. 'Go on with you,' she chided him. 'Who's going to notice me?'

Victor looked serious. 'Don't you underrate yourself,' he said. 'You're a very pretty girl, and just what our lads want to see when they're lonely and far away from home with all sorts of horrible things going on around them. A bit of glamour's exactly what they need to cheer them up, remind them of what they're fighting for.'

Moira looked impressed. 'I never thought about it like that,' she murmured, a trace of pride in her tone. 'So what I'm doing is patriotic, almost, helping the war effort?'

'Very much so,' Victor assured her. 'And what's more, it pays well.'

Moira smiled. 'Certainly better than what my family thinks I'm doing,' she agreed. 'I've told them I'm waitressing in a tea shop.'

Victor was thoughtful for a while, wondering if the time was right. He decided to take the plunge. 'It could pay even better,' he said, eventually. 'You let me guide you, Moira – and you'll be able to own a whole string of tea shops by the time we're finished.'

Moira climbed down from the stool, regarding him with one pencilled eyebrow raised slightly. 'What are you talking about, Victor?'

The question was phrased out of curiosity rather than suspicion, Victor thought, smiling inwardly. It was a better reaction than he could have hoped for.

'Artistic poses,' he expanded. 'That's what the punters'll pay big money for. I could probably pay you a quid a session for them.' Having dropped the bait, Victor paused. 'Course – it takes a very special kind of model to do them well,' he went on eventually. 'And you'd need to trust me – but I really think you've got what it takes, Moira, I really do.'

Moira was flattered – and it showed. 'Oh, Victor, of course I trust you,' she promised him.

It was all going perfectly, Victor thought. There was just one last little touch which would seal matters to his professional – and personal – satisfaction. He adopted a look of tender concern which might have impressed Marlene Dietrich herself. 'Of course, I wouldn't want you to do anything that

you weren't happy about,' he murmured. 'I really am becoming quite fond of you, you know.'

Moira giggled. 'Oh, Victor, you are sweet.' She danced
across, kissing him affectionately.

Victor had been called a lot of things by a lot of women –
but 'sweet' was rarely one of them. Seizing his opportunity,
he returned the kiss – paternal at first, then with studied,
subtle and increasing passion.

32

Apart from his bandaged arm, Harry looked more like a Southend daytripper than a war casualty. He lolled back in a gaily striped deckchair in the hospital grounds, basking in the June sunshine, almost asleep.

'They didn't waste much time getting you out of the ward, then,' a familiar voice said in his ear.

Harry shook himself fully awake with a start. His mother and father had come up on him from behind, across the lawn. He looked up at his mother's concerned face, putting on a smile. 'I'm "walking wounded". There's plenty worse off than me that need the beds.'

Thomas beamed down at him. 'Well, you're looking well enough,' he observed. 'Good to see you, son.'

'And you, Dad,' Harry told him. 'You're looking pretty chipper yourself.'

Thomas's eyes sparkled with pride. 'I feel like I've come up on the pools. Two of my lads back as heroes. Be getting a call from Mr Churchill, I shouldn't wonder.'

The smile faded from Harry's face. 'There was nothing heroic going on over there, Dad, believe me,' he muttered quietly.

His mother frowned at him. 'Now, Harry – don't spoil his day,' she warned. 'I haven't seen your father as happy as this for ages.'

'You wait till I tell all the boys at the dockyard,' Thomas went on enthusiastically. 'Slaters 2, Jerries nil.'

'What about Clifford?' Harry asked. 'Does he count as a draw? And would you be crowing like this if Frank had managed to get himself and Geoffrey blown to bits?'

His father refused to be brought down. 'Well, they weren't, were they?'

Harry sighed. 'So you'll be happy to see Geoffrey marching off to war in two years, will you?'

The suggestion wiped the smile from Thomas's face for a second, then he brightened again. 'It won't happen, will it? We'll have it won by then.'

Harry shook his head sadly. 'Dad, you didn't see it. I doubt if we could beat the Germans at tiddly-winks right now.'

Thomas was edging on to the defensive. 'All right, so they caught us on the hop this time. But it'll still be the same result as the last one, you wait and see.'

'What, twenty million dead?' Harry asked with a bitter laugh.

Thomas's eyes narrowed, his mouth tightening into a grim line. Recognizing the danger signs, Ellen stepped in to mediate. 'Come on, don't you get your father going,' she said to Harry. She turned to Thomas. 'I think we ought to leave Harry to get his rest, don't you?'

It was too late. His anger rising, Thomas glowered at his son. 'You're beginning to sound like a bloody pacifist,' he accused.

Harry smiled, distantly. 'I always was,' he said simply. 'I don't see anything gallant, or heroic, or glorious about war. Well, now I might finally have the courage of my own convictions.'

Thomas looked bemused, almost apprehensive. 'What are you saying, son?'

There was no easy way to break it. 'I'm not going back,' Harry announced firmly. 'I'll refuse to rejoin my regiment. If necessary, I'll register as a conscient –'

Thomas could not bear to hear the word. 'Don't say it, don't you dare say it,' he cut in sharply, his face wracked with pain. 'You can't do this to me.'

Harry was incredulous. 'Do it to *you*?' he echoed. 'For God's sake, Dad – it's my life.'

'It'd be the end of mine,' Thomas retorted bitterly. 'Bad

enough having Tom spivving, but at least he does something for the people. What does a bloody "conchie" do? Nothing!'

'Maybe I can help people see there's an alternative to war,' Harry suggested.

Thomas regarded him with scorn. 'You think that bastard Hitler's open to a bit of friendly persuasion, do yer?'

Harry shook his head. 'No, but the German people may be.'

His father's face was contorted into a mask of loathing. 'Don't make me puke,' he spat out. 'They're a bunch of mangy, mongrel dogs. Bite you as soon as look at you. We should have put 'em down the last time – then none of this would have happened.'

In the face of blind prejudice, Harry tried reason. 'It's governments make wars, Dad – not people. The Germans have been bullied into this, and the same thing's happening over here.'

'Bloody communist,' Thomas shot back scathingly. 'What do you know?'

Harry held his ground. 'I've read the history books. It's always been the same. Power, money, propaganda – that's all it takes to make a war.'

Thomas clenched his teeth. 'You're no better than that bastard Mosley,' he hissed contemptuously. He drew a deep breath, trying to control his anger. 'I'll tell you one thing right now, son. You go back and fight like a man, or I never want to see you in my house again.'

Ellen had been listening to the angry exchange feeling totally helpless, but now she could stay out of it no longer. 'Don't be stupid, Thomas,' she cut in sharply. 'Do you know what you're saying?'

Thomas whirled on her, transferring his rage. 'Don't you ever call me stupid, woman,' he snarled. 'I'll say what I want to say, and I'll say what I mean.'

'For Christ's sake!' Harry blurted out, his own temper snapping. An argument was one thing, but he would not sit

184

by and watch his mother bullied. He glared at his father. 'You're supposed to be my father, damn it. What kind of sons do you want? What kind of a family are we?'

There was no response from Thomas, who felt himself being sucked into a vortex of confusion and self-doubt. Everything he had grown up believing in, every simple faith, suddenly seemed to be turned about, mocking him.

Ellen had already turned away, to hide the shock and hurt on her face. 'I want to go now, Thomas,' she murmured, forcing herself to sound calm. 'Harry's been through a lot – he's been wounded. He needs time to recover himself.'

She began to walk away. After a moment, Thomas turned after her, stumbling in her wake, leaving Harry sitting there. He was reminded, oddly and poignantly, of a starfish shedding its arms rather than be captured. An organism disintegrating. Destroying itself out of sheer bloody-mindedness.

Kaye and Toby lay in the long grass of one of the fields surrounding RAF Hornden, well away from the perimeter fence. Toby lit a post-coital cigarette, took a few puffs and passed it over. 'What are you thinking about?' he asked, as Kaye stared dreamily up towards the heavens.

'How clear and beautiful the sky is today,' she answered him. 'So peaceful and harmless. How it's so hard to even believe there's a war on just now.'

Toby sighed. 'Not for much longer, I'm afraid. Now Mussolini's committed Italy to their side, the Jerries will have Paris in a few days. That only leaves us left to fight.' He fell silent for a while, taking back his cigarette and pulling on it fiercely. 'The CO's stepping up our missions from tomorrow,' he added, almost as an aside.

Kaye's dreamy reverie was shattered immediately. She rolled over on to her side, regarding him anxiously. 'Why did you wait to tell me?'

Toby smiled ruefully. 'Might have spoiled the mood somewhat, don't you think?' He saw the fear in her eyes, and rushed to reassure her. 'It'll be all right, Kaye, I know it. Having you makes me sure of that. When I'm up there, however sticky it gets, I just think of you and know that I have something to hold on to, someone worth living for.'

Despite her fears, Kaye smiled. 'So that's what I am. Your lucky mascot. I did wonder.'

Toby frowned slightly. 'Don't joke about it, Kaye. You're much more than that to me, surely you must realize that?'

His sudden intensity was both touching and slightly embarrassing, Kaye thought. She flushed slightly, feeling a sense of guilt, knowing that she had been begging the words she wanted to hear him say. 'Tell me that again when this little lot is over and all the young debs are back on the social scene,' she murmured, still taking refuge behind humour.

Toby regarded her seriously. 'Can't you get it into your head?' he asked. 'I want you. I love you.' He sat up, suddenly. 'Let's not wait for the end of the war. Let's get married – now.'

Kaye felt like laughing with happiness and crying at the same time. Her heart screamed out 'yes', but the fear was still in her mind.

'Your friend Beaumont has proposed to five girls to my certain knowledge,' she pointed out. 'I believe three of them have accepted.'

Toby gave her a curious stare. 'What are you saying?'

Kaye smiled wistfully. 'That I don't want to talk about it, not now. Just for the present, I want you to know how much I care for you, and I mean *really* care for you. Can't we just hold on to that?'

Toby was thoughtfully silent for a long while. 'You're a very wise woman, Kaye,' he muttered eventually. 'Just what I need right now.' He tossed away the cigarette, rolling towards her. They huddled together like Siamese twins, bonded together in a cocoon against the outside world.

33

Harry stood over the baby's grave, his back to the house, lost in his own thoughts.

'You missed breakfast,' Mary murmured quietly, coming up behind him.

Harry turned at the sound of her voice, nodding absently. 'Wasn't really hungry,' he muttered. He stared up into the sky again, deeply contemplative.

'What is it, Harry? What's wrong?' Mary asked after a while.

He sighed, shaking his head slowly from side to side. 'Did we do as much thinking as this before the war? I can't remember.' He delved into his pocket, pulling out an opened, buff-coloured envelope. 'It came this morning,' he said quietly, handing it to Mary.

There was no need to read the contents. Mary knew. She handed the letter straight back, her face falling. 'Recall?'

'In no uncertain terms,' Harry told her, with a nod.

Mary looked both bewildered and angry. 'But this is stupid. You're wounded. Your arm still hurts, doesn't it?'

Harry shrugged. 'The occasional twinge. Obviously the powers that be regard five weeks' convalescence as enough for any fighting soldier.'

Defiance blazed in Mary's eyes. 'Well, you'll just have to fight them, won't you? Appeal on medical grounds or something.' She paused thoughtfully. 'Perhaps Daddy could help you somehow.'

Harry's smile was gently mocking. 'You think writing to them on headed notepaper might make a difference, do you?' He saw Mary's lips tighten and felt ashamed. 'I'm sorry, that was unfair. Your parents have both been very good to me, taking me in like some sort of homeless waif.'

Mary managed a faint smile. 'It wasn't quite like that,' she pointed out. 'You *are* my husband.'

'Well, for a month I was, anyway,' Harry said, unable to keep a slightly bitter edge out of his voice.

It returned them both to immediate reality. 'So what will you do?' Mary asked. 'You said you wouldn't go back.'

Harry shrugged hopelessly. 'I said a lot of things. They shoot deserters, you know. Is a British bullet any cleaner than a German one, I wonder?'

Mary clutched at his good arm, fear in her eyes. 'Don't talk like that, Harry. You've got an alternative, what we talked about. You can register as a conscientious objector.'

The bitterness was hardening now. 'The word is *conchie*,' Harry muttered heavily. 'And it's pronounced like someone coughing up a mouthful of phlegm.'

Mary stared at him in bewilderment. 'But back in the hospital – you seemed quite certain.'

Harry placed his finger over her lips, silencing her gently. 'Look, I know you're trying to help, but it doesn't make things any easier. This is something I have to think through, work out for myself.' He broke off, his face registering his own confusion. 'The trouble is, I'm just so full up with it that I can't think straight. Being here makes it worse. Detached from my own family, an outsider. It's like my very roots have been cut away from me.'

'Your father is a stubborn, stupid man,' Mary said quietly.

Harry let out a thoughtful sigh. 'Stubborn, yes,' he agreed. 'But stupid? No more so than most people of his generation, the majority of the working classes. They've all been manipulated, controlled – force-fed a whole set of phoney values and ideas by the people with the power to keep them down, keep them subservient.'

He broke off as a lone Spitfire screamed overhead, flying low, making them both look up suddenly. 'And now they're doing it to a whole new generation,' Harry continued bitterly, returning to his theme. 'Like those poor little bastards up there, the Death or Glory Boys. More bullshit, more propaganda, more gung-ho into the breach dear friends and don't think about any of it. It just goes on.'

He turned, taking Mary's hand and starting to walk back towards Albourne House as William, attracted by the sound of the Spitfire, came bounding out of the front door.

William stared after the plane, which was by now dwindling to just a distant speck in the sky. 'Damn, I missed him,' he muttered peevishly. Seeing Harry and Mary approaching, he moved to intercept them, a grin spreading across his face again. 'Did you see him? Did he do a victory roll?' he asked eagerly.

Harry shook his head, a patronizing smile on his face. 'No, William, he didn't do a victory roll.' He glanced aside at Mary with a hopeless little laugh. 'See what I mean?'

'Anyway, glad I caught you both,' William went on, suddenly becoming serious. 'I hope you haven't forgotten about the weekend. Absolutely no excuses.'

Harry looked confused. 'What?'

William regarded him with a look of censure. 'What do you mean, what? The cricket match with the aerodrome pilots, of course. We need all the support we can get.'

Mary touched Harry's injured arm, glaring at her brother. 'For God's sake, William,' she admonished him. 'Harry's hardly in a condition to be thinking about a cricket match.'

William was contrite, but not apologetic. 'Well you can both be spectators, can't you? They also serve who only stand and watch.' He sniffed, indignantly. 'Anyway, it's not just *a* cricket match, it's *the* cricket match. We missed it last year because of your rotten wedding, so the least you can do is support us now.'

'Us?' Mary queried.

William puffed up with self-importance. 'I've made myself

189

fixtures secretary, as no one else seemed to be bothering. Someone's got to show a bit of leadership.'

There was a thoughtful, faraway look in Harry's eyes. 'Yes, someone's got to,' he agreed, almost to himself.

34

The war might have been a million miles away, for this was England at play on an idyllic summer Sunday, the stuff of greetings cards and biscuit tin lids. It seemed as though the entire population of Chittenden had turned out for the match, held, traditionally, on the village green.

William made his run-in to deliver the last ball of his over. It was a near-perfect delivery – medium-paced and well-pitched and directly on line for the off-stump. It might as well have been a careless toss from a five-year old as far as the burly batsman was concerned, who swiped the ball clear to the boundary.

William was not happy. 'It's a rotten swizz,' he complained to his father, serving as team captain. 'He's not even aircrew, just a cook.'

Arthur smiled indulgently. 'Well, the ball doesn't know that, does it?' he pointed out. 'Try pitching it up a bit.'

The advice did nothing to cheer William up. 'I've been looking forward to this for ages,' he muttered bitterly. 'And now there's not even a proper pilot in the whole side.'

The slightest trace of a frown crossed Arthur's face. His son did have a point, he realized, for the RAF Hornden team did have a somewhat makeshift quality about it. Well short of the full eleven men, it consisted of mainly fitters and main-tenance crew, the odd officer and even the station chaplain, who was currently chatting to Mary and Harry as he waited for his turn to bat.

'Shame about the lads,' he was muttering, apologetically. 'But there seems to be a bit of a show in the offing. They were scrambled twice this morning.'

'I'm sure they'd be here if they could,' Mary put in politely.

The chaplain nodded in agreement. 'Oh, very much so. In fact, my orders are to stonewall until they can get across here, which they fully intend to do.' He paused, with a little smile. 'Of course, I'm not much of a cricketer, as you can imagine,' he went on. 'Played a bit of tennis and hockey at theological college, so I'm counting on that to help me through. That and the power of prayer, of course.'

The man was a talker, Harry realized. Given the slightest encouragement, he would probably buttonhole them for the rest of the day. Bored, he gazed around the green, finally picking out Kaye, who was sitting on her own near the refreshments table.

Harry climbed to his feet, muttering excuses. 'Just need to get a drink. I'll be back in a minute.' Leaving Mary to fend for herself, he strolled round the perimeter of the field.

Kaye looked tense and nervous, her eyes darting frequently from the field of play to her watch. She glanced up irritably as Harry approached and stood over her.

'Please, Harry – go away and leave me alone,' she said quietly and sadly. 'I need to be on my own just now.'

He ignored the request, sitting down on the grass beside her. 'Don't push me away, Kaye. I couldn't bear to think that it was finally all over between us.'

Kaye's eyes flickered across to Mary, still bearded by the chaplain, then sideways to meet Harry's.

'I thought that was a decision you made when you got married,' she said, coldly.

Reading the pain of rejection on his face, she softened slightly. It was a decision she was to regret almost immediately. 'I'm sorry,' she apologized. 'I'm just worried about the boys. They should have been here by now.'

'The boys – or just one of them?' Harry demanded petulantly. 'Still Toby, is it?'

Kaye was instantly aloof again. 'What's wrong with you, Harry?' she sighed wearily. 'What's wrong with you and Mary? Why can't you let go, leave me alone?'

It was a direct question, and Harry gave her a direct answer. 'Because I still love you,' he said simply.

Kaye's eyes blazed furiously. 'I hate you for saying that,' she told him. She jumped to her feet, looking over towards Mary, who had finally managed to shake off the chaplain and was staring across the field in their direction. 'Go back to your wife, Harry,' she muttered, without looking at him.

He looked totally wretched. 'I don't want to be with her – I want to be with you,' he said, sounding like a lost and lonely little boy. He stared miserably towards the cricket pitch as Kaye began to walk away.

The cookhouse batsman had finally been dismissed with a catch in the slips. A ripple of polite applause broke out, dying away almost as soon as it had started as a one-ton RAF truck came screaming up through the village and slewed to a halt with a squeal of brakes beside the green.

All eyes turned towards it, expecting to see the long-awaited cricket team. The applause started up again, punctuated by a few cheers. Again, it was short-lived, for save the driver and one warrant officer in the passenger seat, the truck was empty. They both clambered out, walking slowly and grim-faced towards the pitch. A deathly hush fell over the village green as the crowd read their body language.

William turned towards his father, a bemused look on his face. 'What is it, Dad? What do you think's happened?'

Arthur didn't answer him. There was no question in his own mind, for he had seen that look, that walk, before. Instead, he turned to address the Chittenden team as a whole. 'Let's all take a break for a minute, chaps. Leave them to it, just for the moment.' Signalling William to follow him, he walked off the pitch to rejoin his wife.

The RAF team were returning to the truck now, bowed and disconsolate. The warrant officer stayed behind, addressing the crowd. 'On the last sweep, there was a bit of a dust-up with the enemy, ladies and gentlemen – and as you'll understand, the lads must get back now.'

The chaplain caught Arthur's concerned eye, and detoured across the pitch to intercept him. Although he appeared outwardly calm, Arthur could read the sadness in his eyes. 'Bad news?' he inquired sympathetically.

The chaplain nodded. 'We lost a fine squadron leader and two pilots, I'm afraid. Another one of the lads, young Toby Andrews, apparently managed to scrape his plane down on the runway, but it was already on fire by the time they pulled him out.' He paused, taking a breath. 'Please apologize to all your chaps and tell them how sorry we are to miss the opportunity of thrashing you.'

'Yes, of course,' Arthur muttered politely. 'I'm sorry,' he added, rather lamely.

The chaplain walked away. Arthur turned to greet Evelyn and Mary, who had hurried across to meet him. 'I'm afraid that's it for the day,' he announced sadly. 'I'll just tell the chaps to pull stumps and we might as well all go home.' He glanced curiously at Mary, who was staring past him, a look of pain on her face. 'Where's Harry, by the way?'

She said nothing, but the answer was in her eyes. Swivelling on his heels, Arthur followed her point of view across the green to the little mime being enacted there.

Harry stood oddly alone and awkward, rock-still although his body seemed poised for movement. His eyes followed Kaye, as the warrant officer escorted her towards the waiting truck, one arm wrapped around her shoulders.

Kaye boarded the truck, which coughed into life. With a grating of gears, it jerked into motion.

Harry unfroze, suddenly. He broke into a run, chasing the departing vehicle even as it pulled away and began to gather speed. There was no way he could catch it, but he continued to run after it anyway, seemingly oblivious to all else. He was still running, hopelessly, as the truck rumbled clear of the village centre and disappeared round a corner. Only then did Harry pull himself to a halt, continuing to stare after it as though a sheer act of will could make it return.

Arthur looked down at his daughter's face, numb and bewildered. Tears were starting to bubble up in her eyes. He placed his hands gently on her shoulders, turning her away. 'Leave him,' he murmured quietly but forcefully. 'Let's go home.'

35

In his office at the back of the aircraft factory, Tom looked up from his desk to greet his unexpected visitor. His initial look of surprise was quickly replaced by a cheeky grin.

'Well, this is an honour,' he muttered sarcastically. 'Been mentioned in the King's List, have I?'

Frank glowered at his brother. 'You bloody know I wouldn't come here to see you,' he muttered darkly. 'It's only because of Moira.'

The grin fell away from Tom's face. 'Moira? What's up?'

'She's been sick the last few days,' Frank told him.

Tom looked genuinely concerned now. 'What's wrong with her? Nothing serious?'

Frank shook his head. 'She ain't ill,' he emphasized, making the distinction. 'Just sick — you know, in the mornings.'

There was a brief silence as Tom took this in. 'What does Gran think?' he asked finally.

Frank shrugged. 'You know Gran. She refuses to worry till something happens.'

Tom was thoughtful for a while. 'People can just get sick,' he murmured at last, uncertainly.

Frank nodded. 'Yeah, that's what I've been telling meself. Just thought you ought to know, that's all.'

Tom's eyes narrowed. 'Who's she been seeing, d'you know?'

His brother shook his head. 'She don't talk to me much these days. Keeps herself to herself most of the time.' He turned awkwardly towards the door. 'Anyway, I've told you, and now I gotta go.'

Tom stood up, walking round his desk to confront his

brother directly. 'Look, you'll keep me in touch, won't you?' he asked, a rare tone of humility in his voice. 'I'll do anything I can – money, whatever. But you'll have to let me know, 'cos she won't.'

Frank nodded. 'Sure.' He moved to the office door, opening it.

'Here, wait,' Tom called after him. 'While you're here, you can do something for Mum as well.' He crossed to the rear of his office, pulling a filing cabinet away from the wall. Behind it was a large, oblong hole. Reaching inside, Tom flipped on a concealed light switch.

The wall was false, screening off a secret storage area. Inside, Tom's cache of black-market goods were neatly sorted and stacked into piles. Tom climbed inside, quickly re-emerging with two bags of sugar in his hands.

'I promised Mum I'd get her some sugar, ages ago,' he explained. 'Just haven't had a chance to deliver it.' He thrust the two bags into Frank's unwilling hands.

Sandra's voice called out from the corridor outside. 'Oh, Tom. Mr Crabtree from the Ministry's here. Come to check on the production schedules.'

Tom panicked. 'Christ!' he blurted out. He snatched the sugar back and tossed it away, trying to bundle Frank out into the corridor, but it was too late. Sandra, with Crabtree immediately behind her, was already framed in the open doorway.

'I don't know what you're so worried about,' Sandra said gently. She had never seen Tom quite so shaken and upset, and she was deeply concerned.

Tom sat at his desk, his head buried in his hands. Pale-faced, he chewed nervously at his lower lip, shaking his head miserably. 'You don't understand, love,' he muttered quietly.

Sandra slipped her arm over his shoulder, bending down to kiss the top of his head. 'So what if old Crabtree saw your goodies?' she murmured, comfortingly. 'The Ministry of

Aircraft is hardly going to get too concerned about a few boxes of stockings and some sugar, are they?'

Tom refused to be consoled. 'It's more than that,' he sighed wearily. 'He'll be suspicious now, and I just can't afford any kind of investigation.'

Sandra still didn't understand. 'So you do a bit of business on the side, so what? They're not going to haul you off to the Tower of London for that.' She paused, brightening. 'Anyway, you could phone your mate Bernie and get him to take the stuff away tonight. Then if anyone did come snooping, there'd be no evidence, would there?'

Touched by her concern, Tom managed a thin smile at last. He reached up, grasping her hand, squeezing it affectionately. 'You really care for me, don't you?'

Sandra smiled back. 'I love you, you daft bugger,' she told him. 'Even if you are a bit of a wide boy on the quiet.'

Tom rose from his chair, facing her with a look of fondness. 'And what if there was more?' he asked. 'What if there were things about me that you didn't even know?'

The girl looked aggrieved, even maligned. 'Blimey, Tom – don't you know me well enough by now?' she demanded. 'Don't you trust me?'

Tom nodded. 'Yes, of course I do,' he said, meaning it. Over the past few months, Sandra had become about the only person he did trust. Perhaps it was finally time for the truth, he wondered, uncertain of how to go about it.

Sandra saw the hesitancy in his eyes. 'Well?' she prompted. 'Are you going to tell me your deep dark secret or not?'

Tom took the plunge. 'Before all this, the factory – I had a bit of trouble with the law,' he said, sheepishly.

Sandra shrugged. 'So you wasn't Mr Lily White. What's that got to do with now?'

Tom paused before the final revelation. 'I'm still hiding from them,' he admitted finally. 'I'm even pretending to be someone I'm not. My name's not Tom O'Malley at all – that's just someone else's identity card I pinched.'

It was all out in the open now, and Tom felt both relieved and apprehensive. He scanned Sandra's face anxiously, seeking the faintest sign of rejection.

There was none. The girl wrapped her hands around the back of his head, pulling his face towards hers. She kissed him lingeringly on the lips. 'I don't care if you're called Mickey Mouse,' she told him. 'You're still you – and I still love you.'

Tom hugged her, briefly, before pulling back slightly. 'Well, now you know,' he said simply.

Sandra nodded. 'And nobody else ever will – not from my lips, anyway,' she promised him. There was a long, thoughtful silence. 'So who are you, really?' Sandra asked eventually.

A flash of his old self-assurance came back. Tom grinned at her. 'It's still Tom,' he said. 'But it's Slater, Tom Slater.'

36

Hearing the faint slap of the letter-box flap, Ellen hastily wiped her hands on her kitchen apron and hurried down the hallway to the front door. The envelope which had dropped on to the mat bore an unfamiliar foreign stamp, seeming to confirm her best hopes. Her heart surging, Ellen bent down to pick the letter up, scanning the writing eagerly.

Her face fell as disappointment crowded within her. It was not from Clifford after all. Written in a totally unknown hand, the letter was addressed to Mrs Moira Barnes, c/o Frank Slater. Sighing deeply, Ellen was about to walk back to the kitchen when the sound of a car pulling up outside drew her attention. More out of curiosity than anything else, she opened the front door and peered outside. Harry and Mary were just climbing out of her father's Rover.

A look of worry crossed Ellen's face. 'Yer dad's not left for work yet,' she hissed warningly, glancing nervously back over her shoulder towards the stairs.

Harry smiled faintly. 'It's all right, Mum,' he said quietly. He nodded down the front of his freshly pressed uniform. 'I'm going back. Mary's dropping me off at the station, so I thought we'd pop by and say cheerio.' He stepped forward, over the threshold.

Torn by conflicting emotions, Ellen embraced him, acknowledging Mary with a polite nod. 'Come on through to the kitchen, I'm just making yer Dad's breakfast.' On afterthought, she glanced awkwardly at Mary. 'Unless you'd like to wait in the parlour, that is.'

Mary shook her head, smiling although she seemed particularly stiff and formal. 'The kitchen's fine, Mrs Slater.'

Ellen led them through, dropping Moira's letter on the

table before resuming her work. 'So, when you off, then?' she asked, trying to sound bright even though she was acutely conscious of a strained atmosphere.

'Eight o'clock,' Harry told her. 'So we can only stay for a short while.'

Ellen nodded understanding. 'Well, at least you've time for a cuppa and a bite to eat,' she suggested. 'What can I get you?'

Harry tried to lighten things with a joke. 'Six rashers of bacon and three eggs would be nice.'

It helped, at least temporarily. Ellen smiled, despite herself. 'Oh yes, be nice for a fortnight's rations, that would.' She slid two slices of bread under the grill, reaching in the cupboard for the dripping bowl. 'I don't suppose you've heard the sad news about Kaye,' she muttered, conversationally, over her shoulder – failing to see the jumpy expression which flashed between Harry and Mary as she spoke the name. Unaware that she had said anything wrong, she carried on innocently. 'The poor kid, it's terrible for her. The young pilot she'd been seeing died yesterday. Ivy says it's a blessing in disguise in a way, because he'd have been horribly scarred if he'd pulled through.'

Harry needed time to pull his thoughts together. 'Tell her I'm really sorry when you see her,' he said finally. 'Tell her we're both sorry.'

Granma came into the kitchen from upstairs, singing happily to herself. Dressed up in an ornate Edwardian gown and wearing a huge-brimmed hat trimmed with ostrich feathers, she brightened up the room like a ray of morning sunshine.

'Hullo, darling,' she said cheerily, seeing Harry. She stepped forward to give him a hug. 'Mind me bleedin' feathers,' she warned, as he embraced her.

Harry was astounded. 'Blimey, Gran – off to the Palace, are you?'

She flashed him an outrageous wink, putting her finger to her lips. 'Drury Lane,' she whispered. 'ENSA Headquarters, to see if they'll take on an old trouper. But don't tell your father, he'd go barmy.'

Ellen gave her an indulgent smile. 'Well, you'd better get going then,' she pointed out. 'I'm just about to call Thomas down for his breakfast.'

Granma grinned. 'Well, wish me luck, then,' she cackled, doing a little jig on the kitchen floor before hobbling off down the hall. Breaking into song again, she let herself out of the front door, having failed to notice Harry's uniform or even Mary's presence for that matter.

Ellen called up the stairs. 'Thomas, yer breakfast's ready. And make sure you're decent, 'cause we've got company.'

Thomas duly appeared in the kitchen, still adjusting his collar and tie. His face darkened, momentarily, upon seeing Harry, then the uniform registered. He turned his attention to Mary, smiling politely. 'Hello, Mary.'

He sat himself down at the table before looking up at his son again. 'You're going, then?'

Harry nodded. 'We ship out this afternoon. Advance party.'

'Do you know where?' Ellen put in, sounding anxious.

Harry shrugged faintly. 'They're issuing us with khaki drill and sunhelmets, so it's somewhere hot. I'll write as soon as I can,' he added.

There was a silence as Thomas sipped at his tea. He seemed to be putting his thoughts in order. When he spoke again, at last, there was just the faintest hint of apology in his voice. 'You've got to understand, son. I just wanted you to do right. It isn't easy for your mother or me – sending a son off to war.'

Harry said nothing. There was still a rift between them, that might never be closed completely.

'I doubt if Cliff'll be called upon to fight again,' Thomas continued. 'I suppose that's one good thing.'

Harry's face brightened slightly. 'So you've heard from him, then? How is he?' Briefly, he noticed a look of anguish cross his mother's face, and was immediately concerned. 'He's all right, isn't he?'

His father sounded guarded. 'We had a letter from his Welfare Officer. Cliff's had another bout of this fever he keeps getting. And they had to cut away some of the bone in his leg. I'm sure it'll be all right, but it's your mother who keeps worrying, you know what she's like.'

Mary was glancing anxiously at her watch. 'There's not much time,' she murmured warningly.

Harry nodded. 'Yes, you're right.' He climbed to his feet, smiling at his mother. 'Sorry, Mum, but we've got to go.'

Tears glistened in Ellen's eyes. 'Yes, of course,' she agreed. She stepped across to hug him again, then kissed Mary on the cheeks. 'You come and see us,' she told her. 'Any time you can.'

Thomas stood up, fumbling in his top jacket pocket. With an awkward, almost embarrassed smile he pulled out his old pocket watch and thrust it towards Harry. 'Here, I want you to have this,' he muttered.

Harry looked at the offering in surprise. 'But that was your dad's,' he pointed out.

His father nodded. 'Given to me for good luck. It got me through the Dardanelles. Now I want you to have it.'

'Thanks, Dad,' Harry said quietly, genuinely touched. He took the watch, a symbolic offering of peace between them.

He began to move down the hallway towards the door, shepherding Mary in front of him, feeling the warmth of his mother's tears on his back.

'You watch out you don't get sunstroke,' Thomas called after him, with forced humour. He turned to his wife, knowing that she needed his comfort.

The station platform and the waiting train were both crowded, service uniforms predominating. In stark contrast to the many kissing and cuddling couples, Harry and Mary stood apart from each other, almost as though an invisible Kaye filled the gap between them.

'It seems ludicrous to send us away at all,' Harry observed, just making conversation. 'They need the army here, at home.'

Mary smiled thinly, seizing at the chance of light-hearted banter. 'Perhaps it's all just a ploy to fool Hitler into some rash invasion,' she suggested jokingly. 'You're not really going anywhere at all.'

Harry tried to grin and failed. He looked at her with genuine concern in his eyes. 'I wish you weren't so insistent about staying in London,' he muttered.

Mary tossed her head, a trace of bitterness creeping into her voice. 'Well, we all do what we think's for the best, don't we?' she demanded.

Harry stiffened, the gibe striking home. Glancing sideways, he saw the railway guard stepping to the front of the platform, raising his flags in readiness. He sighed. 'Time to go,' he pointed out, flatly.

Mary nodded, moist-eyed. She leaned forward, putting her face to his. Their lips met, but the kiss was almost perfunctory.

It was only after the last door had slammed, and the train was already moving out of the station in a cloud of steam, that Mary felt truly in touch with herself.

Her lips moved, framing the words 'I love you' in silence, almost as though she did not even want to hear herself say it.

37

The normally quiet and peaceful Belgravia square was a buzz of activity as Dorothea drove into it. She stared, aghast, through the windscreen at the trio of flat-bed lorries half-blocking the street, already piled high with great sections of metal fencing torn from the perimeter of the central park. Elsewhere, workmen scurried about lifting gates from their hinges or unscrewing numbers and name-plates from the posts. Two other men struggled with the prodigious weight of a park bench, which had been unbolted from its concrete foundations. Worse, there was a man wearing a protective welding helmet and wielding an oxyacetylene torch crouched in front of her own house, busily demolishing the orna-mental wrought-iron railings.

Dorothea pulled the Talbot to a halt with a scream of brakes, jumping out to confront him.

'What the devil, may I ask, do you think you are doing?' she demanded indignantly, raising her voice to a scream above the roar of the torch.

The workman snapped off the flame, raising his visor. He grinned up at her. 'Scrap iron for battleships,' he explained cheerily. 'Government orders.'

Dorothea's face was almost apoplectic. 'Scrap iron? This is a private garden. Those are my railings.'

The man shrugged carelessly. 'Not any more they ain't, lady. Property of the Crown. Anyway, don't worry, we won't be touching yer garden.' He flipped his visor back down, flamed up the torch and resumed his work.

Dorothea continued to stand there impotently for several seconds, her body trembling with fury. Finally, realizing that the man was not going to pay her any more attention, she stormed into the house.

Edward was in his study, seated at his desk.

'Are you aware that there is a man out there wreaking total devastation on our front garden?' Dorothea demanded imperiously.

Edward didn't answer. Suddenly aware that he was staring at her coldly, his face devoid of emotion, Dorothea's tone changed abruptly. 'Are you all right?' she asked, curiously.

He rose to his feet slowly, confronting her. 'I was teaching first-aid to the Home Guard near Albourne yesterday, so I popped in,' he said quietly. 'You weren't there.' It was a flat statement, not quite an accusation.

Dorothea was flustered for a moment, but rallied herself quickly. 'Didn't Evelyn tell you? I went over to see Bunty Ellison, stayed the night with her. You know how nervous she gets, now that Godfrey is away.'

Edward's expression gave no clue whether he believed her or not. 'Evelyn just said you were out,' he muttered.

Dorothea strove to keep a sense of relief from showing on her face. Her sister had at least partially covered for her, whether consciously or not. She took the opportunity to change the subject. 'Have you seen anything of Rose?' she inquired.

Edward shook his head, the faintest of smiles brightening his face at the mention of his daughter's name. 'A phone call, that's all. Mostly about this new young captain she's been seeing.'

'So, are you home again now for a while?' Dorothea asked. 'I won't go back to Albourne if you're staying here.'

A faintly mocking smile played over Edward's lips. 'That's unusually caring of you, my dear,' he observed, with irony rather than sarcasm. 'As it happens, no such sacrifice will be called of you. I'm off again this evening. The Medical War Committee directs, I go. I'm being assigned to the free hospital at Battersea.'

Dorothea's nose wrinkled in disgust. 'Battersea?' she echoed. 'That's hardly more than a workhouse.'

Her husband regarded her with an expression of exaggerated patience, refusing to be riled even though her snobbishness infuriated him at times. 'It's a perfectly bona fide hospital,' he muttered heavily. 'And I expect I shall soon have very serious work to do there. Now that Churchill has ordered night bombing raids on Berlin, the *Luftwaffe* aren't going to restrict their raids to RAF airfields and oil storage facilities for much longer.'

Dorothea flashed him a sad, distant smile. It was difficult to tell if it was affection or pity.

'Poor Edward,' she murmured. 'Still rooting for the wrong side, even though your old chum Mussolini has let you down.'

Moira stood outside Victor's photographic studio for a long time, trying to pluck up the courage to go in. Finally, realizing that she had very little other choice, she braced herself and made her way up the stairs.

The outer office was empty, although there was a woman's handbag on the sofa. Moira looked about uncertainly. 'Victor?' she called out.

Victor appeared from behind the studio curtains, looking slightly furtive. Seeing Moira, he managed a half-smile which was not at all convincing. 'Look, I'm really busy right now,' he muttered. 'Why don't you come back later, after I've closed up?'

Despite his aloofness, Moira smiled at him. 'It's all right, I'll wait,' she announced, moving towards the sofa.

Victor's expression hardened, becoming almost hostile. 'You can't,' he snapped. 'I told you I'm busy.' He moved to intercept her, grasping her by the arm and turning her towards the door.

Moira shook his hand off, taking a defensive step back to stare at him incredulously. 'What's the matter with you?' she asked, sounding hurt.

He might have bluffed it out. Instead, Victor glanced back nervously towards the curtained-off studio.

Moira's eyes narrowed suspiciously. 'What's going on? Who you got in there?' she demanded. Without waiting for an answer, she ducked past him and ran to the curtains, pulling them back.

The girl curled up on an imitation tiger-skin rug was probably even younger than Moira. Naked, apart from a pair of ostrich-feather plumes held in front of her breasts, she glared up at Moira in mute insolence.

Moira dropped the curtain, turning back to face Victor with a mixture of pain and disbelief in her eyes. 'Who's she? What's she doing here?' she wanted to know, a sob in her voice.

Victor shrugged. 'My new model,' he announced. 'The public needs new faces.' He paused, sighing. 'Look, you were getting browned off with posing anyway, admit it.'

Moira looked at him sullenly. 'Only with the dirty stuff,' she said with deep bitterness. 'But I did it, didn't I? Because you said you loved me.'

It wasn't a subject Victor wanted to get into. 'What you doing here, anyway?' he demanded.

'I had to see you, talk to you,' Moira told him. Conscious of the girl behind the curtain, she dropped her voice to a mere whisper. 'I'm expecting.'

Victor looked rattled for a second, quickly covering his dismay with a doubting sneer. 'And what – you thought you'd try to pin it on me?'

Moira looked as if he had slapped her in the face. Her eyes opened wide, glistening wetly. 'There weren't anyone else, Victor – honest,' she whimpered.

The change of mood from aggression to defence was subtle, but more than enough for Victor. His self-confident grin returned. 'You must think I was born yesterday,' he said scornfully. He nodded his head towards the door. 'Now bugger off, and don't ever come back here again.'

Moira was frozen, unable to move, for some time. Then the tears started. Determined to retain something of her pride, she ran for the door before she broke down completely.

38

Evelyn found it difficult to cope with anything vaguely me-
chanical. Looking totally flustered, she crouched over the
Soyer heater at the back of the mobile canteen, parked just
outside the perimeter fence of RAF Hornden. Following Miss
Cardew's garbled instructions, she fed in lumps of wood and
hoped for the best.

Behind her, peering over a row of sandbags, the entire
eight-man crew of an anti-aircraft gun emplacement watched
with mild amusement, each one willing her skirt to ride a
little further up her legs.

Evelyn straightened at last, wiping her hands together with
a gesture of vague satisfaction. The heater appeared to be
doing its job, as thin wisps of steam started to curl from the
safety valve on top of the hot-water urn. She turned to face
the gun crew, smiling apologetically. 'Tea shouldn't be long
now. I'm afraid we had so many ports of call, we ran out of
hot water.'

A well-built corporal of about forty clambered over the
sandbags and sauntered over, still munching one of the sand-
wiches Evelyn had distributed earlier. 'Be a bit quicker if you
screwed down the valve a bit,' he suggested helpfully, making
the necessary adjustment.

Evelyn smiled at him. 'Thank you.'

The corporal grinned. 'Always willing to help out a real
lady.' He took another bite of his sandwich, smacking his
lips. 'Lovely fillin' in this,' he mumbled appreciatively.
'Better'n the usual stuff they dish out.'

'It's only Gentlemen's Relish,' Evelyn told him. 'I brought
it from home.'

The corporal turned back to the rest of his crew, calling

out to them with a huge grin on his face, 'Hear that, lads? We're all gentlemen now.' He returned his attention to Evelyn, eyeing her up. 'I haven't seen you on this run before,' he observed. 'Be coming here regular now, will you?'

The man appeared to be flirting with her, Evelyn thought, beginning to flush with embarassment. It was a long time since she had had any experience of such a situation, and she wasn't sure how to deal with it.

She was rescued – if that was the right word – by the tooting of a car horn. She whirled round to see Dorothea just pulling the Talbot to a halt. As usual, she was in full warpaint and dressed to the nines.

The corporal had also turned in her direction. 'Blimey,' he muttered, his eyes popping. 'First we get a lady, and now it's the bleedin' Duchess herself.'

'She's my sister,' Evelyn told him flatly. It was almost an apology.

'Blimey,' the corporal said again. Deciding that discretion was the better part of valour, he scurried for the cover of the sandbags again.

Evelyn regarded Dorothea warily as she approached. 'What on earth are you doing here?' she asked, with a weary sigh.

Dorothea smiled, although she did not seem quite so ebullient as usual. 'William told me where to find you,' she explained. She cast a quick glance over the mobile canteen. 'Doing our bit for the war effort, are we?'

Evelyn's eyes flashed a warning. 'Now don't start being patronizing, Dorothea. I'm just helping out until they can get a regular rota established again. There's been so many bombing raids, everything's knocked out of kilter.'

Dorothea pouted. 'Patronizing, darling?' she repeated, sounding affronted. 'I came to see if I could help.'

Had she announced she was going down the mines, Evelyn might have been more convinced. She looked her sister squarely in the eye. 'What do you want, Dorothea?' she demanded.

The last trace of guile dropped from Dorothea's face, realizing that Evelyn had her measure perfectly. 'Edward told me he dropped in to see you the other night,' she murmured.

A knowing smile spread across Evelyn's face. 'And now you're here to find out if I gave away where you were?'

Dorothea said nothing, just looking rather sheepish.

Evelyn sighed with exasperation. 'Well, you might as well have saved yourself the trip,' she said irritably. 'I couldn't tell him anything because I didn't have the foggiest idea.' She paused, momentarily. 'God dammit, Dorothea – are you having an affair?' she asked finally.

Her sister looked down at the ground. 'No – but yes,' she murmured ambiguously.

Evelyn rolled her eyes, fast losing what little patience she had left. 'What on earth does that mean?' she demanded.

Dorothea looked genuinely upset. 'Please, don't be angry,' she whimpered.

Evelyn's eyes blazed. 'Why the hell shouldn't I be? You put me in a position where I have to lie for you, you use my home as an alibi.' She broke off, fighting a losing fight to control her rising temper. 'God, but you're just so vain and self-centred. So long as you enjoy yourself the rest of the world can go hang. You don't seem to care who you hurt, or how.'

Dorothea wilted under her sister's attack, looking like a spoiled little girl. 'I don't want to hurt Edward,' she murmured, defensively.

Evelyn's anger was fast dissipating into helpless resignation. 'Well, you're going about it in a very strange way,' she pointed out.

Dorothea nodded miserably. 'I know,' she admitted. 'But you don't really understand. I was only trying to help him, you see.'

The tea urn was hissing away like a minor demon now, but Evelyn ignored it. For all her faults, Dorothea was still her sister and obviously in some sort of trouble. Blood being thicker than water, she had little choice but to help if she could. 'Perhaps you'd better try to explain,' she suggested.

Dorothea sniffed, wetly. It was the nearest she had ever seen her sister to tears, Evelyn reflected.

'A few months ago, Edward was under investigation, about his contacts with the British Union,' Dorothea started, uncertainly.

Evelyn nodded. 'Yes, Arthur mentioned it. So how does that lead to you having an affair?'

'I thought he was going to be arrested,' Dorothea went on. 'I was desperate, so I turned to the only person I thought might be able to help.' She paused for a moment. 'You remember Cecil Mortimer, don't you? I used to date him when I was about nineteen.'

Evelyn did remember him. The ghost of a smile played across her face. 'I remember what a frightful ass he was,' she said.

Dorothea bristled, momentarily. 'Well, he's not an ass any more. He's quite high up in the Home Office now. Anyway, I went to see him to ask if he could call off the surveillance on Edward, for old times' sake.'

Evelyn was beginning to get the picture now. 'But he expected a favour for a favour?' she prompted.

Dorothea nodded. 'That's about the size of it. I was willing to do anything to save poor Edward from ending up in some ghastly internment camp, or being shipped off to the Isle of Man. I did it for him, Evelyn, so you see I'm not totally selfish.'

'And you were with Cecil the other night?' Evelyn asked. 'You've been carrying on this affair ever since?'

Dorothea nodded. 'That's why I was so worried. He mustn't suspect. I could never go through the dreadful scandal of a divorce.'

This final admission blew away the entire sham of Dorothea's supposed altruism. In the final analysis, she had acted out of self-interest, Evelyn realized. Just as she always did.

She regarded her sister with an expression of pity. 'God, Dorothea – you'll never change, will you?' she asked sadly.

39

The sound of the front door opening and closing shook Granma out of a light doze in Thomas's favourite chair. She sat up with a start as Moira walked into the parlour, her eyes red and puffy and her cheeks stained with tears.

'Blimey, gel – you look like the wreck of the Hesperus,' Granma told her candidly. 'Where've you been all afternoon and evening, anyway?'

There was no answer. Moira slumped on to the sofa, staring at her own knees, avoiding Granma's eyes.

Granma smiled hopefully. 'I got something might cheer you up,' she said, gently teasing. She fished down the side of the chair cushion, pulling out the letter which had arrived that morning and holding it out. 'Yer nan must have forgotten to give it you.'

Moira made no move to take it. Granma wasn't even sure if her words were even registering with the girl, she seemed so distant and depressed.

'Look, love – anything you want to talk about?' she inquired gently. 'It's just you and me. Yer nan and grandad's down at the Plaza seeing the new Gracie Fields film, Frank's on fire duty and Geoffrey's in bed.'

Moira spoke for the first time, in little more than a choked whisper, 'Ain't got nothing to talk about.'

Granma sighed, trying again. She waved the letter. 'Well, ain't you even interested in who it's from?' she asked. There was no response.

'It'll brighten you up, I promise,' Granma went on. She looked a bit guilty for a few seconds, realizing that she'd given the game away. 'All right, I'm sorry – but I steamed it open and read it,' she admitted. 'But it's wonderful news. Yer hubby's coming home on leave.'

A look of shock and horror crossed Moira's face as she promptly burst into a fresh bout of sobbing.

It was not the reaction Granma had expected. 'Blimey,' she muttered, half to herself. 'I might have well said in a box.'

Moira pulled herself together with an effort. She looked up through tear-filled eyes. 'I don't want him to come home, not now,' she said wretchedly. She paused, tensing her body against a new wave of emotion. 'I'm up the spout, Gran,' she blurted out, finally.

After the bouts of morning sickness it was not a total surprise, but still shocking. 'Oh, you daft girl,' Granma said, reprovingly. She sighed deeply, her tone softening. 'Whatever made you do it?'

Moira choked her words out between sobs. 'He said he loved me, Gran. Now he won't even believe that it's his.'

Granma snorted. 'Bloody men've been saying that since they learned to walk on their hind legs,' she observed laconically. She pushed herself from her chair to go and sit beside Moira, hugging her. 'Luckily us women have learned a few tricks an' all.'

Moira sniffed back her tears. 'You gonna help me?' she asked uncertainly, as though hardly daring to believe it.

Granma nodded, a determined look on her face. 'It'll be all right, darlin'. Yer Gran'll look after you.'

The kitchen table had been dragged against the back door, sealing it off. Behind a folding screen, Moira sat back in an old tin bath, up to her shoulders in hot water and gulping down cups of neat gin – both of which Granma replenished frequently. The girl was already well past the point of mere drunkenness and in a state of near-stupour, hardly aware of what was going on and no longer even able to control the hiccoughs which racked constantly at her body.

'Try holding yer breath, girl,' Granma told her helpfully,

but it was highly doubtful if Moira even heard her. She topped up the girl's cup with more gin, lifting it to her mouth.

The handle of the back door rattled suddenly, accompanied by the sound of someone pushing against the door. Tom's voice came from outside.

'Mum? Gran? Anyone in there?'

Granma swore under her breath, taking a large swig of gin from the bottle in her hand and grimacing at the raw taste.

The door was pushed again, forcing the table back and opening a few inches. 'Come on, it's me, Tom. Let me in, for Christ's sake.'

'Bugger off,' Granma shouted back at him. 'Come back termorrer.'

Tom's voice was wheedling. 'Aw, please Gran, let me in. I've come to see Moira.' He pushed at the door again, but the table was now wedged under the handle and it refused to budge any further. Starting to lose his temper, Tom began pounding on it with his fists. Oblivious to it all, Moira continued to hiccough loudly.

There was a new sound, suddenly. A throbbing, wailing sound which built up quickly to an all-pervasive crescendo. Granma swore again, louder this time.

Geoffrey came pounding down the stairs, carrying Shirley. He burst into the kitchen, sounding panicky. 'It's an air-raid, Gran,' he shouted, urgently.

The 'Moaning Minnie' sirens were going full-pelt now, the sound almost drowning out Tom's increasingly furious battering on the back door. Geoffrey stared at it and the wedged table, looking totally baffled. 'It's Uncle Tom,' he shouted at Granma. 'What's going on?'

In the midst of pandemonium, Granma fought against being sucked into it. She pulled the folding screen closer to Moira's bath, shielding it from Geoffrey's eyes. 'Don't you let him in, for Gawd's sake,' she yelled at him, meaning Tom. 'And stop getting yerself all in a tizz. It'll only be another bleedin' false alarm.'

Outside, Tom's voice rose to a scream. 'They're dropping flares, for Christ's sake!' Seconds later came the first faint *crumps* of distant explosions. The windows rattled – but it was a different kind of shockwave which rippled through the population of London that night. This air-raid was for real – the 'Phoney War' was finally over.

Granma raised her eyes to the ceiling. 'Picked yer bleeding time, didn't yer?' she demanded bitterly. She turned to Geoffrey, thrusting the bottle of gin into his hands. 'Get that bloody door unblocked.' She bent over Moira, struggling to haul her limp body out of the bath.

Tom finally burst in as Geoffrey slid the table out of the way. Assessing the situation at a glance, he took control. 'Go on, take Geoffrey and the kid to the shelter,' he told Granma. 'I'll take care of Moira.' He dragged his daughter to her feet, swathing her in a towel. Scooping her up in his arms, he manhandled her through the door and stumbled across the back garden towards the Anderson shelter.

The explosions were much closer now. Tom carried Moira down the steps, laying her next to Granma. 'Where's Mum and Dad?' he hissed urgently, suddenly noticing their absence.

She looked shaken. 'They went out to the pictures.'

'Christ!' Tom blurted out. To his knowledge, there was no public shelter between the Plaza and Nelson Street. He ran back up to the top of the shelter steps, peering out across the garden.

His parents were just running through the back gate, Thomas pushing Ellen in the direction of the shelter and turning towards the house. Tom yelled at him, 'Come on straight down the shelter, Dad – I've got 'em all safe.' He jumped out into the garden, clearing the way for his mother.

The sound of exploding bombs was almost constant now, each resultant shockwave more powerful.

'The buggers must be coming over in droves,' Thomas observed, morbidly, reaching the shelter entrance. He froze, suddenly, glaring at Tom as though he had just noticed his presence for the first time. The two men held each other's eyes for several seconds, wrapped in a small cocoon of silence despite the bedlam all around them.

Tom broke it, finally. 'Now's not the time, Dad,' he said quietly. He lay his hand on his father's shoulder, pushing him down the steps. They both dived into the shelter together, Tom pulling the door into position.

The 'all clear' signal faded away at last, leaving an eerie sense of quiet in which the loudest sound was Moira groaning. She began to retch violently, giving the shelter's occupants the incentive they needed to emerge into the outside world again.

Tom pushed open the door, clambering up the steps into the garden, staring out over the fence and beyond. Next door, Reg Collins's greenhouse was completely demolished, shards of broken glass strewn all over his precious marigold beds. Perhaps two or three streets away could be seen the orange flames of isolated fires, the odd shattered rooftop silhouetted against their light. But further towards the heart of the city was an almost solid red glow that lit up the horizon as though the sky itself was on fire.

Tom pulled his silver cigarette case from his pocket, extracting one and lighting it as his father stepped out of the shelter to stand beside him. 'We were lucky,' he observed, proffering the case.

The offer was not even acknowledged. 'You'll be safe to go home now,' Thomas muttered thickly, looking away.

Tom sighed wearily. 'I came to see my daughter, Dad.'

'So you've seen her,' his father said. He lapsed into silence, compressing his lips into a tight, thin line.

Something snapped inside Tom's head. He turned on his father suddenly, seizing him by the shoulders and shaking him. 'For Christ's sake, what is it with you? Even if you feel bugger all for me except hate, try to accept that she matters to me.' His anger evaporated as quickly as it had erupted.

Dropping his arms, he took a step back, staring into his father's eyes, forcing confrontation. 'If it means anything to you at all, I was glad to be with her through all that. In fact, wiv all of you.'

Thomas's face remained impassive. 'You always did have the gift of the gab,' he murmured, unimpressed.

Sheer disbelief made Tom laugh out loud, albeit bitterly. 'Christ, Dad, is that all there is – your bloody grudges?' He nodded down towards the Anderson shelter. 'For a while, I thought we were close in there, like family again. Do there have to be bloody bombs falling out of the sky? It could've been us.'

Any reply which Thomas might have made was interrupted by Geoffrey, who came scrambling out of the shelter at that moment with Ellen close behind him.

'Stop him, Thomas,' Ellen called out, as the boy appeared to be about to make a bolt for the gate.

Thomas grabbed at his arm, restraining him. 'Where do you think you're going?'

Geoffrey struggled to free himself. 'Let me go, Grandad. I've got to go and see if me Dad's all right.'

Ellen had reached him now, and held his shoulders. 'Don't be silly, Geoffrey. What if there's another wave of bombers?' She glanced at her husband for support. 'Tell him, Thomas.'

Thomas looked up into the empty night sky, shaking his head slowly. 'They won't be back tonight,' he said confidently. 'Something tells me that was just a taster.' Considering what was to come, it was a remarkably prophetic statement.

Ellen looked unconvinced. 'Well, at least someone ought to go with him,' she muttered uncertainly,

Tom stepped forward. 'I'll go,' he offered.

To his great surprise, as well as Ellen's, Thomas pulled him back. 'I'll take him,' he said firmly. 'You stay here – with your family.' He noticed the look of happiness which passed across his wife's face and knew he had done the right thing.

Granma's face appeared at the top of the steps, glaring up at them. 'Well, is someone going to help me out of this hell-hole?' she demanded indignantly. 'And get young Moira out before she turns it into a bleedin' latrine?'

Tom bent over to give her a hand, grinning. He turned to his mother. 'Take her back into the house and give her a stiff drink,' he suggested. 'I'll bring Moira.'

He plunged back into the gloom of the shelter, snapping on the emergency flashlight kept by the door. Moira was huddled in the corner, her body shuddering from the after-effects of nausea. Tom knelt beside her, stroking her hair tenderly. 'Come on, love. It's all over now.'

Moira sat up slowly, still hopelessly groggy from the gin. She stared at her father through eyes which refused to focus properly. 'What' you doin'ere?' she slurred.

Tom smiled. 'Waiting for you to wake up. We had a few bombs, but you was out for the count most of the time.'

Dimly, Moira started to remember. Her hand strayed under the towel to her stomach, stroking it. 'Din't work, did it?'

Tom shook his head sadly. 'No, love,' he murmured.

Moira's bottom lip began to tremble. 'Gran said it'd be all right,' she said miserably.

Tom held her by the shoulders, forcing a smile. 'It will be,' he promised. 'I'll make it all right.'

Post-alcoholic depression was settling upon the girl quickly. She began to whimper. 'He told me I was a forces' sweetheart, Dad. He said he loved me.'

Tom slipped his fingers under her chin, lifting her face. 'Who?' he asked. 'Who told you that, love?'

Moira shook her head, the tears starting to flow. 'I can't tell you, Dad,' she murmured sadly. 'We both got enough troubles as it is.'

40

It was all rather exciting, Geoffrey thought – a bit like a Sexton Blake story but without the danger. He stalked Moira at what he considered to be a discreet distance, every ready to duck into the nearest doorway should the girl turn round, or suspect that she was being followed.

Luckily, neither of these eventualities happened, for Geoffrey's skill as a private detective was largely inside his own head. Set upon her quest, Moira led him straight to Victor's photographic studio.

Geoffrey watched her pause outside the entrance, summoning her courage before striding purposefully inside. Hurrying forward, he peered cautiously round the corner of the doorway just in time to see her disappear through the door at the top of the stairs, closing it behind her.

Geoffrey frowned, not at all sure what to do now. His instructions from his uncle Tom had been simple and specific – to keep an eye on Moira and report back on anywhere she went or anyone she met. The possibility of prying beyond closed doors had not been mentioned.

Eventually, caught up in his own sense of adventure, Geoffrey decided on a compromise. Tip-toeing up the stairs, he pressed his ear against the door, hardly daring to breathe. Though muffled, it was just possible to pick out the sound of voices.

Victor glared at Moira angrily. 'I thought I told you never to come here again,' he said, nastily.

Moira stood her ground, defiant. 'Don't worry, I ain't gonna pester you or anyfink. I just want you to help me this once and I'll never bovver you again, I promise.'

'Help you?' Victor was guarded.

'I've found this woman,' Moira went on. 'She can get rid of it, but she costs fifteen pounds.'

Victor smiled craftily, mocking her. 'But that's against the law, Moira. You can go to prison for that.'

'That's my bloody business,' Moira shot back. She was silent for a moment, a pleading tone creeping into her voice. 'I promise I won't bring you into it, Victor. It's just that I ain't got that kind of money.'

He sneered at her. 'So what makes you think I have?'

Moira was bitter. 'You must've made plenty out of me and all them pictures,' she pointed out.

Victor laughed in her face. 'Well, that's business, isn't it. You got paid good money, didn't you?'

Moira was becoming increasingly desperate. 'Please, Victor. I'll never ask you for nuffink ever again.'

The girl's persistence was beginning to tax Victor's patience. 'Damn right you won't,' he retorted viciously. 'And you're not lumbering me now. So clear off now, before I bloody throw you out.'

Moira was stunned by his sudden vehemence. She gaped at him in disbelief. 'But you've gotta help me,' she whimpered, hopelessly. 'My husband's coming back.'

Victor laughed again. 'Well, that makes it his bloody problem, doesn't it, love?' he demanded.

Pushed against the wall, Moira's desperation erupted into sudden blind anger and panic. 'You bastard,' she spat at him. Hurling herself forward, she ran past him to the filing cabinet, yanking open the drawer. She began to pull out files and sheaves of photographic prints, throwing them to the floor.

Victor had been caught off-guard for a moment. Now he reacted furiously. He ran forward, seizing Moira by the arm. 'What the bloody hell do you think you're doing, you little tart?' he yelled at her.

Moira struggled to free herself, continuing to pull out bundles of photographs with her free hand. 'You ain't gonna sell any more of them dirty pictures,' she screamed back.

Victor struck her across the face with the back of his hand, making her shriek with pain. She fell back, clutching her own file. Prints of her in various poses spilled out on to the floor.

Outside the door, Geoffrey had been listening to their heated exchange with mounting concern. Now, hearing Moira's scream of pain, he burst in to the rescue.

'You take your hands off her,' he shouted at Victor, running to Moira's side and trying to help her to her feet. She shook him off, scrabbling about on the floor and trying to gather up as many of the photographs as she could before he saw them.

She was too late. Geoffrey's eyes widened in shock as they fell upon one of the pictures. Utterly naked apart from a Carmen Miranda-style head-dress of plastic fruit, Moira knelt on a rug in an obscene pose, her knees splayed apart and her hands cupped under her breasts as though holding them out in offering.

Geoffrey had never seen a naked girl before, let alone his own cousin. He was temporarily stunned. Victor took his opportunity to grab the boy by the throat, slamming him back against the front of the filing cabinet. 'Who the hell are you?' he demanded savagely.

'I'm her cousin,' Geoffrey managed to grate out. He kicked out at the man's shin, making Victor jump back with an angry roar of pain. Making the most of her temporary respite, Moira scooped the rest of the photographs together, stuffed them in her bag and made a run for the door.

Recovering himself, Victor began to advance on Geoffrey again, his face dark with menace. 'Seems to me I'd better teach you a bloody lesson, you little toe-rag,' he hissed nastily.

Geoffrey was not prepared to wait and find out what form this lesson might take. With Moira safely out of the way, self-preservation appeared to be the order of the day. Side-stepping, he ducked out of Victor's reach and followed Moira's escape route.

Victor did not bother to give chase. All in all, it was not a bad outcome, he told himself. He had got rid of Moira in no uncertain manner and she would be highly unlikely to ever bother him again. As far as the photographs were concerned, she had taken only a few pounds' worth of prints, and he still had all the negatives. And if the heaviest support the girl could manage was her fourteen-year-old cousin, he was in little danger of recrimination.

Geoffrey caught up with Moira some hundred yards down the street. She stopped dead in her tracks, glaring at him angrily. 'What the hell were you doin' following me?' she demanded. 'Who put you up to bloody spying on me?'

Geoffrey had not been expecting gratitude, but Moira's antagonism still threw him slightly. Feeling defensive and slightly guilty, he bluffed it out as best he could. 'I was just looking out for you, that's all.'

Moira didn't believe him. 'Oh, yeah?' she muttered sarcastically. 'On whose orders? My bloody Dad, was it?'

Geoffrey shook his head. 'No,' he lied, thinking that his promised sixpence might not materialize if he revealed too much.

Still unconvinced, Moira decided to let it drop. She was unlikely to prise the truth out of him, and now she had another worry on her mind. She put on her most vulnerable look, appealing to him. 'Look, Geoffrey – you won't say anything to anybody about them pictures, will you?' she pleaded.

Geoffrey didn't quite understand. 'But you gotta have someone to stick up for you,' he protested. 'He can't treat you like that – not after he put you in the club an' all.'

It was Moira's turn to lie. 'It weren't nuffink to do wiv him,' she maintained. 'Anyway, it's my business.' She clutched at his sleeve, wheedling again. 'You got to promise not to say anything, Geoffrey. You got to swear.'

Confused, Geoffrey struggled with his own thoughts, trying to work out where his loyalties actually lay.

'Promise me, Geoffrey,' Moira pleaded with him again. 'Your grandad'd kill me if he found out.'

She probably had a point there, Geoffrey conceded. Eventually, he nodded in agreement, still unsure if he was doing the right thing.

Moira managed a thin smile. 'Thanks,' she told him. 'And thanks for trying to help me back there an' all.'

Tom was still reeling from the bombshell which Sandra had dropped in his lap upon his arrival at the factory. He sat at his desk, looking up at her with deeply troubled eyes.

'And you're sure they were regular police, not Government inspectors?' he asked carefully, needing to check the facts.

'Oh, they was coppers all right,' Sandra confirmed, sadly and apologetically. 'One detective sergeant, one in uniform. Can't have missed you by more than ten minutes.'

Tom sighed deeply. 'Did he give you his name?'

Sandra nodded. 'DS Howard.' She noticed the sudden look of anguish which passed across Tom's face. 'Know him, do you?'

Tom let out a bitter half-laugh. 'Oh yeah, I know him all right. Him and me go way back.' His face became serious again. 'Tell me again – exactly what sort of questions he was asking.'

Sandra drew a breath, thinking for a moment. 'How long I'd worked for you? Was the factory your only line of business? Did I know the names of any of your friends?'

Tom tried to take encouragement from this information. On the face of it, the police were only fishing, with nothing solid to go on. 'Did they say anything about coming back?' he asked finally.

Sandra shook her head, giving him a comforting smile. 'No, and there's no reason why they should, is there? You've cleared out all your stuff, and I'm pretty sure they was satisfied with what I told 'em.' She paused, grinning proudly. 'I said I'd known you for years. Tom O'Malley, that is.'

Tom smiled gratefully. 'You're a good girl, Sandra,' he told her. 'I don't know what I'd do without you.'

She slipped her arm around his shoulder. 'Do you mean that?'

Tom reached up to pat her hand. 'Yes, I do. I really do,' he murmured, tenderly. He climbed to his feet, walking across to his office window to look down over the factory floor.

'I've built all this up from nothing,' he muttered over his shoulder, a distinct hint of pride in his voice. 'I've made something of meself, proved that I wasn't the shiftless bugger some people thought I was. I'm even doing my bit for the war.' He turned back to face her, a deep sadness in his eyes. 'I couldn't bear to lose it all now, Sandra. In a way, that'd hurt even more than going back to prison.'

The girl ran over to him, clutching his hand. 'Don't you even talk about going back to prison,' she scolded. 'Like I said, there's no reason them coppers should ever come back. Anyway, if you needed to you could always come to my house, lie low there for a bit.'

Tom exploded into sudden defiance. 'But that's it – I don't *want* to lie low,' he blurted out. He pulled his stolen identity card out of his pocket, staring at it wistfully. 'I like being Mr O'Malley. He's got a much better life than poor old Tom Slater ever had. He is somebody – I'm somebody.'

Sandra squeezed his hand, starting to murmur words of consolation. Outside, the sirens wailed into life, drowning her out.

'Bloody hell!' Tom cursed. He ran to his office door, opening it and staring down to the factory floor. The workers were already panicking, dropping tools and paintbrushes and snatching up gasmasks, tipping over their workstools in their rush to get away from the benches.

'Oi – what the bleedin' 'ell do you think you're all doing?' Tom yelled down at them. 'Get back to work – don't you know there's a war on?'

Sally, who had set herself up as official shop steward,

glared up at him. 'You must be bloody loony,' she scoffed. 'Bleeding death-trap, this place, with all this paint and dope lying around. One bloody bomb and it'd go up like an inferno.'

Tom was about to hurl back a retort, but there was a frightened gasp from Sandra, who had run to look out of the far window at the first sound of the sirens. 'Christ, Tom – there's hundreds of 'em,' she said, her voice shaking. 'Hundreds of bloody planes. The sky's full of them.'

The girl looked frozen with panic. There was a growing buzz in the air, like a swarm of angry hornets, rapidly swelling above the wail of the sirens. The windows rattled, the very floor and walls of the office starting to vibrate. He ran across to her, shaking her back to reality.

'Come on, love – there's a public shelter in Bale Street. We'll be safe there.'

Sandra still seemed too frightened to move. 'Do you think this is it – the invasion?' she asked shakily. Rumours that Hitler would order a major paratroop drop had persisted for weeks now.

Tom's mind raced. On sudden impulse, he ran across to his desk, pulling Edward's stolen gun from its hiding place. 'We'll be ready for the bastards if it is,' he told Sandra, starting to bundle her towards the door.

41

The hospital operating theatre was reminiscent of a factory production line, with rows of wheeled stretcher trolleys ferrying a constant stream of wounded towards the operating tables as though they were items on a conveyor belt.

Heading one of the three surgical teams which had been working flat out for the past three hours, Edward looked more like an abattoir worker than a surgeon. His cap, mask, gown and rubber apron were all liberally splattered with blood, with more of the sticky red gore sucking at the soles of his rubber galoshes every time he moved his feet.

He bent over his newest patient, scalpel in hand, peering uncertainly at a grotesque swelling the size of half a tennis ball on the man's chest. Pouring blood from a single jagged hole in its centre, it was unlike any wound he had ever encountered before.

Edward looked up at the young Scots house surgeon assisting him. 'Ever seen anything like this before, Gordon?'

The young man shook his head. 'No, sir.'

Edward managed a grim smile. 'That makes two of us, then.' He lowered the scalpel, making a single diagonal incision and calling on the scrub nurse for a pair of retractors. The wound made a strange crackling sound as he prised it open.

'Glass,' Edward observed. 'Hundreds of tiny splinters.' He called for a scoop, cleaning the bloody mess out as best he could before backing off, glancing aside at Gordon again. 'Swab out and stitch him up. I'll get on with the next one.'

He peeled off his surgical goves and discarded them, accepting a new pair. Sidestepping to the next trolley in line, he inspected the damage. Already anaesthetized and stripped from the waist down, the victim was female, probably no more than twenty-three and with the slender, shapely legs of a dancer. The frilled bolero top of the Latin American outfit she was still wearing appeared to confirm this non-medical diagnosis, but the gaping wound in her knee, revealing the whiteness of bone, did not speak well for her professional future.

Edward smiled wanly, speaking gently to the unconscious girl even though he knew she could not hear him. 'Well, young lady – you won't be dancing the night away for a month or so.' He looked up, briefly, scanning the line of waiting trolleys. 'But then I don't think any of us will, for that matter,' he added, purely to himself.

Gordon had finished stitching up the previous patient. He moved to Edward's side, regarding the man with concern. Already weary himself, he could only guess at the heavy toll such an intense workload must be having on someone of Edward's age. He glanced down at the girl's injured leg, assessing his own professional competence. It was not an easy operation, but well within his capabilities.

He touched Edward gently on the shoulder. 'Come on, sir – you really ought to take a break,' he urged. 'Even if it's only for an hour or so.'

Much the same thought had already occurred to Edward himself. Ever the realist, he was fully aware that his hand and eye co-ordination was starting to slip. Gordon's intervention was almost confirmation of his fears. Reluctantly, he nodded. 'Yes, I think you're probably right,' he muttered. 'It's probably best if I take a bit of a rest.'

Holding a handkerchief delicately over her nose, Dorothea made her way hurriedly down the chaotic hospital corridor, ducking and weaving past stretchers and trolleys and trying very hard to ignore the tide of human misery all around her. She was already beginning to regret her rash decision to come, but the brief telephone call from Cecil Mortimer had rattled her, and Dorothea was not very good at coping with a crisis on her own.

She reached the end of the corridor with a sense of great relief, finally leaving behind the mass of injured people with their pitiful groans and cries of pain. A flight of stairs led down into the hospital basement, where she had been told the staff rest rooms were situated. Peering down into the gloom dubiously, Dorothea started to descend.

The 'rest rooms' were in fact no more than cleaning material stores, which had been hastily cleared out, furnished with single iron cots and pressed into emergency use. In a small cell barely larger than a broom cupboard, Edward half-dozed on a thin, bare mattress, his bloody gown and apron thrown over the end of the bed.

He sat up with a start as the door opened, revealing a blurred human shape. His mouth dropped open in astonishment as he identified his visitor by the smell of her perfume, rather than by sight.

'Dorothea?' he muttered in disbelief. He reached for his spectacles by the side of the pillow, slipping them on. Dorothea settled into focus, confirming his suspicion. He continued to gape at her dumbly, quite thunderstruck.

'I thought you might be hungry,' she said brightly. 'I managed to get hold of some caviare.'

Edward shook his head, not sure if he was having a lucid dream or a nightmare. 'Caviare?' he echoed, hollowly. 'My God, Dorothea – have you seen what's going on out there?'

She tossed her head dismissively. 'Of course I've seen it. It's absolutely ghastly. I don't know how you can bear it.' She paused, frowning at him. 'I must say you don't seem very pleased to see me.'

It was a near-classic piece of understatement. Edward regarded his wife with a thin, cold smile. 'Pleased, my dear? Perhaps astounded might be a better word. I'd rather assumed that you would be with your lover right now.'

Dorothea's face froze into a mask of shock. 'Lover?' she

demanded, bluffing it out. 'What on earth are you talking about, Edward?'

The smile was still on his lips, now tinged with a resigned sadness. 'Please don't insult me, Dorothea,' he murmured wearily. 'Do you really think me such a poor fool that I don't know what's been going on? All those furtive phone calls, unexplained trips into town, not being where you're supposed to be?'

A denial seemed pointless, Dorothea thought, an explanation too complicated and an apology worthless. She settled for something in between. 'It wasn't like that at all,' she said flatly. 'I was trying to help you, whether you believe it or not.' She broke off, an expression of real concern on her face. 'I'm here to help you now, as a matter of fact.'

Edward sighed. 'Fine, then you can help by leaving me to get some rest. I have to be back in the operating theatre in less than an hour.'

It was not so much a dismissal as a rejection. Dorothea bristled, her anger rising. 'Damn you, Edward. There are other doctors. This is important.'

Edward shook his head, slowly. 'No, Dorothea. My work here – that's what's important.'

It was time for the blunt truth. 'I had a telephone call – from someone I know in the Home Office. You're going to be arrested at any time now, Edward. Now that the powers that be consider an invasion imminent, they've started to round up anyone who might be considered a sympathizer.'

Edward took the news with calm fatalism, shrugging his shoulders. 'Then they will arrest me. At least in an internment camp I shall be free to say what I feel. That if the fools had listened to people like me in the first place, I wouldn't be making these pathetic attempts to patch up these poor creatures now.'

Dorothea stared at him aghast, failing to understand his coolness. 'But it needn't come to that, don't you understand what I'm saying? We have warning, that gives us time. I have the car outside – we can go up north, perhaps find a way of getting over to Ireland.'

Edward smiled at her indulgently. 'Poor Dorothea – you never really understood me, did you?' he murmured. His voice took on a firmer tone. 'I won't run away, slink off like some cringing dog with its tail between its legs.'

Nothing seemed to affect him, Dorothea thought. With a sense of rising desperation, she tried to appeal to his sense of chivalry. 'Don't you care about me – about us?' she demanded.

Edward merely smiled again. 'You already do all the caring about you which could possibly be necessary,' he pointed out. 'And as for "us", I'm not even sure if there is such a thing anymore.'

Delivered almost gently, the words nevertheless had the force of a physical blow. Dorothea reeled back under their impact, the colour draining from her face. She was silent for a long time, coming to terms with herself, plumbing her own depths for an ounce of fight, but there was nothing left.

Finally resigned to the inevitable, she let out a long, drawn-out sigh. 'Then there's nothing else I can say or do,' she said in a tired little voice. 'If you need to get in touch, I'll be at Albourne.'

She turned towards the door and began to walk away, leaving Edward another thousand miles behind her with every step.

42

The smell of burning greeted Thomas as he walked in through the back door to the kitchen. Glancing around the room in alarm, he noticed a thin plume of black smoke curling from the top of the oven. He moved to switch it off, hurrying down the hallway to the parlour.

Frank was curled up on the sofa, reading the latest Raymond Chandler thriller. Granma was at the piano, tinkling away happily. Of Ellen, there was no sign.

'Something burning in the oven,' Thomas announced. 'I hope it's not my tea.'

Granma started at the sound of his voice. She slammed her hands down on the piano keyboard with a crash of discordant notes. She jumped to her feet, a black look on her face.

'My bleedin' sausage rolls,' she said bitterly. 'Ellen said she was going to take them out for me. Practically had to go down on me bloody knees for that sausage meat as well.' She stormed off out to the kitchen, muttering under her breath.

Frank looked up at his father, grinning. 'Mum had a letter from Clifford this morning,' he said by way of explanation. 'She's upstairs reading it – yet again.'

Thomas's face glowed. 'Cliff's written, eh?' He moved back to the door, calling up the stairs. 'Ellen? Frank says we've had a letter from Clifford.'

Granma reappeared in the hallway, having consigned the spoiled sausage rolls to the bin. 'Must have been a bleedin' full-length novel, judging by the time she's spent reading it,' she observed sarcastically.

Ellen started to descend the stairs, holding the letter in her hand. Smelling the burnt pastry, she flashed Granma an apologetic glance. 'Sorry, Gran – I'll make another batch.'

'Well, how is he?' Thomas wanted to know, impatiently.

Ellen managed a thin smile. 'They got his leg sorted out now, and they're sending him to a convalescent home. He says he's got a new plaster and all the nurses have signed it with love and kisses.'

Granma smiled, forgetting about the sausage rolls. 'Always said your youngest was going to be a ladies' man,' she muttered.

'Anything else?' Thomas prompted.

Ellen nodded. 'They're giving him a medal,' she said, managing to sound almost resentful.

Thomas looked impressed. 'Here, let me see.' He reached for the letter, taking it from his wife's fingers and scanning it eagerly. His face began to shine with pride. 'Blimey – Distinguished Service. You didn't tell me that.'

Ellen regarded him sadly, unable to share his enthusiasm. 'He's twenty years old, Thomas,' she reminded him. 'He'll have a bad limp and he'll probably suffer from bouts of fever for the rest of his life.'

Thomas was vaguely aware that he had said or done something wrong, but couldn't understand what it was. He gave Ellen a cheering smile. 'Well, he's got to be better or they wouldn't be moving him. This convalescent home isn't too far away. I could try to get some time off and we'll go and visit him.'

Ellen would not be comforted. 'I don't want to visit him,' she complained. 'I want him home.'

Finally, Thomas thought he understood. He slipped his arm around his wife's shoulders, hugging her. 'I'll write back and ask if they can discharge him,' he promised. 'Don't worry, love – we'll have him back just as soon as we can.'

This seemed to cheer Ellen up somewhat. At least, she put on a smile. 'Anyway, I'll get tea ready,' she said, getting back to business as usual. 'Thomas, go and call Geoffrey in, will you? He's out in the back garden.'

Thomas looked slightly puzzled. 'What's he doing out there on his own?'

Frank looked up from his book. 'Well, if you find out, perhaps you'd tell me,' he put in. 'He's been in a funny mood all day.'

The lad certainly seemed strangely withdrawn, Thomas thought, finding Geoffrey standing at the very end of the garden, staring moodily up into the evening sky. It was probably the bombs, he decided, moving up to stand beside the boy in silence for a while.

'Worried?' he asked eventually.

Geoffrey turned to face his grandfather, his eyes distant and troubled. He shook his head. 'Not about them,' he said, with a trace of defiance.

There was another silence, in which Thomas could sense that the boy had something he wanted to get off his chest, but needed prompting. No master of subtlety, he went straight to the heart of things.

'Are you in some kind of trouble?' Thomas asked directly.

Geoffrey gave a barely perceptible nod.

'So, want to talk about it? A trouble shared, as they say?'

The boy was cautious. 'You got to promise me you won't get cross,' he urged.

Thomas smiled gently. 'You do think I'm an old ogre, don't you? Come on, lighten the load.'

It was an enticing offer, Geoffrey thought. Something he had wanted to do all day. Making up his mind, he drew a breath. 'The thing is, it's not my trouble, it's Moira's,' he blurted out eventually. 'There's this bloke – and he's selling these dirty pictures. . .' He broke off, suddenly alarmed at the black look spreading over his grandfather's face. 'You said you wouldn't get angry. I promised Moira I wouldn't tell anyone,' he said, sounding frightened.

But Thomas wasn't listening to him anymore. Grim-faced, he was already marching back towards the house.

*

This was men's talk. With a woman's natural sense of discretion, Ellen had vacated her precious kitchen for the parlour, leaving them to it. Geoffrey had been despatched to an early bed. Even Granma, who would normally have made sure her nose was in the thick of it, had had the sense to retire upstairs, on the pretext of comforting Moira.

'So where's this toe-rag's shop?' Tom thundered. 'I'll soon sort the bastard out.'

Thomas shook his head. 'I'm not having you get involved in this, Tom. Frank and me will handle it.'

It was not good enough. 'Dammit, she's my daughter,' Tom spat out angrily. 'That makes it my business.'

'We could go to the police,' Frank suggested.

Tom shot his brother a scathing glance. 'Don't talk bloody daft. If the flamin' police find out she's my daughter, I'd never be able to see her again.' He turned back to his father, appealing to him. 'Look, Dad – we're supposed to have buried the hatchet. So why can't you and me be on the same side for a change?'

Thomas faced him squarely. 'We are on the same side. I had Frank come and fetch you, didn't I? I thought you deserved to know – but not to take things into your own hands.'

'So meanwhile this bastard carries on selling photographs of your granddaughter in the buff,' Tom pointed out. 'Is that what you want? He's got to be stopped.'

Thomas sighed, feeling confused. They were at an impasse, and he didn't know what to do about it. Frank just felt rather helpless and embarrassed, knowing that it really wasn't anything to do with him. With Tom and his father more or less in broad agreement for once, he didn't even have a role as a mediator.

Tom's next move, however, was to drag him right into the front line.

'Bloody Geoffrey – he's the key to all this,' Tom announced suddenly. 'I'll get the truth out of him, even if I have to shake it out.' He darted to the closed kitchen door, wrenching it open, preparing to run up the stairs to the boy's bedroom.

Pre-empting the move, Frank rushed past him, taking up an aggressive stance at the foot of the stairs. 'You leave my son out of this, Tom,' he hissed warningly. 'You lay a finger on him and by God I swear I'll floor you.'

The two brothers faced each other warily, eyeball to eyeball.

'Get out of my way, Frank,' Tom muttered, with grim determination. 'You want to protect your son – you make him tell me how I can help my daughter.'

The atmosphere was fraught with tension, the threat of violence almost crackling in the air like static electricity. Suddenly, it was Thomas who was cast as mediator. He eased himself between his two sons, holding them apart. 'Get hold of yourselves, the pair of you,' he barked, sternly. 'We want to end all this trouble, not make it worse.'

His words went unheeded. 'Tell him to get out of the way, Dad,' Tom said, stubbornly defiant. He looked up the stairs, shouting angrily out over Frank's shoulder, 'Geoffrey – you get out here this minute.'

The threatened violence broke. Frank drew back his fist, throwing a punch at Tom's head. He reeled back, blood dripping from his nose, poising himself to return the attack. Thomas jumped into the fray, pushing Frank back with his shoulders, fending Tom off with his arms.

There was a knock at the front door, Ellen coming out of the parlour to answer it. She froze in the hallway, appalled by the sight of her whole family brawling.

Geoffrey appeared on the top landing, looking down with equal shock. 'Stop it,' he screamed. 'I'll tell you what you want to know. His name's Victor D'Arcy, place in Miller Street.'

The three men quietened down almost at once. Tom backed off, dropping his arms to his sides, breathing heavily.

The knock on the front door was repeated. Ellen glanced at them all nervously, satisfying herself that the trouble was over before answering it.

Opening the door, she stared blankly at the young man standing there in Merchant Navy uniform. He smiled at her nervously. 'Hello, I'm Jack,' he announced. 'Moira's husband. Have I come to the right house?'

It was not the right time to greet one's son-in-law, Tom decided. Taking advantage of everyone's stunned surprise, he footed it out of the back door.

'I can't face him, Gran, I just can't,' Moira sobbed. She lay face-down on the bed as though she wanted to burrow into it, bury herself.

'You love him, don't yer?' Gran asked gently. 'You want a proper dad and a decent life for your Shirl?' She sat on the edge of the bed, pulling Moira up into a sitting position and cradling the girl's head against her shoulder.

Moira nodded, miserably. 'But I can't have it, can I?' she asked bitterly, patting her stomach.

Granma's eyes twinkled. 'You got a young man downstairs who's been at sea for nearly a year,' she pointed out. 'He loves you, and he's come all this way to see you and Shirley. Seems to me you're going to have a reason to fall for a baby pretty soon.'

For a moment, a bright spark of hope showed in Moira's eyes as she clutched at an impossible dream. It faded, slowly. 'I couldn't do that to him, Gran,' she murmured, hopeless again.

Granma stood up and hauled the girl to her feet. 'He won't be the first, or the last, not in this war,' she muttered seriously. Her face brightened into a grin. 'And don't you tell me you can't tell a white lie,' she said, almost reprovingly. 'You're good enough at the other sort.' She began to lead Moira over towards the dressing-table. 'Now, let's wash those tears away and get you all prettied up, shall we?'

43

Tom pulled the Humber Hawk to a stop outside Victor's studio. The street was quiet and deserted, with only the odd faint chink of light showing past the blackout curtains in some of the flats above the shops. It was getting on for ten o'clock, and most people had started to learn that the night bombers would be coming soon. Getting bedded down early in the shelters was becoming part of life's routine.

Tom climbed out of the car, approaching the studio entrance. It was closed, of course – but then locked doors had never been much of a problem. Pulling a long, thin-bladed knife from his pocket, Tom slipped it neatly between the door lock and the latch, pushing the door open with a faint click. He closed it behind him again, creeping up the stairs.

The second door at the top was, surprisingly, unlocked. Tom pushed it open cautiously, stepping furtively into the outer office and snapping on his torch.

'What the hell?' a voice blurted out, suddenly. The black curtains separating the office from the studio were pulled back abruptly, spilling a dull red light into the room.

Victor regarded his intruder warily, sizing him up. They were both about evenly matched in weight and height, he thought, and Tom did not look particularly strong or fit. If it came to a fight, Victor fancied his chances.

He made a grab for the telephone but Tom beat him to it, ripping the cord out of the wall. Victor backed away into his darkroom, half-expecting an attack. 'Look, there's nothing here worth stealing,' he blurted out. 'You're wasting your time.'

Tom regarded him coldly. 'I'm not here to steal anything. I'm Moira's father.'

A brief look of panic flitted across Victor's face. He moved tentatively forward again, away from the darkroom, suddenly and uncomfortably reminded of the dozens of fresh prints of the girl hanging up to dry just a few feet behind him. Moira was, in fact, the reason he had been working late, replacing the pictures she had taken from his filing cabinet.

He forced a smile on to his face, trying to bluff it out. Reaching behind his back, he tried to slide the blackout curtains back into place discreetly. 'Oh yes, Moira,' he muttered. 'She was one of my models. Unfortunately, I had to let her go.'

His attempt to screen off the darkroom had not gone unnoticed by Tom. He stepped forward smartly, pushing Victor in the chest and ducking past him. He looked up at the still-dripping photographs of Moira in the fruit hat, his mouth curling into a sneer of disgust.

'You call that modelling, you piece of filth?' he demanded in fury. 'What sort of a bastard makes a girl do those sort of pictures?'

Still tensed for a fight, Victor tried a verbal defence first. 'She was quite willing to pose for them, and I paid her good money.'

Tom was incensed that the man was trying to justify himself. 'And seducing her was all part of the deal, was it?' he demanded angrily.

They were entering hostile territory, Victor realized. A firm denial seemed appropriate. 'I never seduced her.'

'So who was it, then? The Archangel Gabriel?' Tom spat out. He made a threatening move forward, clenching his fist.

Victor cowered back against the wall. 'Look, do you want money? Is that it?'

Tom's eyes narrowed to mere slits. There was a dangerous edge to his voice. 'Are you calling me a bloody pimp for my own daughter?'

'I thought you were here on her behalf,' Victor said hastily, backing off. 'Just tell me what it is that you want.'

'I want the negatives,' Tom told him. 'And then I want to watch you burn every single one of them photographs.'

Victor shrugged, spreading his hands, humouring the man. 'Fine, all you had to do was ask.' Eyeing Tom warily, he edged around the wall towards a cupboard and opened the door, reaching inside.

His hand came out again almost immediately, clasping the handle of a small but razor-sharp craft knife. Cradling it in his palm, he spread his legs, balancing himself. Holding the blade out on a level with Tom's throat, he began to advance, slowly.

'Don't be a bloody fool,' Tom said, half-crouching into a defensive position.

Victor wasn't listening. Thinking he had his man on the run, he made a couple of tentative lunges with the knife.

Tom ducked away from the first, tried to grab Victor's wrist on the second. He was a split second out on his timing. The scalpel-like blade sliced up the back of his hand, making him pull back his arm with a grunt of pain. Victor's foot lashed out in the direction of his groin, connecting high on the inside of his thigh. His leg half-numbed, Tom was off-balance as he backed away from another knife-thrust. He stumbled and crashed backwards to the floor, the force of the fall knocking the wind out of his lungs.

Grinning savagely, Victor closed in for the kill. A few disfig-uring scars and the man would never come bothering him again, he thought. He stepped over Tom's supine body, jab-bing the point of the blade down towards his face.

In a purely reflex action, Tom's hand snaked into his coat pocket and came out clutching Edward's gun, aiming and firing in a simple act of self-preservation. The bullet took Victor high in the chest, the close-range impact throwing him right across the room and through the darkroom curtains. He lay there unmoving, a look of idiotic surprise on his life-less face.

Tom scrambled to his feet, his body shaking. 'Oh, Christ,'

he muttered, hopelessly, under his breath. Totally shaken, he stumbled over to Victor's body and looked down at it, praying for a sign of life.

Tom stood there for several minutes – long after he had satisfied himself that the man was dead. With a cold and sickening sense of finality, he realised that there was nothing left of his own life, either – except for the haunting shadow of the hangman's noose.

Outside in the streets, Moaning Minnie was wailing out her defiance against the drone of approaching bombers, but the man who was Thomas O'Malley heard nothing.

He sat stiffly in his office chair, dressed in his best hand-tailored suit and wearing the gold wristwatch he had bought only two weeks previously. His hands rested on the top of his desk, one of them clutching his monogrammed silver cigarette case. A mixture of paint, fabric dope and petrol washed the floor around his expensive two-tone alligator-skin shoes.

In the darkness of the empty factory, a match flared, briefly, then dropped to the floor. A wall of flame leapt up, moving forward rapidly, devouring everything in its path.

44

Finding an unexpected and unwanted Dorothea on one's doorstep was not the best start to the day, Evelyn decided. She could only hope that her surprise successfully masked her displeasure.

'I thought you were spending a few days with Edward,' she said finally, when she had pulled herself together.

Dorothea stepped over the threshold without waiting for an invitation. 'Slight change of plan,' she announced. 'So I thought I'd come and keep you company instead.'

Evelyn's face fell. The next bit was going to be very tricky indeed. She forced a look of apology on to her face. 'Well, of course, it's nice to see you, Dotty – but I'm afraid you can't stay here,' she said awkwardly. 'They bombed the barracks at Hornden last night. We've been commandeered as an emergency billet. I've got six pilots arriving some time this afternoon.'

An expression of theatrical tragedy crossed her sister's face. 'Please don't turn me away,' she begged. 'My whole life is in ruins.'

Evelyn was flustered. This was Dorothea playing a part she had not seen before, and she wasn't sure what her supporting role was supposed to be. Playing it by ear, she tried sympathy. 'Well, you'd better come in to the sitting-room and we'll talk about it. Would you like a cup of tea?'

Dorothea rolled her eyes, snorting. 'Tea, darling? I want hemlock.' Making the most of her invitation, she swept past Evelyn and headed for the gin supply.

The hall phone began to ring. Evelyn's eyes flitted between it and her sister's back uncertainly. William came bounding down the stairs. 'I'll get it,' he offered helpfully. He glanced at Dorothea and looked back at his mother, feigning a look of horror.

Trying hard not to smile, Evelyn followed her sister into the sitting-room and installed her on the sofa. She sat down in the chair opposite. 'Now, suppose you tell me what's happened?' she murmured sympathetically.

Dorothea's eyelashes fluttered delicately. 'It was terrible, darling,' she gushed. 'I went to see Edward yesterday and he was horrid to me. He wouldn't even listen when I tried to explain about keeping him out of prison.'

There was a sinking feeling in Evelyn's stomach. It sounded as though it was going to be a long and depressing story. William's return from the phone was almost like a rescue mission.

'They've strafed Hornden again,' he announced gravely. 'Hit the NAAFI rather badly, from the sound of it. They need the mobile canteen as soon as possible.'

Evelyn jumped to her feet, immediately concerned. 'Were there any casualties?'

William nodded. 'Some. I didn't ask for details.'

'I'll have to go,' Evelyn said quietly. She started to head for the door. Dorothea looked up in horror. 'You're not going to just abandon me?' she pleaded.

Evelyn was incredulous. She turned back to stare at her sister almost pityingly. 'You heard what William said. They need me, Dotty.'

Dorothea pouted. 'So do I,' she muttered, petulantly.

Evelyn regarded her for another few seconds, wondering why she was still constantly surprised by her sister's selfishness. She pushed the thought out of her head, returning to more urgent matters. 'William will look after you while I'm gone,' she snapped, turning away and leaving the room without another word.

Numbed with shock, the image of the burned-out and gutted aircraft factory still fresh in her mind, Sandra sat in the police station interview room. Across the desk, DS Howard faced her, sympathetic but efficient.

'I understand how distressing this must be for you, but we don't seem to have any next of kin,' he said gently. 'You seem to have been the closest person to him.'

Sandra nodded, choking back a sob. 'I was,' she managed to whisper.

DS Howard nodded understandingly. 'Then you'll appreciate why I have to ask you to do this? Help us with formal identification?' He slid open a drawer, pulling out two bulky brown envelopes and emptying their contents out on to the top of the desk.

Sandra's eyes refilled with tears as she looked down on the pathetic, charred remains of the man she'd loved. What was left of an identity card, a blackened scrap of a ration book, a watch, a cigarette case, a lump of burned leather which had once been a shoe.

DS Howard smiled thinly. 'Not much, is it?' he murmured. 'But with all that inflammable stuff laying around, the place would have gone up in seconds. Must have been hit by an incendiary.'

Sandra wiped at her eyes, nodding. 'They're all his,' she confirmed. 'All Tom's.'

Howard digested this information thoughtfully for a second. 'But Tom who?' he asked finally. His tone was still sympathetic, but there was the faintest suggestion of pressure behind it.

The change was subtle, but enough to make Sandra tremble suddenly.

'Your loyalty can't help him now, Sandra,' DS Howard went on. 'Our records show that Thomas O'Malley reported his identity card missing over a year ago. So who was he, really?'

The man was right, Sandra realized. There was no point in maintaining the lie. There was nothing left to protect. At least the truth would let him be buried with his own name.

'His name was Slater,' she said, with a sigh. 'Tom Slater.'

A thin smile of satisfaction passed across Howard's lips. He rose from his desk slowly, walking round it to the girl's side. 'Thank you for your help,' he said simply, helping her to her feet and escorting her towards the door.

Dorothea was on her fifth gin of the morning and well into a mood of maudlin self-pity as Evelyn walked in. She stared up at her sister sullenly, too tipsy to notice the strain on her face.

'Oh, so you're back at last,' Dorothea said reproachfully. 'Feel guilty about abandoning me, did you? Even your precious son didn't have the good manners to stay and console me for long. One phone call and he was out of the house without so much as a simple good . . .'

'He came to fetch me,' Evelyn blurted out, cutting in abruptly and stunning her into silence.

Dorothea stared at her glassy-eyed, only now becoming dimly aware of the grim, shocked expression on her sister's face.

'The phone call was about Edward,' Evelyn went on. 'I'm afraid there's some terrible news.'

A flicker of concern pierced Dorothea's alcoholic stupour. 'Has he been arrested?'

Evelyn was as gentle as she could be. 'I'm afraid he's dead, Dotty. There was a direct hit on the hospital, just as he was about to go back into operating.'

Dorothea stared at her in incomprehension, her glass slipping out of her fingers to the floor. The shock couldn't quite penetrate. Grotesquely, she let out a nervous little giggle. 'But that's silly, he can't be dead. I was with him, last night.'

'I'm sorry, Dotty,' Evelyn murmured sadly. She sat down beside Dorothea on the sofa, placing her arm around her shoulder. 'It must have been instantaneous. He'd have known absolutely nothing.'

There was a long silence, before Dorothea's body began to

quiver with dry, pathetic sobs. 'I was going to put everything right, Evelyn,' she murmured distantly. 'I can't, now.'

The tears began to flow, finally. Evelyn hugged her consolingly, finding herself wondering who she was actually crying for.

45

The train pulled slowly into St Pancras station, uniformed figures hanging out of the doors and windows, each one eager to catch the first sight of their loved ones.

Thomas and Ellen stood waiting on the platform, both dressed in their best clothes which hadn't been worn since Harry's wedding. Granma, as usual, had gone way over the top, sporting an impossibly large floppy hat festooned with red, white and blue ribbons.

Ellen was edgy and nervous, scanning the train with anxious eyes as it inched, slowly, towards the buffers. She glanced up at her husband, chewing at her bottom lip. 'Oh Thomas, I'm so happy and frightened at the same time,' she whimpered. 'Worrying how he's going to look, how it might have changed him.'

Thomas squeezed her hand comfortingly. 'He'll be fine, love,' he promised. 'He'll be just fine.'

The train doors were opening, disgorging a motley crew of soldiers, matelots and civilians on to the platform.

'Can you see him yet?' Granma asked insistently, aware that her old eyes weren't fully up to the job anymore.

Ellen was too excited to answer her, concentrating upon the rapidly thinning crowd of discharged passengers. For a terrible moment, she though that the train was finally empty, that she would have to face the bitter pill of disappointment.

Then Clifford appeared in an open train doorway, being helped down the steps by another sailor. Finally on the platform, he stood there awkwardly, balancing himself on his crutches, his left leg encased in a huge plaster cast.

Ellen sobbed with relief, rushing to greet him, screaming out his name.

Clifford's pale face came alight at the sight of her. 'Mum,' he yelled back as she ran towards him, her arms outstretched.

She reached him, stopping in her tracks, the ecstatic smile on her face momentarily clouded by uncertainty, desperately wanting to hold him but not knowing how.

Clifford grinned at her. 'It's all right Mum. You can hug me if you want to. I've learned the trick of keeping me balance now.'

Sobbing with relief, Ellen took him at his word, throwing her arms gratefully around his waist as Thomas and Granma walked over to join them.

'Hello, son,' Thomas said warmly. He stooped to pick up Clifford's knapsack. 'I'll carry your bag.'

Granma kissed him on the cheek. 'Hello, love.' She nodded down at his crutches, grinning cheekily. 'Need any help wiv yer pogo sticks?'

Clifford smiled back, drawing himself up stiffly, proudly. 'Thanks, but I think I've got the hang of it now,' he told her. 'Though I still have a bit of trouble getting me shoe on.'

To back up his words, he took a few hobbling steps forward, looking pleased with himself. 'Did I tell you I was getting a medal?' he asked proudly. 'I'll be in the *London Gazette*.'

'That's grand, son,' Thomas said. He fell into awkward step beside his son, his face glowing with pride.

Half-hidden behind a news stand, the man who was now Victor D'Arcy stood observing the happy little family group with an expression of tender affection on his face. He watched them all the way to the exit before turning towards the station office and walking over to buy a ticket on the next departing train. The destination didn't matter, he told himself – it was just a place to start a new life.

He patted his top pocket absently as he walked, checking the presence of his new identity card.

'Victor D'Arcy – photographer,' he reflected, grinning to himself. Now all he had to do was to steal a camera.